THE
LAND WHERE
SINNERS
LOVE

Edited by Jenny Sims

Proofread: Rumi Khan

Cover Design: Hang Le

To the power of love.

AUTHOR'S NOTE

The Land Where Sinners Love is a dark romantic suspense.
It mentions abuse, rape and graphic violence.

PROLOGUE

Take me to the land where sinners love...
Where sins are forgotten and bad memories don't show.
There your past does not matter,
And you get a second chance to atone for the wrong use of your power.

Take me to the land where sinners love...
Where laughter echoes through the space.
There cruelty does not exist,
And people live in harmony as their souls heal.

Take me to the land where sinners love...
Where love is a cure.
There it's the only salvation,
And your soulmate who holds your hand tight and never lets go.

Take me to the land where sinners love...

CHAPTER ONE

"Take me to the land where sinners atone..."
Phoenix

*N*ew York, New York

*P*hoenix
A butterfly-like kiss touches my neck, the plump lips sliding down my warm skin and leaving goose bumps in their wake while sending shivers down my spine.

I smile, my fingers curling into the sheets as the light breeze from the open balcony door nips on my flesh, bringing much-needed relief to my heated form.

The hot mouth moves lower, the teeth scraping over my collarbone when his hands find mine, raising them above my head, lacing our fingers while he makes more room for himself between my legs. His hard length rubs up and down my center before entering me with one hard thrust.

He catches my gasp with his lips, his tongue pushing and roaming inside my mouth. Seeking my tongue, he locks us in a deep kiss, driving me insane with each swipe and lick.

He sways back, and then slowly, agonizingly slowly, he enters me again, stretching me around his length, connecting us in the most primal way. I sigh into the kiss, arching my neck to give him better access.

Scorching heat rocks my entire system. Shivers rush down my spine as fire burns inside me, boiling my blood and awakening every hair on my body, losing me in the pleasure this man delivers to me with each hard yet deep thrust.

As birds chirp loudly along with the bright sunlight streaming from the windows, I soak in lust and passion so strong, it has the power to block everything and everyone away, holding me tightly in its tempting clutches and making me crave this man in ways I never thought possible.

He consumes me, owning my body and soul.

Gradually, his pace changes. His thrusts become deeper, pushing me closer and closer to the edge until I finally erupt in his arms. He swallows my moans as my core spasms around him.

He tears his mouth away from me, both of us gulping for breath, and then hides his face in the crook of my neck, still moving inside me to chase his own peak.

One. Two. Three more thrusts and he bites my neck, groaning and finding his own release.

Running my hand down Zach's spine, I squeeze my legs around him harder while pressing my head to the pillow and grinning at him. His handsome face watches me intently from above while our skin glistens from the lovemaking.

Sweet, sweet but oh-so hot lovemaking that only my husband can give me.

"Good morning, Mr. King." I rise a bit and meet him halfway, his tongue dwelling deep and mingling with mine in a passionate kiss that sends tremors rushing through me despite the pleasure still rocking my entire system.

"Good morning, Mrs. King," he says right after tearing his mouth away and thrusting into me again. His dick slowly hardens inside me, and a moan slips past my lips. "Today, we're going to spend the whole day in bed," he informs me while laughter bubbles up inside me. Happiness spreads through me in waves at what my life has become now. I'm ready to grab him again to feel his mouth on me, when the annoying ringing of the phone penetrates through our lustful fog.

Our heads swing to the nightstand, where my phone flashes brightly, continuing to ring. My brow furrows when Zachary asks, "Who might be calling you?" I shake my head, silently telling him I have no clue.

After six years of being blissfully married, everyone knows better than to interrupt us on our anniversary. While we don't go away on this specific day, I always make sure our mornings are free, so we can spend the day with the kids, seeping joy from the happiness we have found in the middle of a storm that almost swallowed us both in hate and grief.

Zach reaches for the phone, the muscles of his arm flexing, and he looks at it, an unreadable expression settling on his features. "Who is it, honey?"

"Noah." One single name makes me freeze, coldness sinking into every bone of my body while thousands of flashbacks play in my mind.

On instinct, I jerk to the side, leaving my husband no choice but to roll onto his back and disconnect us while I sit up on the bed, grabbing the sheet to cover myself as if trying to protect me from the inevitable hurt inspired by this name.

Or rather...

Reminds me of the past I wish to forget, yet I cannot forget. The events forever imprinted themselves in my brain and left bleeding scars on my heart.

With trembling hands, I snatch the phone from Zachary's death grip and slide it open. "Hello."

"Phoenix." The deep baritone greets me, and I scrunch my eyes, his tone alone announcing the upcoming doom as an FBI agent never calls you just for the hell of it. "I need your help."

And while everything in my head screams to hang up for my sanity and to preserve the bubble of our creation where the past was nonexistent, I resist the urge and listen to him.

Because in the land where sinners atone...you cannot run away from your scars or past.

Even if the help you need to provide might kill you.

CHAPTER TWO

"Life comes full circle at some point.
And in the most unexpected way possible."
Phoenix

*P*hoenix
Thunder echoes in the air, shaking the sky above me. The birds squawk soundly, flying up high and ruffling the leaves, sending them down in little swirls.

Dark clouds gather, ready to pour heavy rain on this secluded place, trying to wash away the sins of the people residing in it, not that it would help much.

Some sins are so dark and despicable, nothing can wipe them off. As no atonement could make up for their mistakes and actions because they are and always will be irreversible.

The harsh wind whooshes over my form, flapping my coat backward, yet I pay no attention to the frigid air slamming into my lungs and just stare at the grim, granite building with an electric fence.

"You'll get what you deserve here. Because hell is too good of a place for people like you," she whispers into my ear and tightens her hold on the rope wrapped around my neck. "Are you ready to die, Phoenix?"

Gulping for breath, I rub my fingers over my neck and bite on my lower lip, holding back the sobs threatening to escape.

I scrunch my eyes at the harsh voice echoing in my ears, pulling me back to the most difficult time of my life where goodness died and only evilness remained.

Evilness that at some point destroyed my soul, leaving only scattered pieces for everyone to stumble on, and they gladly did. Forcing me to burn in the hell of their creation as thousands of demons tore my flesh over and over again, finding satisfaction in my every painful groan while inflicting even more scars on my body.

A body that became a canvas for their cruelty and sadistic cravings.

Someone gently touches me on the shoulder, shifting my focus back to present, and I look at the dark-haired muscled man in a suit. He oozes confidence and calmness that almost makes you believe you could trust him and lower your guard around him.

Almost as his FBI badge proves otherwise because his every move and word holds a different kind of meaning, and if you aren't careful enough, you might get trapped in whatever he has on his agenda.

Or at least it's like that for me.

After my past, I have a hard time trusting anyone in the federal forces. The jurisdiction system failed me all those years ago, and I'm still living with the consequences.

"We better get inside," Agent Noah says, motioning with his hand toward the prison's gates, where two guards wait for us. "It's going to start raining any minute now." He glances up before twisting his wristwatch. "Not to mention that we have our appointment scheduled in five minutes."

Despite nodding at his words, I stand still, frozen in time, as my eyes roam around the place that holds so many memories.

Painful, agonizing, hurtful memories that still find their way into my nightmares, awakening me at night and not letting me forget.

Truth be told, I even stopped hoping and temporarily gave up on my therapy because it brought no results.

As a psychiatrist, I should know better and continue my treatment, but how much can a person really take?

All these sessions brought me back to the hurt and agony, and I cannot stand it.

Maybe that's a part of my destiny too. Forever remember the hideous crimes committed toward an innocent woman between these walls as a sort of reminder to never be fully happy.

I know better than anyone how everything might change in the blink of an eye, and those you call your loved ones will turn their backs on you faster than your enemies.

"Phoenix." Noah touches my shoulder again. "Breathe."

Only after his soft command do I realize I've been holding my breath and exhale heavily. My heart beats wildly as my hold on the folder in my hands tightens to the point of my knuckles turning white.

"I'm sorry." I clear my throat. "It's harder than I thought."

Or rather I didn't think about it at all when I agreed to this charade my husband strongly suggested against.

In fact, we had our very first serious fight this morning because of it.

If it can be called a fight, that is.

"Absolutely not," Zachary spits, his emerald-green eyes flashing in anger as he gets up from the dining table. Our kids glance at us, surprise written all over their features. He's never raised his voice at me in their company, so his behavior must confuse them. "Call them right now and tell them you've changed your mind."

I bristle at the command. Judging by his tone alone, he expects me to do as he says because that's what he's used to.

Dishing out orders that people blindly follow as angering him has severe consequences.

You don't marry a King and then expect a great temperament. Even my kids share his character and can be a force to be reckoned with if something happens against their wishes.

Keeping my grin intact for the kids, I run my hands through our daughter's hair and grit through my teeth, "I won't." My eyes must send daggers his way because he straightens up and lifts his chin, indicating to me he won't budge on this one.

Well, tough luck because I won't either.

"Let's go, sweetie," I tell Emmaline. Our nine-year-old daughter jumps up

from her chair, the ballet shoes hanging from her shoulders as her ponytails sway from side to side. "Mommy is going to drop you off at practice before she goes to work." I walk around the table and kiss my twin sons on the cheeks as they giggle soundly, their faces smeared in jam. "Behave, my darlings."

"Yes, Mama," they reply in unison and then share a glance, letting me know they have no intentions of doing so.

While my daughter is the perfect child every parent dreams of...my boys are ready to cause chaos wherever they go.

And I love them all so much, sometimes my heart is ready to burst from it.

Since Emmaline already runs ahead toward the hallway, I spin around, ready to ignore my husband and leave.

Only for him to catch my elbow and pull me toward him, my yelp reverberating through the space as he wraps his hand around my neck and our chests bump against each other's.

His powerful frame completely hides me from the boys' view while his thumb rubs over my lips, and I frown at him. "Let go of me, you difficult man." Although my voice holds heat, it doesn't really sound sincere, and my body already reacts to his closeness, the blazing heat traveling through my entire system and sneaking into my every cell. "Zach, I'll be late."

Instead of answering, he puts his mouth on mine, his tongue piercing through my lips and dueling with my own.

On a sigh, I allow him to deepen the embrace as he delivers his hot and passionate kiss in which he owns my mouth, playing it like the most skilled musician with his beloved instrument.

His fingers slide to my throat, lightly grazing my skin and breaking goose bumps on my flesh, earning himself a moan while annoyance lingers at his earlier words.

He brushes his tongue against mine one more time, then ends the kiss, our breaths mingling between us. He puts his index finger on my lips when he sees I want to say something. "You don't leave our house without kissing me, my love." He gives me one more peck, then steps back, his warmth leaving me while fire burns in his gaze. "Be careful."

My heart contracts inside my chest at the worry detected in his voice and self-loathing while he returns to our boys, who chatter about their upcoming play in kindergarten. He always makes sure to spend some time with them before work, and it's adorable.

And even though I'm still mad he wanted to forbid me to go to the prison that gives both of us nightmares, I understand.

What man would want his woman to go back to the place where he hurt her the most?

"It's normal to feel this way. You've been wrongly accused of murder and went to prison for a crime you didn't commit." Noah snaps me out of my thoughts as we start moving toward the gates. "Your emotions are valid."

A smile shapes my mouth despite my surroundings. "No need to use psychological tactics to calm me down, my friend." I shake my ID in the air. "I'm one of the best psychiatrists in the world, remember?"

"Still. You're human, and in light of our tragedies, experience and professionalism don't matter."

"True."

Although, in my opinion, my knowing the human mind so much somehow lessened the blow from the shit happening in my life. It made me see it in a different light, not less painful but at least...less something.

Otherwise, what explains my going back to being normal in such a short span?

They freed me from prison after three years and caught the real killer shortly afterward, the identity of whom shocked all of us. Despite the turmoil it brought to the family, I married Zachary within months and had twins, staying at home for two more years.

The first day I got back it felt like coming home as if nothing happened, which allowed me to dig deep into it, and I've been lost in it for three years now.

Which means six years in total after getting my freedom back.

I'm surprised it took me this long to come back, but then I avoided any cases that had to do with murder. When you have wealth and power, choosing which patient you want to handle is easy, and no one can tell you what to do.

The perks of being a King I gladly use if it meant avoiding prison.

When Noah called today asking for help, though, I couldn't refuse after everything he did for me back in the day. I might not like agents, but at least he has integrity.

"Have you read the file?" Noah shows his badge to the guards, who nod and let us in, where we put all our things on the scanner and remove our coats. "I'm sorry for not giving you more of a heads-up."

Walking through the gate, I gather my coat and reply, "Yes. The woman stabbed her husband several times, then called the police herself." The report was quite short and didn't give me any significant details on the case. "I'm not sure why you need my help, though." Throwing the coat over my arm, I follow Noah as he walks through the narrow path led by a prison guard, already recognizing the surroundings.

My pulse speeds up, and I press the folder harder to my chest while we pass by the hallway filled with cells occupied by women. They stare at us with hatred and malice; some even spit on the ground to inform us about their distaste toward us.

They can't say anything because that might bring punishment. However, they use everything else in their arsenal to make their emotions loud and clear.

Keeping my head held high, I focus only on the door in the distance leading to the interrogation room and ignore the various cries and hisses shot our way because they inspire such conflicted emotions within me.

As a society, we judge all these people for crimes they have committed and strip them of their basic human rights because, in our eyes, they do not deserve atonement or a second chance.

However, when you were one of them with the whole world taking away everything from you...you don't share such sentiments.

How many of them are actual monsters, and how many were just unlucky enough to be at the wrong place at the wrong time?

Or worse.

How many of them were someone's sick obsession like I'd been?

Once we reach the door, the guard presses on the keypad and opens it, letting us in, and Noah finally replies to my earlier question.

"The report was a bit incomplete. I didn't want to scare you." I blink at this, dread filling my chest while chills run down my spine. Incomplete never means good in our professions. "She tortured him for sometime before finally stabbing him in the heart. That was the fatal wound based on the autopsy."

So the murder was not done in cold rage but a calculated strategy to bring the most suffering before she ended the life of her husband. The final wound is too specific, maybe indicating some kind of betrayal?

"Oh."

Her husband must have done something unforgivable, according to her. I tried finding some information on the man to understand her profile better and provide much-needed help. However, all the search engine showed was that he was a perfect man who doted on his wife and three daughters while dividing his time between his surgical career and charity events. He even flew to other countries to operate on countless children, and one of the newspapers called his death a loss of talent for humanity.

Not that it made him innocent. Sometimes the hideous people wear the most mesmerizing masks in order to fool everyone around them about their sainthood. After all, monsters love nothing better than to play the perfect person because it allows them to hide their rotten nature and indulge in their sadistic cravings to the fullest.

However, sometimes perfect people *do* marry psychos, so without really knowing the woman or talking to her, it's impossible to even predict what was really going on in her brain.

We enter farther into the room where a correctional officer rises from his seat, extending his hand to me. "Dr. King. It's nice to meet you." I shake his hand. "I've heard so much about you."

"I guess it was impossible not to," I say, and he tenses a bit, stepping away while casting his gaze down, maybe feeling guilty for what his colleagues made me go through in the past. God knows they showed me no kindness either and didn't mind delivering their own blows after prisoners were done torturing me. "How is she?" I ask and then look at the two-way mirror, studying the interrogation room.

A blonde woman with a messy bun wearing an orange jumpsuit sits on the chair, her hands chained to the table, her eyes closed and her head thrown back.

My hold on the report tightens when I notice various scars on her neck and under her chin, bruises on her cheek, and a black eye. They're fresh. "She got into a fight with another inmate in the middle of the night," the correctional officer quickly explains while the ringing in my ear buzzes louder. "We had no choice but to isolate the two."

Of course. That's how they handle all this, right? Just isolate them until the next time because no one gives a shit what happens to these women since they are dirty murderers who deserve no mercy in their eyes.

Silence greets his statement; the only sound echoing through the space is the clock hanging on the wall, and every ticktock of it pulls at the strings of my mind, forcing it to bring up unwanted flashbacks, one after another.

I will become your worst nightmare. You will bleed and cry...but even then, it won't be enough for me.

How can this cruel and angry voice that rings in my ears to this day belong to the same man who owns my heart now?

"Phoenix." I peel my eyes away from the woman and look at Noah. "If you're not—"

"I'm fine." I place my coat on the nearby chair. "What do you need me to do?"

"We cannot find the kids." I know this much; it was the only reason I agreed to take on this case. My soul couldn't bear thinking about the little ones struggling somewhere. "She refuses to talk about them, and we're on the clock here."

I quickly scan the file. "She's been in custody for three days. Why are you questioning her about them just now?" As a rule, when children are missing, they have twenty-four hours to find them alive because they usually end up dead.

Granted, in the current situation, the killer involved is the mother, but with her unpredictable behavior, only God knows what she decided to do with them.

Anger crosses Noah's face, and by the annoyance coating his voice, I know it's addressed to whoever initially handled this case. "The detective assumed they were with their grandparents." My brows rise at this, and he chuckles, although it lacks any humor. "The idiot believed what she told him. The grandparents found out from the news. They were on a cruise, so once they informed us about the kids, we were called in. Needless to say, the case is handled by a different detective now."

I'm a bit confused with all this information because it makes zero sense to me. Why did they call in profilers?

For all the help they provide during an investigation, they never go out and chase criminals, and considering that they caught the murderer already, there isn't much for them to do.

Regular agents to find the kids? Yes. But profilers? No.

Noah must read it all on my face because he elaborates, "We believe that her husband was just a decoy, and she still plans to kill her kids."

"They need your help to learn her character and, in this, find the clues that might lead them to the kids," I finish for him, and he nods. "Okay. I'll do my best to evaluate her state because if she's crazy, I don't think we'll get much out of her." It can certainly help us understand why she committed the crime, not that it matters much.

Our priority are her children, who already lost their father due to their mother's madness. They shouldn't die because of it too.

Instantly, guilt washes over me, and I rub my stomach or, rather, the scar hidden under all the clothes that almost screams at me to show the woman compassion and the benefit of the doubt.

A benefit of the doubt no one showed me.

Sometimes even if all the evidence points at a certain person, it doesn't mean they're guilty and deserve all the hate.

"Anything else I should know?" They shake their heads, and I motion with mine toward the interrogation room. "Let's go then. You will evaluate her profile while I just study her reaction, yes?" I haven't done this in a while, but at least that was the procedure a decade ago. I walk to the door, ready to press the pad but pause when Noah makes no move to follow me. "Noah?"

"There is a reason I reached out to you, Phoenix."

"Yes. Because I'm the best in my field." It took me a long time to get used to saying this without feeling as if I'm trying to show off, but a fact is a fact.

I worked my ass off to be where I'm now, and I'll make no apologies for it.

His mouth curves in a smile before becoming a straight line once again. "That you are, but it's not the reason. Knowing your history, I would have never put you on this case by choice." I blink, still not really following. "Miranda requested you specifically."

Everything inside me goes still at this, my heart speeding up while uneasiness slides in my veins, alerting every protective instinct in my body. "You should have told me that," I grit through my teeth, barely resisting grabbing my coat and bolting away from all this mess as the bile rises in my throat, slowly announcing the panic attack and my desire not to be dragged into yet another situation where the rules of the game require me to sacrifice my soul.

Once upon a time, I was used as a pawn in a serial killer's game, and it almost cost me everything, including my life.

I refuse to be used again.

"Phoenix, please." Noah steps closer, and our gazes clash, the fury swirling inside me and demanding an outlet although I try to rein it in and remember what's at stake here. "Just one meeting that might help us find them. If she tries to manipulate you into anything, we'll end it. I promise you it won't be like the last time."

"You cannot give me such promises. She requested me, Noah!" I yell the last part, running my fingers through my hair. "You should have told me this on the way here, so I could prepare myself." My bitter laughter rocks off the walls. "Now I understand why your team was called in. No killer requests anyone unless it was a plan and a game all along. A puzzle that needs to be solved. With my brain." I hit the table next to me, the correctional officer's mug spilling coffee, but I don't give a shit. "I've given enough to the judicial system of our country. I won't be a pawn again, Noah."

"Phoenix, the kids."

I spin around, placing my splayed palm on the door while breathing heavily, doing my best to calm my nerves and focus on the fact that it's okay to be selfish once in a while and choose yourself. People sure as shit will always find an opportunity to screw over whatever happiness you find.

I have every right to walk away from this case and tell them all to fuck off with their plans and let them figure out this mess on their own.

Just as this thought enters my mind, though, I know I cannot do this because I'm a mother too. Which means I have little ones at home, and if, God forbid, anything happened to them...I'd want everyone to do their best to find them.

How could destiny put me in such a position once again? Haven't I suffered enough?

"I'll do it. But pray Zachary doesn't find out about it, Noah." He tenses, as he should. I might be forgiving, but my husband?

No such bone in his body, and if he ever finds out Noah put me in danger? Well, let's just say we all know what his wrath and hate entail.

I bite on my lip, shaking my head to clear the fog in my mind, and take a deep breath. I press on the keypad, letting the door slide open, and enter, the door quickly shutting behind me.

Miranda slowly opens her eyes, their crystal-clear blue freezing me on the spot for how cold and hollow they are.

Her mouth curves into a smile that must hurt her bruised lips, and she winks at me. "You came." A beat passes. "Phoenix King." She pronounces my name as if she's tasting it on her tongue and exhales in pleasure. "Welcome to my nightmare."

Yes.

I'm once again playing someone else's game without knowing the rules.

But I'll be damned if I'll allow anyone to destroy the life I have this time around.

CHAPTER THREE

"Past sins have the tendency to cause you nightmares.
Even if the one you hurt has forgiven you."
Zachary

Zachary

Leaning back in my chair, I pick up the latest marketing report on one of my companies and peruse it, frowning when the numbers don't add up.

Pressing the intercom, I wait for my secretary, Prudence, to speak up. "Yes, sir?"

"Who brought in the report for our Texas company?"

"Howard, sir."

My brows shoot up at this because the man has been working with us for the past twenty years and has never made a mistake. In fact, he's won awards as the best employee several times in a row. While I don't have the best relationship with the guy, finding his approaches slow and boring, my father still values him, so he kept his high position through the years. "The numbers don't add up. Set up a meeting for me with him."

"He's currently on vacation but should be back on Monday. Would that work?"

Vacation? In the middle of the takeover, he decided to take a vacation without my permission?

Everyone knows that when we are in hunting mode, nothing gets in the way, and we get rid of all the distractions. That includes family and vacations.

And he expects me to wait three days after his recent fuckup?

"No." Insanity. I hear her typing on the keyboard, probably preparing the necessary arrangements to bring the man here. "The latest I have to see him is tomorrow morning." I glance at the clock, estimating the damage his miscalculations have done. "Call the team in Texas and tell them to prepare all the information for me. We need to act fast to fix this mess. Otherwise, all our work in the past few months will be for nothing."

She types more. "All done, sir. Should I inform him of the problem? Or do you prefer for me to come up with some other excuse?"

Ah, the perks of working with someone who understands the game and has been by your side for years. She was one of Phoenix's patients who needed a helping hand after getting out from her abusive relationship and was desperate for a job.

Initially, I refused. While I admire my wife's good heart and love her desperately, business is business.

I don't give chances to incompetent people without any experience where there is already competition to work at my empire. But she insisted, so I agreed to give Prudence a chance because of her kid.

I've committed enough sins to last me a lifetime without adding someone losing their child in a custody battle because I didn't give them a chance.

It turns out my wife was right, and we make a perfect match. She's always on top of things and handles everything like a pro, although she's still skittish around me.

"No details."

"Got it, sir. I'll make all the changes on your schedule to fit in the meeting." She continues to type. "And a reminder that Dr. King has a gala to attend next week on Thursday so I blocked off your evening."

Phoenix got invited to give a speech to young doctor graduates with the highest grades at a gala, and while she refused at first, hating all the attention on her, she relented after some convincing from me. No one deserves that more than her, and I won't allow my past mistakes to hinder her present happiness. "Thank you, Pru."

I disconnect us and walk to the window, hooking my thumbs in my pants pockets while studying the scenery opening up to my view. The mesmerizing beauty of New York from such a height is almost blinding.

Countless cars drive in the traffic and pedestrians hastily walk to their destinations along with various activities happening on the street. I can almost smell the delicious food sold all over the place with endless queues as people get a five-minute break to grab a bite. Tourists snap pictures, influencers create content, and finally, someone who soaks up the beauty around them, moving here expecting everything to be sunshine and roses without knowing about the rather cruel thorns.

All the while, the city buzzes with energy and chaos that makes one thrive and crave to achieve things no matter what.

One of the reasons I never wanted to live anywhere else. Simply put, nothing feels like New York, the city of dreams where everything is possible.

Even atoning for horrendous sins that deserve no forgiveness.

My mind instantly goes to my wife, possessiveness washing over me and the need to follow her and wrap her in my protection drives me hard, urging me to shield her from the damage that fucking prison would do to her.

Yet I'm powerless to stop her from facing her greatest nightmare, the nightmare that wouldn't have ever happened if it wasn't for me.

She has to face them all alone once again without me by her side, but I think she'd hate my presence anyway. There is no hiding from our beginnings and my crimes in prison, no matter how we both wish it were different.

A part of her still resents me for my actions. She hides it well, but the way she grew cold in bed the minute Noah called is telling in itself.

I've made it my mission to study my wife. I know her every

emotion as if it were my own, attuned to her in ways I never thought possible to connect with another person. She's the air I breathe because living without her has no meaning to me.

However...

We never speak about the past. We closed the subject after that fateful night as if it never happened to us, and despite her therapy, she never opens up to me about it.

I've tried, but she just flat-out refuses any conversations. It's like a Pandora's box, she gives me no access to it as the things spilling from it might destroy our world.

I have no one but myself to blame, but this hopelessness doesn't let me rest as I've been many things in this life; however, hopeless?

Fucking never.

I'm a King. Whatever I want, I get, and what I've wanted for years is my wife.

I will protect her no matter what—even if it's from herself.

That's one of the reasons I pulled all the strings to get information on this current case. I'm watching it closely because the system cannot be trusted when it comes to her safety.

They failed us both once, and I won't give them a chance to do so again.

My power in this city is absolute, and I will not hesitate to use it against anyone daring to threaten my wife in any way, shape, or form.

She's mine, and what's mine shall always be cherished.

Loud voices outside snap me out of my thoughts. "You cannot enter without permission!" Prudence shouts, and my brow furrows when the door bursts open. In the window's reflection, I see a man stepping inside, wearing a three-piece suit and carrying a file in his hand. "I'll call security on you, sir," my secretary warns while the man just shrugs, his shoulder-length hair swaying a little under the strong A/C in the room, and he sends a cocky grin her way. "This is unacceptable."

"It won't take long. Call off your guard, King." Amusement dances on the edges of his tone, and I slowly spin around, coming face-to-face with one of the most assholish people I've ever met. Considering I've met a lot, that says something.

Rafael Wright.

"Learn some respect, Wright," I say instead of greeting him, and he just chuckles at this while Prudence blinks in confusion, her gaze darting between us. Her mind must be swirling, trying to remember where she might have seen him.

She makes it her mission to study anyone who does business with me or walks into my office, always being on top of things and providing me with all the needed information.

"Sir, I'm sorry," she says to me while still sending daggers Rafael's way. "He just barged in." She sighs in exasperation, clearly as stunned with his audacity as the rest of the corporate world. "He wouldn't stop!"

I bet he didn't. The fucker has little regard for rules and prefers to set his own.

"It's all right, Pru. You can leave us alone." She shifts her focus on me and shakes her head in disbelief, so I repeat, "It's all right."

She waits a minute and nods, although she still throws a glare his way. "I'll call security anyway. They'll be outside, so just let me know, sir." With this, she walks out and quietly closes the door behind her.

"Zachary King." He addresses me for the first time and, without invitation, grabs the chair opposite mine and drops on it, sitting down comfortably while his elbows rest on the chair's arms. "We finally meet. The Cruel King of New York whose wrath knows no mercy." He proclaims my title that no one dares to utter in my presence and clicks his tongue. "Sounds so pompous." He sighs dramatically as he scans me from head to toe. "I guess I expected something better."

Well, the time has come to teach the little shit a lesson.

"Disrespect my staff again, Rafael, and you will know why they call me the Cruel King." His brows rise. "You might behave as you please, but in my domain? My word is law. Next time, your ass will be thrown on the streets before you can open your fucking mouth." His lips twitch at this scenario. "What do you want?"

While we haven't been officially introduced to each other, I've seen him in action countless times as a newly hired attorney in Lauren's firm. Rafael graduated with honors earlier than most people due to the brilliance of his mind. His shark-like tendencies made him the most sought-after graduate in his class, so it wasn't a surprise Lauren trapped him in his clutches.

Simply put, the man makes offers no one can refuse. He probably promised Rafael fortune and fame, which is a temptation to every cub out there who wants to prove something to the world.

Rafael has been a menace ever since, going after anyone who so much as looked at their clients wrong. He's won every single case, quickly earning himself a reputation of his own.

I despise Lauren and his methods. That's why we always played in the opposite fields. So Rafael's visit means nothing but the announcement of an upcoming war.

"I'm here because of this." He throws the folder on the table where it lands with a loud smack, and I see the name Miller written on it.

The name rings a bell.

A company specializing in jewels experienced difficulties with its finances when its leadership changed. Their reputation was stellar, though, so a lot of companies didn't mind buying up shares when they went public with them. They first came to me for help, but I refused because even good staff won't save your ass if you have a shitty leader.

You don't build an empire out of charity.

"What the hell does this have to do with me?"

"We'll be suing you for unlawful acquiring of Miller's company." I freeze at this, because what? "Unless you will agree to settle. In this case, we will keep this information private."

Picking up the folder, I flip it open and scan the document, my eyes widening the more bullshit I read. According to this, I bought it for three hundred million and assigned Howard as my CEO while promising the Miller heir additional shares in my corporation. He'd also remain the main shareholder while still getting a salary from me. "You bought it but didn't keep your promise. Per clause fifty-six, the contract in this case is null and void, which makes your rule over their company illegal." A beat passes. "And we are allowed to sue in this case and go public with this information."

If the situation wasn't so serious, I would have laughed at this pile of crap, but instead, I throw it back at him. "I have no idea what you're talking about. I haven't bought this company, and if I did, I sure as fuck wouldn't have promised anything to Tim. Especially any shares in my company."

No one owns shares in the King empire but my father, me, and my kids. Even my father's stepchildren don't get any say. He set them up for life, but actually giving anyone but us reins to our family legacy?

Never.

In order to have access to what's ours, you have to be born a King.

"Yet your signature is on it," he points out and shakes the folder. "So I'm afraid your words mean nothing." He takes out a paper from it, placing it between us on the table. "Like I said, all this can be avoided. Just let's agree on a settlement." His green eyes flare in anticipation of his upcoming victory. His cheek twitches, and by how excitement almost pours from him, I know the man lives for this thrill.

Of cornering his opponents and leaving them no choice but to play to his tune in order to avoid what the powerful and wealthy are afraid of the most.

Social scrutiny that might cost them their fortune.

After all, every lawsuit is a gamble that might not end up being in your favor.

I quickly go over the document, and this time around don't stop the laughter slipping past my lips, which, in turn, makes Rafael narrow his eyes. Clearly, that's not the reaction he expected from me. "One billion settlement? Now I see why Tim lost his company. He's an idiot." Holding his gaze, I tear the paper in two and throw it away in the nearby trash. "I won't pay a single cent in settlement."

"If we take it to court, you might end up paying more. Not to mention, no one would want to do business with Zachary King afterward."

Too bad for him, I don't give a fuck what anyone thinks about me. "Any expertise would prove I haven't signed it."

He shrugs. "Maybe or maybe not. Howard signed it as a witness as well, and he has been overseeing the merger along with a couple of other things. We even have photos of him dining with Tim."

Fury glides through my veins and tastes bitter on my tongue at the obvious betrayal Howard has shown to my family by deciding to scheme against me, which explains the numbers on their earlier report.

Tim must have promised him the world in order for him to try to trap me.

Howard could be a dick sometimes, I just didn't think he would end up being a snake. And a stupid one at that.

My retribution would be absolute. Howard's name will be synonymous with disaster, despair, and devastation. No one will associate with him, or they'll be tainted.

His career and social life are over as far as I'm concerned.

No one goes against me and remains unscathed.

"Your entire case is bullshit."

"Is it?" he hisses through his teeth. "One might argue that Howard was an unwilling participant in all this. A working-class person used in order to get what you want." He cocks his head to the side, something crossing his face, but he masks it with indifference. "With the right strategy, he'll be the victim, and you'll be the villain in this story. All this legacy of yours"—he swirls his index finger in the air—"might be gone in a second." He takes out one more paper from the folder and sends it flying on the table, another copy of the settlement contract. "Sign it, Zachary. One billion won't even put a dent in your company."

I have to give it to him—no one dares to come to my office and order me around, but this little cub in the corporate world isn't afraid to face me.

Everything I've heard so far about this man, though, has shown that while he was a vicious hunter when it came to his prey, he never punished the innocent or went against his moral code in order to win.

A fair lawyer who used all the knowledge in his arsenal to bring the victories to his clients and never put his integrity in question.

So why is he risking it all now? Because no one can convince me he believes this bullshit. Only a crazy person or an idiot would ever sign a contract like that.

"What did he promise you?" He blinks in surprise at my question. "What did Lauren promise you if you win this case?" Lauren's had it out for me ever since I fired him almost a decade ago and hired Sebastian Hale as his replacement.

Although this was a part of my revenge plan, looking back at it now, I've made the best choice. I might hate Sebastian because he serves as a reminder that my wife loved someone before me and married him. The idea of her entertaining the forever with someone else just sends rage into every part of me, which makes me a hypocrite, considering my first wife was brutally murdered, a case that brought Phoenix and me together. So it wasn't like I never loved anyone but Phoenix, even if it sometimes feels like it due to the sheer intensity of my emotions.

However, the possessive beast living inside me gives no fuck about logic. It just despises Sebastian sharing any space with my wife, but thankfully, she isn't his biggest fan either.

Still, though, Sebastian is a damn good lawyer who always has my back despite our personal differences since he married my stepsister, and they recently welcomed a baby girl.

Needless to say, the family gatherings are awkward at best, but we try to keep it civil. His saving grace is his character and love for Felicia.

"Nothing. My clients come first. Always." His tone stays even. I don't miss how traces of emotion lace it, announcing he hides something from me.

"Your client is lying. And we both know it. This case sounds laughable."

"Does it?" He slaps the folder on the table's corner. "From my point of view, we have enough evidence to take it to court, and your chances of winning it are very slim. It might be news to you, Zachary, but a lot of people don't like you and wouldn't mind seeing your downfall."

My mouth twitches, and I sigh. "I don't know how I'll sleep at night with such knowledge." A beat passes, and I fire another question. "I thought you valued your integrity above anything else? It must have been a lie."

This time, his eyes flash with anger, and his hold on the folder tightens while he clenches his teeth before calming enough to reply.

Ah, the little cub doesn't like when his ethic is questioned. Too bad for him, the corporate world isn't fair. We use all the weapons available to us in order to reach our goals. "My client has a stellar reputation and is deeply loved by his community. He's a man with a dream who always wished for the best when it comes to his people. And they got screwed over by a billionaire."

We share a long stare with each other. Maybe if we had met under different circumstances, I would have respected the guy, but he decided to come to my den and threaten my empire.

There can never be respect after that.

Splaying my palms open on the table and leaning forward, I drop my voice a few octaves while anger laces my tone, leaving no room to doubt where my emotions lie. "You want a war with me, Rafael? Make sure you're ready for the consequences."

He slowly rises from his seat and comes closer, absolute determination written on his features. "Oh, I'm ready. And I've never engaged in wars I can't win."

Either he's too naïve for his own good and truly believes Tim or he has an agenda and a goal in mind worthy of him to risk everything, his career included.

As talented as he is, he's still new to the scene, and his newfound career won't survive the blow this court case would do to him.

Lauren must have known that and still fed him to the wolves, which just proves that he has always been an asshole.

"Very well," I say, straightening up and flicking the settlement agreement on the floor while our gazes clash. "I shall see you in court. From now on, you'll speak to my lawyer."

"It doesn't need to be complicated, Zachary."

"Mr. King," I correct him and motion with my hand to the door. "Get the hell out, Mr. Wright. You aren't allowed on my properties, effective immediately."

"I'll win this case, *Zachary*." He emphasizes my name and winks at me before turning around and going to the door.

"What he had promised you, he has no intention of giving to you. Otherwise, he wouldn't have assigned this case as a bargaining chip and a test." His movements halt for a split second before he resumes his walk. "Think hard about this, Rafael. This case will be a defining moment in your career."

"Yes. My victory will be a defining moment in my career indeed." With this, he leaves, shutting the door loudly behind him, and I shake my head.

This kid will bring me a lot of problems before he realizes he plays for the wrong team, and it's a shame that such talent will go to waste. Once it's all said and done, his best shot will be working as a nonprofit lawyer because no one will want him in their firm.

I don't get the chance to dwell on it much, though, because my phone rings, and I pick up when I see my head of security's name, Zeke, flashing on the display. "Yes?" I gave him two hours to get all the necessary information about my wife's case so I could be prepared to face all the shit with her.

And the information he shares with me sends rage through my system.

CHAPTER FOUR

"I've never dreamed about a prince.
Everything I got, I earned with hard work.
Funny how destiny works, though, right?
Because I ended up with a king.
And a cruel one at that."
Phoenix

P hoenix
  Turning all my emotions off and locking away my internal turmoil, I will all my self-control and experience to let me withstand this without losing my shit.

My professionalism and skills are legendary because, unlike a lot of people, I know how to dissociate myself from the situation.

"Miranda." I address her, ignoring her earlier comment so she wouldn't think she has power over me.

Ironically, her greeting already answered my question. She isn't mentally unstable and shows the signs of psychopathy, which only worsens her case.

Walking farther inside, I drop the folder on the table with a loud smack. "It's nice to meet you." Her brows shoot up at this, and confusion crosses her face for a second before she quickly masks it with indifference.

As someone who spent almost four years behind bars, I know better than anyone that everyone treats you like shit between these walls. Any sign of humanity would work in my favor and shift her toward my direction.

"Is it?" She grins, flashing her white teeth at me.

"Yes." Pushing the chair out, scraping the legs against the floor and making her wince, I sit opposite her, making sure our bodies do not touch. My eyes remain glued on her and hold her stare. "After all, you requested my presence. I have to say I'm intrigued." The words taste bitter on my tongue because I feel no such thing. However, to determine how deprived her mind truly is, I need to see her reaction to my various statements to have the clear analysis.

She clicks her tongue. "You aren't a good liar, Phoenix." She laughs, although it lacks any humor. "You probably don't play poker."

Mentally, I note that she's good at reading people's emotions, so there is a high probability she also possesses the skills that allow her to manipulate anyone as she sees fit.

What is manipulation if not knowing which buttons to press or what to give to a certain person in order to achieve what you want?

"You're right." Pleasure flickers in her eyes at the praise, so we can also add her narcissistic tendencies to the profile. Maybe this meeting can end sooner than I expected, considering in the first three minutes, she almost fully convinced me she fits the psychopath criteria. "Lying is a skill life hasn't granted me." A beat passes. "However, I have other talents."

"Yes. I've heard. That's why I wanted you. Nothing but the best for me." She drums her fingers on the table, bringing attention to their rather miserable state as the nails are almost nonexistent on them. She must have bitten them all off. "It's my life's motto."

I open her file and briefly glance at it. "Did this motto help you climb the social ladder?" Her drumming stops at my question, her fingers hovering over the surface while she looks to the side. I study every little detail on her face, trying to determine her thoughts.

Miranda grew up in a small town and a poor household. The family struggled to survive due to their father's alcoholism, which resulted in him beating his wife daily until he passed out and died from a heart attack.

Things got better, but then their mother once again picked up an asshole for herself, and he kicked the kids off the farm, leaving them on the streets to fend for themselves.

Her sister married the pastor's son, birthing him ten kids before they joined some kind of cult and were never heard from again. Miranda, though, ran away to the big city at the age of fifteen and joined a modeling agency. Due to her connections in the fashion world, she met her husband, Matt, three years later.

"I had no choice. Mama loved the dick more than her daughters. She gave us a fifty-dollar bill each and told us to get the fuck out. She didn't like to upset Johny, and our existence alone annoyed him." Judging by the rage lacing her tone, she hates her mother and hasn't forgiven her for this, despite the woman being dead for ten years. Then again, forgiveness is not a given right, and certainly being blood-related to someone doesn't make them special.

"You must have been very angry with him." I wait a beat before adding, "After what your father subjected you to, you probably expected better from your mom's new man." According to the file, Johny was quite a respected citizen in their neighborhood.

Her early experience with men would explain why she might have pent-up anger at them and how it could have escalated to rage with her husband, although such cases are extremely rare. Usually, for the trauma to debut itself like that would require the husband to display abusive behavior that would, in turn, push the little girl inside her to retaliate.

She rolls her eyes, leaning back on her chair and resuming her drumming. "Daddy was a saint compared to Johny. I mean, he'd hit us here and there, but usually, he'd shut up right after we'd give him the booze." She shrugs. "I don't consider him a monster."

It isn't rare for the victims of child abuse to paint their parents in a better light over the years in order to heal the bleeding wounds inside them. Plus, the stepfather kind of replaced the abuser, and since he kicked them out of the only home they knew, he ultimately transformed into a bigger monster, and they could have redirected all the anger at their father on to him.

My mind swirls with all these possibilities, and I fire off my next question. "But Johny was a monster?"

She nods. "Johny loved to spy on us in the bathroom and bedroom. Sometimes he'd even grab us, and when we would object, he'd get angry." Her drumming becomes more erratic, and her foot taps on the floor while rage fills me at the implication here. That asshole worked in the school for thirty years before passing away a decade ago. "Once we were alone in the house and he ripped my shirt off and threw me on the couch, pressing his body to mine." She digs her fingertips on the table and slowly clenches her hands into fists. "He covered my mouth and told me to be quiet as he gets his fill." Her eyes become glazed, her voice dropping a few octaves. "He then proceeded to bite me until I bled before raping me. Over and over again. No amount of crying helped." Her breathing speeds up, and she leans down in order to rub her neck as if still feeling him touching it. "He told me over and over again it was my fault. I tempted him, so he acted on his urges." She mimics his voice. "All these fucking short skirts, you practically begged for it." She bangs her fists on the table, rattling it. "And he laughed. All the time laughed and asked me to tell him I liked it. He wouldn't end it until I said it." She finishes on a loud exhale.

This is not going where I thought it would. The only reason I even started talking about her past was to open her up to me and establish an emotional connection before going in for the kill and interrogating her about the children.

Contrary to what most people believe, you don't start conversations with psychopaths by saying, *Hey! Heard you killed someone. Where are the kids? Confess or else!*

Everything is a game to them, and we have to play it if we want to win it. Without understanding their motivations, we are doomed to fail. They exist in a different reality where compassion, mercy, and empathy are just empty words they cannot understand. Instead, they live for the suffering they inflict on others.

And the worst part about it?

They won't hesitate to use any weapon available in their arsenal in order to bring as much destruction as possible.

Before I can comment on what she's told me, her laughter reverberates through the space, her entire body shaking from it. She throws her head back, such joy etched on her features, one might think she got the news of a lifetime. "Is this what you expected to hear from me?" she finally asks, grinning at me. "A sad story that led to my downfall and killing my beloved husband for no reason?" She shakes her head. "Ah and you ate it all up. Spoiler alert, I lied. Johny was just an asshole who didn't want to deal with all our drama. But it was a nice story, wasn't it?" she asks, waiting for my reaction.

My face stays blank. However, I notice how her hands still shake slightly and the drumming resumes once again while she keeps her focus on me, craving my disappointment, so I give her the exact opposite.

Praise.

"Brilliant acting, Miranda." The grin slips from her lips, and she frowns at me, her mood souring instantly when I clap several times. "You could have fooled me." I rest my elbows on the table. "So I guess your mom kicking you out was a blessing? It brought you to New York where you met Matt." I take out the photo of her husband from the file and place it between us, the one with him lying on the floor covered in blood from all his wounds with a knife stabbed in his heart. "Your husband."

She drops her gaze to the photo, her lips curling a little bit before she raises it back on me, seemingly not interested in studying her victim.

No displays of fascination with her "art" or the desire to seek pleasure from it chasing some unknown high; however, she shows no signs of regret or remorse either.

She's rather indifferent, and I don't like it as it complicates things even further.

"Yes. Matt was the prince everyone dreams of." How does she keep her tone so even if she killed him in such a rage? "He swept me off my feet, and the rest is history."

Okay.

Glancing at my watch, I realize we've already spent thirty minutes on it, and the clock is ticking. I need to speed things up because we haven't moved an inch on this investigation. Instead, she plays in circles with me without stating her agenda either.

Why is she stalling the process?

"You got noticed by his father's modeling agency. They hired you at the age of sixteen. Your beauty attracted a lot of companies, and due to your talent, you became quite famous." Nothing on worldwide level but enough for her name to mean something. "Two years later, you met the owner's son, and you guys fell in love. Is that correct?"

"Yes. They called me Cinderella. He proposed two months later. According to everyone, I was lucky." She cocks her head to the side. "We share that in common, don't we?"

Oh, she's good.

"You had a name and a career when you met him. Arguably he got lucky too, didn't he?" I shift back the conversation to her, rebutting her attempt to direct it at me and try to manipulate me into playing her game. "Not to mention that he was thirty. Way too old for you."

She bites on her lower lip, studying me for several moments, then sighs. "Some people said that, but I didn't mind. He was nice, caring, and promised me the world."

"Did he deliver on his promises?"

"Sometimes and sometimes he failed. Over the years, his failures outnumbered his promises."

"Is that why you killed him?"

The atmosphere changes instantly after my question, coldness sinking into every bone while her demeanor shifts from amused to anger, and she pulls at her wrists as if wanting to free herself. "You have no idea what you're talking about!" She shouts the last part and kicks her chair, pulling at the restrains once again while rage pours from her, and at this moment, I think she wishes to stab me as well.

I raise my finger in the air, a sign to Noah to stay put and not inter-fere with my process because I have the situation under control.

"I wouldn't kill that fucker just because he forgot our anniversary," she spits and then clenches his photo in her palm.

"Why did you kill him then?"

"Because he deserved it!"

"What did he do to deserve it?"

She opens her mouth, ready to shout something, when she blinks and drops the photo. Another smile shapes her mouth, and I know she went back to her cocoon, her mood shifting like the wind. "Wouldn't you like to know?" She motions with her chin toward my file. "Don't you have our relationship history in there?"

"No. I have nothing besides some bullet points. I prefer for you to tell me if you want. What I do know, though..." I snatch another photo, this time of three girls laughing into the camera in the flower field and holding ice creams in their hands. I slide it to her. "Is that you have three beautiful daughters. Catriona, fifteen; Kayla, ten; and finally Peggy, five. Daughters you both loved and adored."

"Ah, my girls," she whispers, rubbing her fingers over the photo, and a single tear slides down her cheek, landing on Catriona's face. She covers her mouth with her other hand while continuing to stare at her daughters. "My beautiful girls." Her voice trembles, and she exhales heavily, gazing at them with so much love it astonishes me.

Psychopaths are capable of attachments, obsessions even. But love? No. Never that.

In fact, most of them have no idea what it is because they've never had it, so they despise it and wish to destroy it.

"Where are they, Miranda?" I ask softly, and she scrunches her eyes, shaking her head while still rubbing their image. "Where are the girls? Are they alive?" After a beat, she nods, thank God. We still have time then. "Where are they?" I repeat, and she grabs the photo, kissing it before sliding it to me. Our gazes clash, hers hollow once again as she wipes away her tears. "Miranda, where are the girls?"

"I won't tell you. Not until you figure it out." She laughs, and the sound grates on my nerves. "Why do you think I requested you on this case?" When I stay silent, she elaborates. "You know better than anyone what it's like to sit here"—she points at her seat and then swirls her finger in the air—"while the entire world judges you. When no one believes you and thinks you're a cold-hearted monster who should die."

Even though I know it's a ploy and a dangerous territory, I fire back nevertheless. "I haven't killed anyone." Maybe when she discloses why she needs me on this case, I'll have a better understanding of what she's trying to achieve.

She isn't denying killing Matt, so what is the agenda here?

"No. But the system failed you. And it will fail my girls unless you figure out why I killed Matt." I freeze at this, and she taps on their picture. "Because if you find them before you figure it out? They might as well be dead. I will not subject my daughters to it." She covers their image with her splayed palm. "I might be cruel, but death is easier than living in a nightmare."

Oh no.

She's mad and unstable after all. Unfortunately, her daughters will have to pay the ultimate price for that.

During my vast experience, I've encountered several cases where madness consumed a person so much they truly believed their hideous crimes were justified. In this, they saved their family from some illusive danger. Their delusions destroyed any rational thinking and pushed them to do the unthinkable.

The worst kind of criminals are the ones who don't even comprehend they've committed a crime. In their eyes, they are heroes and not monsters.

And how do you explain to a hero that their actions transformed them into a creature they rebelled against in the first place?

"Tell me why you killed him, and I will do everything in my power to help you. I give you my word." Not for her, for these three girls who still need a mother despite everything.

We stop being children the minute we become orphans. That's the kind of loneliness nothing and no one can fulfill as the pain attaches itself to your heart and never lets you forget.

My life is a true testament to that.

"No." She leans back in her seat, gripping the edge of the table so hard her knuckles turn white. "You have three days counting today to figure it out, or my daughters will die." Panic and fear envelop me whole, my heartbeat speeding up at the outrageous statement that tells me we are in more trouble than we originally thought.

If she can control the lives of her children from prison, she has an accomplice, and the plan has been in motion for some time to think about all routes. The little ones might just not survive this sick game of hers!

Several flashbacks assault me at once—the honking of a car and the maniac voice of a serial killer who, for some reason, thought I owed them and should help them and pay for the sins only they knew about.

Because I spoke to them on some level, and they felt righteous to shatter my life into tiny pieces until nothing but despair remained.

Only sheer will allows me to keep my voice steady when I ask, "And if I refuse, then what?" If she wishes to play the justice system that she clearly doesn't trust, she must have a plan B in motion in order to prolong this as long as possible.

I'm no coward, but I'll gladly give this case to someone else, salvaging my soul in the process. However, destiny isn't that kind to me because her answer almost makes me rip my hair out for how nonchalant it sounds.

"That shall be it. The fate of my daughters lies in your hands, Phoenix. And the clock is ticking." She snaps her fingers. "Ticktock. Ticktock. Ticktock." She bursts out laughing and cocks her head to the side, winking at me. "We're playing a dangerous game, and the strongest one will win."

"The lives of your daughters are nothing but a game to you?"

Something crosses her features, but it's gone so quickly, I have no chance to examine it. "They'll understand. They know Mommy loves them." She rolls her lips and continues, "I gave all the clues you need today. I'll give you more tomorrow." A beat passes as we stare at each other. "We're done for today."

The message is clear—she enjoys toying with me and my mind. For whatever reason, she seeks a connection with me because, in her damaged mind, we are alike.

Kindred spirits who got punished for a crime we didn't commit except, in her case, she hasn't committed a crime only in *her* eyes.

"It's a great plan, Miranda. Cunning and cruel with a splash of confusion." She grins at this, and I get up, gathering the pictures and files. "Except in all your planning, you missed one crucial thing."

Her brow rises. "What?"

"For it to work, I have to agree to be a willing participant in this game of yours. And last time I checked, I desire no such thing." For the first time, fear flashes in her eyes. Her hands clench once again, and she sits up straight. "But maybe that doesn't matter to you anyway? As you said, then it is fate. A fate that will be unbearably cruel to you." She swallows hard at this and opens her mouth to say something, but I beat her to it, hammering my point home.

"If your daughters die, you will have to live with the consequences of your choices, forever trapped here for eternity. And trust me, every second in this place feels like an endless hell. Especially when you lose a child." Despite my efforts, my voice hitches on the last part because nothing brings me greater agony than when I thought I had lost my baby girl. I place my hand on my heart while still holding her gaze, speaking to the gentle part inside her that clearly loves her kids. "You carried them under your heart for nine months, you watched them grow, and you love them. Are you ready to live in a world where they're no more because of *you*?" Tears form in her eyes.

She erupts in manic laughter, the disgusting sound echoing through the space and coating it in misery and anger so strong I can almost touch it. "Don't you dare play your psychological games with me, Phoenix. They won't work. Besides, everyone knows your reputation." She taps on the table. "People here talk even after all these years."

Chilliness rushes down my spine, but I just crack a smile at this, not giving her the upper hand. "Oh, do they?"

"Yes. You're too compassionate for your own good." She sighs dramatically, and I mentally prepare myself for whatever blow she'll aim my way because I dared to rub salt on her gaping wound, which scared her. And what does a scared wild animal do when confronted?

It attacks.

"I mean, you married a man who hurt you so badly. Still have physical scars on your body, don't you? A souvenir of sorts after his order. An order eager inmates didn't mind listening to since he paid enough money for it." She lowers her voice to a whisper and leans as close as the chains allow her. "If I were you, I'd kill him at the very first opportunity. But you're so weak you've forgiven him instead." Her upper lip curls. "I'd rather live with my consequences than ever choose a man who did what your husband did to you."

Her words hang between us, their weight and hideousness urging me to plop back on my seat to face my worst fears in my soul. The fears the press and everyone else love to speculate on while the faded scars reflecting in the mirror remind me every day about the past.

The past that all the magical present cannot wipe away...cannot fix...cannot heal.

I forgot one crucial thing when it comes to inmates and prison. It's a wild jungle where predators search for a way to tear your flesh and feed on your misery. It temporarily numbs the misery that destroyed them from the inside.

Like junkies searching for a fix.

Except all it ever leaves behind is hollowness bordering on insanity.

"I'm sorry, Miranda," I finally say in the stretched silence, and she furrows her brow, a deep crease forming on her forehead. "I'm sorry that a man hurt you at a young age. It wasn't your fault. And you telling him that you liked it so he'd finally end it didn't mean consent to the horrible thing he had done to you." She freezes, her short nails digging into her skin while tears fill her eyes once again. Although her breathing becomes labored this time, I know my suspicion was true. She lied about Johny, but she spoke about a real experience, an experience that must have been a crucial moment in her life. The change in her pitch was a clue for me. "No one deserves what happened to you. I'm sorry you had to experience it."

Her inhales and exhales gradually grow louder. She sinks her front teeth into her lower lip so hard she draws blood. "Get out," she hisses with tears streaming down her face. When I remain, she screams, "I said get out! Get out! Get out! Get out!"

I step back from the table, and with one last glance at her, I go to the door and press the keypad. The minute it opens, I get back into the room where two men gape at me. The correctional officer has the decency to lower his gaze and pretend to be busy with his notes, but Noah does no such thing.

Instead, he meets my silent fury head-on and nods as if agreeing to whatever cursing word I want to throw his way. "Congratulations, Noah. I'm playing a twisted game with a serial killer once again."

"Phoenix—"

"Save it!" I snap, and he shuts his mouth, although by how his cheek twitches, he isn't used to getting orders. Instead, he dishes them out. "I need all the files you have on this family. History, connections, and whatever else I might need to understand her clues. Also, family photos, particularly with her in it."

"They're bringing it to our headquarters as we speak."

If he thinks I will go there, then he has another think coming! That bureau witnessed my emotional outburst all these years ago, and I won't go there again. Besides, he screwed up, so he can damn well now dance to my tunes!

"Splendid. Send it to my home. And a little bit of advice? Make sure to avoid my husband in the foreseeable future. Trust me, he'll want your head on a silver platter."

"Phoenix—"

Without further ado, I grab my things. With my head held high, I walk off alone, ignoring all the hissing sounds and women staring at me.

This is my past and not my present or future. I've lived through a nightmare and survived, which means I won't let anyone touch my peace or my family.

Try as I might, though...

Miranda's words echo in my mind and scrape at old wounds, forcing them to bleed again as resentment fills my soul.

Maybe because deep down...they mirror mine.

We can forgive and move on.

But we can never truly forget.

CHAPTER FIVE

"When life grants you a second chance...
You take it and hold on to it with both of your hands.
Because if you don't and lose it again?
You didn't deserve it in the first place."
Zachary

Zachary
The tires screech on the concrete when I stop the car abruptly, my hands gripping the steering wheel. I get out right in time to see Phoenix running out from the prison, her coat flapping in different directions. She hectically shoves the papers in her handbag, clutching it tightly to her chest.

The wind whooshes around me, sinking cold into my skin. I'm covered only by my shirt because I left the office in a rush, forgetting even my suit jacket.

After Zeke gave me a full report on the case and disclosed how the inmate wanted my wife specifically, I told Prudence to cancel all my appointments and arrange for the nanny to pick up the kids because I knew this would shake my wife.

And on the way here, rage filled my every cell, polluting my blood and mind with one desire.

Vengeance against those who dared to use my wife in their game and risk her life.

No one hurt her and lived, no fucking one, and there will be hell to pay for everyone involved.

She freezes when she sees me rushing toward her, her movements halting, and a raspy breath escapes her before it turns into a sob. She drops her bag and runs to me. I catch her in a second, wrapping my arms tightly around her.

Her palms are trapped between our chests, and she grips my shirt hard, crumpling the cloth in her hold while she hides her face. I hope she seeps all the strength she needs from me at this moment.

Near the place that ruined her beyond repair, all the hideous crimes committed against her are forever imprinted in her mind and carved in her soul. It's impossible to forget the cruelty of such caliber.

I should know since I was the one who ordered the events that forever changed both of our lives.

Gazing ahead, I look at the prison where she spent almost four years of her life, hated and betrayed by everyone from her ex-husband to her work colleagues who believed what every one of us believed back then.

That she was a murderer who deserved no pity when, in fact, it was all a serial killer who made her a pawn in a deadly game.

I feel wetness on my chest, and I still, closing my eyes and despising myself right now more than ever because if it weren't for me, my wife wouldn't be in such pain right now.

And I'll be atoning for her pain for the rest of my life.

"Phoenix," I say gently, palming her head and leaning back until our gazes clash. Her dark eyes fill with tears and despair while anguish blankets them, speaking to me about how much strength it actually cost her to come here and face it all head-on. "I'm here, darling." I wipe away the tear falling down her cheek, and she sighs, leaning into my touch when I press a kiss to her forehead, lingering a bit. "This time around, I'm here." She winces at my words and jerks, wanting to escape my embrace, but my hold on her stops her, leaving her no room to move. "Phoenix."

"This time," she whispers hollowly, her voice sending invisible arrows at me and deepening the hurt intensifying in my system. The beast inside me roars at the idea of her hurting, and my inability to truly help her at this moment because I'm a part of her nightmare. "Zach." She splays her palms on my chest and glides them upward until she circles my neck, stepping closer to me once again, and we share a breath. "I hate this."

Although her tone stays even, the weird notes in them send an alarm through me. It feels as if she's miles away from here, barely holding on to her sanity, and if she could...

She'd run away from me too.

Which, in turn, makes me hug her even tighter, my fingers digging into her waist while we stare at one another. Possessiveness washes over me, my eyes caressing her beautiful face and wishing I could light it up and remove the pain from it.

If I could, I'd whisk her far, far away where no one could find her. I'd cherish her like my most prized possession, away from the fucking world that cannot leave us alone and forget our past.

A past that's a taboo between us as well, the silent axe that hangs over our heads, ready to drop on us if we only dare to rip the bandage covering up the bleeding wounds.

She played the part so well I started to believe that maybe it truly didn't matter to her anymore, and she put it all behind her, blooming in her new world and our marriage while returning to her old self and thriving in her career.

Except I was a fool who wished for the impossible.

Guilt still eats at me every single day and makes me think about the unresolved past. How could I have expected my wife to move on from the experience that scarred her for life?

Literally and figuratively.

Right now, I want nothing more than to drag her to our house and lock her in our room where I can strip her naked and kiss all the scars again, worshipping her body with mine and bringing her pleasure so she'd know I love her with everything in me.

I live and breathe for her, even if a part of her would always hate me.

That's okay, though.

Whatever hatred she feels toward me...can't match the one I feel for myself.

"It's all right, darling," I tell her, and she closes her eyes. I capture her mouth with mine, licking over her lips and nudging for entrance as our tongues entwine in a kiss.

Swallowing her moan in my throat, I probe deep, staking my claim all over again so she has no doubts who she belongs to no matter what.

Fuck anything and anyone who thinks they can stand between us.

My wife is mine. And I will kill anyone daring to think otherwise.

The kiss grows hotter, her nails clawing my nape. Moving my hands upward, I grab her shoulders and forcefully push us apart as we both gulp for breath, and she blinks at me in confusion. "We're in a public place, darling." A ghost of a smile appears on her face, although it doesn't reach her stunning eyes. "Turning me on here isn't a good idea."

"Everything I do turns you on."

Well, that's true.

"Can't argue with that. Let's go home where we can talk." She grimaces. However, it has to be done. I might not be a psychiatrist, but even I know she wanted to use our passion to forget about the turmoil her soul is currently experiencing.

We've run away from the past long enough. The time has come for us to uncover all the pain and finally let us both heal. Otherwise, we'll go insane.

Every illusion, even the most mesmerizing one, can break with the right weapon, and I do not wish for anyone ever to threaten my marriage.

Even Phoenix herself.

"I think..."

Whatever she wants to say dies on her lips when we hear the gates open, and rage comes at me tenfold when I see Noah strolling to us, determination written all over his features. I finally find an outlet for all the pent-up frustration within me. "Get in the car."

"Zach—"

"Get in the car, darling. I'll get your bag." We share a long stare, and she sighs, knowing full well that fighting me over this is useless.

She tamed the beast of my constant rage, but she didn't change me. And as such, I would do whatever I deem necessary in order to protect what's mine.

"Be nice," she warns, and I chuckle although it lacks any humor.

"I've never been nice to anyone but you, darling."

She shakes her head at me, rises on her toes, and kisses me on the chin before doing as I asked. Once she's securely inside the car, I focus my full attention on Noah.

"Zach." He greets me as I go to him. "I should have expected you."

Instead of replying, I speed up my pace and push my elbow back. Delivering a blow straight to his face, I make him stumble back and mutter, "Fuck," under his breath as he holds his nose, the blood seeping through his fingers.

The sight of that doesn't diminish the inferno ready to burn everyone around me, especially the fucking agent who brought my wife to all this mess using deceit.

"I'm an FBI agent, King. I can sue your ass for it!"

The energy around us changes in spades, creating a rather dark and gloomy atmosphere where only darkness exists, giving us full rein to display our vices. "You go ahead, Noah. We both know I have the means and power to go unscratched from it. And I wonder if people in high rank would have approved of what you just did." Resentment flashes in his face, and that's all the answer I need. "What were you thinking when you called my wife to help you with this case?" I ask him while he straightens up, pressing on his nose, probably checking to see if it's broken.

He shouldn't worry. I didn't use all my force.

Yet.

Just enough for him to be in pain for the near future, so he'd think twice before involving my wife in his schemes again.

"She's the best of the best. And if anyone can help us find these children, it's her."

"Don't give me this bullshit excuse. She isn't a profiler. All she has to do as a psychiatrist is determine whether Miranda was sane or not when she committed a crime." He clenches his teeth and takes out a handkerchief from his pocket, covering his nose with it. The white cloth quickly soaks with blood as we glare at one another. "You want her because she's the perfect bait, isn't she?"

"Zach—"

"I thought about this on the way here. All the facts point at it. Miranda killed her husband, yet you found no fingerprints on the knife. She called the cops on herself two hours after she murdered him and then admitted to everything just like that." I snap my fingers. "She was so compliant, the cops didn't even bother checking her story on the children. They didn't expect her to all of a sudden turn into some kind of mastermind." My laughter echoes in the air. "Because such masterminds never give themselves up easily."

"She requested Phoenix. That's the only reason. We had no ulterior motive." His tone stays even; however, something else coats it, letting me know my initial suspicions were correct, and he's lying. "We need to find her children. That's our top priority. In case you don't know, we're on a clock here."

Oh, yes. I do know the rules.

Except I wasn't born yesterday.

"No. If it was about her request, you would have brought in your best agent on the case and tried to crack her. You know better than anyone else that giving a psychopath or a serial killer what they want only feeds their sadistic desires and makes them prolong the game. They get off on the power, and that's one thing you do not give them once you catch them."

He wipes his nose, wincing several times, and then smirks at me. "What makes you an expert on the subject all of a sudden?"

I shrug, putting my hands in my pants pockets. "Well, when justice fails you, you learn everything about serial killers and their habits. Came in handy when you didn't catch the unsub who killed my first love and almost cost me the love of my life. Wouldn't you say?"

He opens his mouth to argue some more but then closes it, a muscle twitching on his cheek while we stare at one another, both of us exuding power. It doesn't work, though, since we're both used to one thing.

Complete dominance. And while Noah might win almost every argument in his workplace, I don't give a fuck about him or his profession.

I respected him for how he handled most situations; however, he had lost all my respect with this one decision and might have gained himself an enemy for life.

Using any member of my family as bait, let alone my wife, is an unforgivable sin in my eyes.

Finally, he exhales heavily while pinching his nose again and tilting his head back, trying to control the bleeding. "Okay, you have a right to be upset with the law and me. However, your past situation has nothing to do with the current case." My brows rise, and he rolls his eyes. "Yes. This case has a lot of variables that we cannot understand. For a cold-blooded murderer, she doesn't fit the profile. But there is no one else to blame. And she isn't emotional either when it comes to her husband." A cold wind whooshes over us, the frigid air nipping on my skin making Noah burrow deeper into his coat, still holding the hand-kerchief. "She only mentioned Phoenix after we tried to find the kids. Somehow it's vitally important to her, and we need to find them before it's too late."

"In other words, you've reached a dead end."

He squeezes his nose one last time and then crumples the handker-chief while I notice several prison guards looking at us and even step-ping closer, probably wanting to hear what we're talking about. I imagine that's the highest entertainment they get to witness in their surveillance job. "She has an accomplice. She admitted this much to Phoenix."

"I hear a *but* at the end of that sentence."

"My team has a theory that's not supported by the head detective on the case. We think there is a chance Miranda hasn't committed the crime but is covering it up for someone else."

I mull over his words, thinking back on everything I've read. "You think the eldest daughter killed her father? And Miranda's protecting her?"

He nods. "Yes. The girl is fifteen and has a history of getting into trouble in and out of school. According to her best friend, her father wasn't happy with her behavior lately and planned to send her to boarding school."

Ah, the favorite punishment of the richest. I should know since my father sent me abroad in order to protect me, only it destroyed our relationship for decades as a result.

Still, though, what he says makes little sense to me. "Why would she need Phoenix on the case, then?" Besides the woman playing a game, would she want to risk it if her child's freedom was on the line?

They come from a wealthy family. She would have been better off sending them somewhere and letting the dust settle, and by that, I mean her trial before they could return and act as if they have no idea what is going on.

"We think Catriona might have accidentally killed her father."

"Wasn't he tortured for days?"

"Yes. Which would explain her angry outbursts at school and her moodiness. They also had three birds in the last ten years, and all of them died due to some kind of accident." I still at this information, uneasiness rushing through me just thinking about a kid harming an animal. This would mean... "She might have shown an early sign of sadistic behavior. And when she finally found a human flesh to let her anger out on..." He trails off, and I understand him at once.

The kid tortured her father for days, and when Miranda found out, she could have delivered that last blow to the heart to end his torture and then save her daughter from the law.

I'd hardly call this accidental.

Try as I might, though, something feels off about this, especially with Noah's voice being so calm and formal, yet...hesitation laces it while he drills his stare into me, gauging my reaction to what he might say next.

"That's the best-case scenario theory, isn't it?" He sighs while my rage hits me with full force once again.

They deal with such cases all the time. It might be horrible for people to imagine a child committing a hideous crime, but for a profiler who sees chopped limbs and vices every single day? Nothing to get bothered about.

Or succumb to deceit in order to get a person on their team to catch the killer.

Unless...

"What's the worst-case scenario theory, Noah?" He stays silent, clenching his fists, and looks to the side. My voice booms around us while clouds gather above us and thunder shakes the sky, the nature's mood fitting my own. "What is it?"

Soft footsteps from behind me alert me that, despite my request, my wife didn't keep her ass in the car and has listened to our entire conversation. She speaks up in the monotone that tells me she has placed herself in the cocoon of her own creation, serving as a shield from the outside world and the upcoming storm that might destroy everything in its wake.

Including us.

"Worst-case scenario is that the accomplice is, in fact, a psychopath who killed her husband, made her watch, and then forced her to take the blame for it by blackmailing her with the safety of her children." My eyes widen at this, and I glance at Noah, who blows out a breath, running his fingers through his hair. "Which means the unsub has left her instructions to follow, and she would play the part because she's terrified." A beat passes. "The kids are not safe. They're in danger."

"Psychopaths aren't known for their patience, especially when it comes to anyone or anything disturbing their comfort. The youngest is five years old. Sooner rather than later, the unsub's control will snap, and the consequences will be severe." Noah adds grimly, "That's why I had no choice but to involve you two."

"Why can't she just tell the cops the truth?" As soon as the question is out of my mouth, the answer pops in my head. "The unsub is watching her." And if he or she has the means to put such surveillance on an inmate and conversations she has with the agents and police officers?

They're smart and powerful.

And smart and powerful serial killers bring nothing but destruction and death along with misery and tragedy.

· · ·

Unsub

The classical music echoes through the space mingling with the TV located on the wall above the microwave blasting the evening news. The stern presenter speaks, "She still hasn't spoken about the whereabouts of her children." The girls' pictures appear on the screen one after another, replacing the presenter while she continues talking, her fucking indifferent tone grating on my nerves. As it lets me know she doesn't give a shit about these children.

She just craves a new sensation that will make viewers watch their program all day long.

I snarl, grabbing the remote and turning the damn thing off right before she announces, "If any of you have any information about these girls, please call this number."

Sighing, I grip the counter and lean backward, resting my head between my shoulder blades, allowing the music to glide over my skin akin to the softest silk and calm the never-ending screams that ring in my ears every single day.

Just temporary numbness that lasts minutes and sometimes seconds, so I cherish classical music above any other sound in this world.

Music is a poetry written with notes that requires no words.

I frown, though, when another sound pierces through my mesmerizing fog, the barely audible whimper turning into a sob. "I'm hungry," she says, louder than she should. Then I hear someone shushing her and probably covering her mouth with her hand.

I told them all not to disturb me, not that it has done any good. If the older one knows how to follow instructions, then the other two are just whining messes who constantly need something from food to the washroom.

I straighten up, huffing in disgust at their weakness and inability to withstand a little discomfort.

These spoiled princesses grew up with love and wealth. They'd have died if they had to live through my experiences.

Where basic necessities were a privilege and not a given right, and

I sure as fuck knew better than to whine because fists and blood followed it.

Among other things.

"I'm hungry, Catriona," Peggy whispers once again before her next words are muffled through her older sister's palm.

Truth be told, I sometimes wonder if Catriona has any emotions at all. She's kept her mouth shut unless it was to shush her siblings or murmur gentle words into their ears, temporarily calming them down.

Impressive, though, she still wet her pants on the way here and had to change into my sweatpants all while holding back tears and blushing brighter than a red light.

Highly disappointing to watch. All things considered, I value bravery while cowardliness inspires nothing but disgust in me.

Picking up a tray from the counter, I open one of the shelves and snag two packs of cereal and cookies along with fresh bread.

I also take three small water bottles before turning around and going to the small living room, hating my whereabouts more than anything else, but it's a perfect place for my plan. It's a small one-bedroom apartment on the outskirts of the city in a building with questionable people where no one gives a fuck what you do in your spare time.

Even the walls are yellowish while the rotten smell brings up nothing but nausea, and the light bulb flickers from time to time, creating a rather gloomy atmosphere straight out of a horror movie.

But as I've discovered...life can be way more scarier, crueler, and filled with more monsters than any horror movie.

The washed-up carpet has several blood stains on it that lead to the small couch in the right corner.

Exactly the opposite of a cage where three girls are trapped. Catriona sits right in the middle, her arms wrapped around her siblings who hug each other tight while their eyes widen at the sight of me.

They hide their faces in the crook of her neck and she blinks at me, fear crossing her face, but she continues to stare as if afraid I might do something to them from a distance.

She shouldn't worry.

When I hurt my victims, I prefer to do it up close so I don't miss the blood slowly dripping from their wounds and watch as the hope shining brightly in their eyes transforms to terror. They always assume someone will come and save them from me.

Such a big mistake because is there a point in kidnapping and torturing someone if you don't intend to kill them?

Serial killers are artists in their own way, except our instruments and brushes are knives, and our canvases are human bodies destined to suffer for eternity because even in hell there is no reprieve from the likes of us.

I guess they call us sick for a reason.

"Dinner is ready," I say, breaking up the silence. Gripping the cage's door, I rattle it a little, and they all jump up. Catriona's hold on her siblings tightens. "You can stop whining now." The little one digs her head deeper into her sister as Catriona glares at me, and for a second, annoyance flashes in her blue orbs that she quickly masks with indifference.

Yet this little act of rebellion...speaks to the dark soul inside me.

Or maybe it's nothing but a myth? People speak highly of souls. Mine, though?

Craves nothing but violence as it's the only peace it knows as contradicting as it sounds.

Opening the cage, I step inside while they all press their backs against the bars, and I lean forward, placing the tray down and kicking it lightly in their direction. "Eat. And then sleep." The little ones glance in my direction before nodding. Catriona bites on her lower lip, bringing attention to her porcelain-clear skin that sports several bruises on it from her trying to fight me at her house.

After she found me standing above her father, my hands soaked in blood while I laughed like a maniac.

Not the most ideal meeting, but still quite unforgettable, I'd say.

Turning around, I lock the cage and walk to the couch, dropping on it and kicking my feet up on the coffee table in front of it while watching them slowly reach for the food, the younger ones snatching the cereal bags. Catriona picks up the bread, tearing herself a piece and chewing on it.

The stupidity of humankind never fails to astonish me. Never once during all these days have they questioned the food and drinks I gave them. I could have poisoned them, and they wouldn't fucking know it.

When I lived in their shoes, I learned the hard way that sometimes food and water can be a poison that slowly kills you from the inside out.

Resting my head on the back of the couch, I take out my phone and slide the screen open, my mouth curving in a smile at the sight of Miranda and Phoenix having a conversation where she lists her terms.

Phoenix King.

A legend in itself if her past is anything to go by, a woman who always intrigued me ever since I've heard about her case. Her countless interviews, her work ethic, the way she always stayed kind despite people being rude to her.

She has this aura of peace that even creatures like me cannot help but be attracted to, not in a sexual way.

Fuck, no.

However, the darkness polluting my mind wishes to get closer to her and observe her under the most challenging circumstances.

High empathy is not something I can ever understand. However, suffering?

I understand it and have respect for her since she withstood all the shit...that being said, her marrying a man who did what Zachary did to her?

That's what attracts me to her the most. She saw him at his worst and still found enough love in her heart to build a life with him.

Love.

It's a concept that is beyond my comprehension but awakens my curiosity. Maybe that's why I like to test its boundaries.

I do it because I love you. I cannot help it. Stop crying! Stop crying, or it will be more painful.

The voice in my head becomes louder, and my fingers curl into the leather cushions, the creaking sound rocking off the walls. Catriona looks in my direction, her brow furrowing. The odd need to come closer slides through me, my self-control the only thing keeping me on my seat.

We share a long stare before she lowers her gaze again, focusing on the food. At least this particular prey is smart enough to know when to back off before the hunter eats her up and leaves nothing behind.

I set a timer for seventy-two hours.

Seventy-two hours for Phoenix to find everything there is about this case and knock on my doorstep.

I close my eyes and inhale deeply before exhaling, silently begging her to find me on time before I commit a crime I could never justify in my eyes.

The timer is ticking, and with each ticktock in my head, my sanity slowly slips away, and with this...my control.

Because nothing is more torturous for a psychopath than to be this close to vulnerable and innocent that inspires anger within me and be denied.

Which makes my hatred toward them even stronger.

The timer is ticking.

And only Phoenix can stop it.

CHAPTER SIX

"He should be the devil in my personal hell.
Instead, he is my salvation in the dark."
Phoenix

*P*hoenix

Zachary pulls by the massive iron gates, and they instantly open, the guards nodding at us in greeting while the car drives onto the narrow road among the endless garden straight out of a fairy tale.

Various rose and orchid bushes spread over the perimeter, creating gorgeous figurines as the sun shines brightly on them, bringing attention to their cold beauty while the neatly cut emerald-green grass surrounds the vast property.

Countless oak trees with their heavy leaves almost invite you to rest under them and not have a care in the world while basking in the nature around us as the birds chirp soundly, creating nests on them.

The wind whooshes so loudly, I can hear in it the car. It sways the smaller trees in different directions, bringing attention to our alcoves in the middle of the garden. Zachary built them specifically for Emmaline, who loves to read in them during the summer when she needs a minute alone. For all the dancing she loves to do, our girl is painfully introverted.

A two-level massive house, though, stands out among this mesmerizing nature. The brick structure has numerous windows made of the finest glass along with the eighteenth century design. The design for which countless magazines ask us to feature our house, but we refuse of course.

We do our best to keep strangers away from our house because we know better than anyone that they rarely have good intentions when it comes to our family.

Despite the sun, thunder echoes in the air, and I rest my head on the window, studying the marble fountain in the middle of the garden.

It depicts Athena, the goddess of war, as water pours around her, the sculpture so vivid and detailed one might truly believe her dress sways right along with the wind, and her eyes stare right into your soul.

And currently, my soul desperately tries to keep all its secrets intact while my husband's brewing anger hits me like a thousand waves, silently demanding for me to confess, but it's one thing I cannot do.

Once you open Pandora's box, there is no going back, and I'm not sure we're currently in the right state of mind for that.

"Do you remember what you told me all those years ago?" Zach breaks the silence that has been present even since we got into the car. Goose bumps cover my skin, and I look at him, frowning. "You're a poison that's slowly killing me from the inside out. A curse I don't know how to break."

The air hitches in my throat at these words, the words I uttered to him during another car ride after we had sex for the first time.

Back then, I hated him so much for everything he had done to me, and I couldn't stand how my body didn't care one bit about it. Loving his every touch and the knowledge in itself was humiliating enough.

Ironic, isn't it?

Sometimes the person you hate the most might become the person you eventually love and can't imagine living without.

Zach parks the car near the house and turns to me, our gazes meeting. "Do you still feel that way? That I'm a poison and a curse?" Torture laces his question, everything in me urging me to soothe it, and I open my mouth to reply, when loud squeals echo through the space, snagging my attention.

"Mama!" The twins emerge from the house, hopping on the stairs and running toward us. Mustering up a smile, I get out of the car, deciding to continue this conversation later. "You're home!" Ian shouts, smacking right into me, and I huff although internally preparing myself for Wyatt, who follows his brother shortly after. "We missed you." He sighs dramatically, and I ruffle their hair, grinning at them.

They look at me with their identical green eyes, Zach's eyes, and joy seeps from them.

My little miracles who remind me each day what a right choice I made all these years ago.

"Hi, my darlings. How are you?"

"Awesome. But our kindergarten teacher isn't happy with us."

Oh, here we go.

"Why is that?"

"We accidentally let the kindergarten bunny out," Wyatt replies. He runs to Zach, who catches him easily, and then his giggle rings in the air when his dad lifts him. "But everyone thinks we did it on purpose." He palms Zach's head and widens his eyes. "Can you imagine?"

Biting on my lower lip and still hugging Ian, I hold back my laughter because the little liars can't lie for shit. Even Zach's lips twitch in amusement.

If we know one thing about the twins, it's this.

No disaster around them is an accident but a strategically planned action executed by them to cause mayhem.

What can I say?

My boys love destruction and playing with people's nerves, and I'm afraid no amount of parenting will fix this craving of theirs.

"Is that so?" Zach wonders, and the twins nod right before Ian goes to his dad, wrapping his hands around his thigh, and Zach runs his fingers through his hair. "So the bunny escaped?"

"He lives a free life now. That's what you say, Daddy, right? Everyone deserves freedom." Wyatt frowns. "They found him shortly after, though, so he still lives in a cage."

"For the bunny, the cage is home, son." Zachary kisses him on the cheek, and Wyatt giggles again. "So when you give him so-called freedom, it seems as if you're throwing him out of the house."

The twins gasp, sharing a long stare, and Ian kicks the pebble from under his shoe while still leaning on Zachary. "There goes the Monday plan, then," they mutter in unison.

"Tragic, isn't it?" their father asks. "Such is life."

"It's inconvenient, Daddy. Not tragic. We still have a parrot in biology class that—"

"No." Even I don't miss how Zach's tone leaves no room for argument, and they sigh, recognizing that as well.

While on most days, they can get away with almost everything when it comes to their father, he has his limits, and the kids never cross them.

"Where is Emmaline?" I ask, reaching for Ian and lacing my hand with his as we go up the stairs to the house with Zach following us, still holding Wyatt.

"They're baking pie for Anthony." Ian lowers his voice to a loud whisper. "It's his favorite."

"Is it now?"

Emmaline's best friend has the biggest crush on her, and he follows her around everywhere. He even attends her ballet classes, which is adorable. These two have been inseparable ever since they met at the age of four. Should they keep this connection going, I can see them eventually falling in love. It's really funny considering he has the same name as Zach's dad.

"His favorite is pumpkin pie, Mama." Wyatt makes a gagging sound. "Imagine."

Oh, yes.

For whatever reason, the twins cannot stand anything pumpkin. During my pregnancy, I suffered a lot from it too, and just the sight of pumpkin made me want to vomit.

The minute we enter the house, we're hit with the delicious smell of cinnamon and coffee while warmth greets us. I sigh, loving the energy around my spacious home.

Beige dominates the color scheme, which goes well with the

exquisite interior design consisting of expensive furniture made of the finest wood from Italy and oil paintings depicting various myths from ancient Greece.

Their worth alone can make someone a wealthy person, yet they casually hang on the walls in our spacious hallway leading to a living room and dining room. Our kitchen buzzes with energy since most of the staff spends the day there.

The staff scatter to their nearby houses when we're around, so we rarely see them; however, they ensure that our mansion is run like a well-oiled machine.

I don't think I've seen an ounce of dust on our furniture, let alone any stains.

"I'll help you with your coat, Mama," Ian says, tugging on my sleeve, so I take it off and give it to him since he loves to help. He huffs, holding the coat in his hands, though most of it drags on the floor, and marches to the nearby table where one of the maids waits for him. "Here, Melody." She picks it up. "Thank you!" He yells the last part and rushes back to me, hugging me close once again, and my brow furrows.

"Everything all right, honey?" While they are both mama's boys through and through, which I think is fair, considering Zachary is Emmaline's favorite, they are never this attached to my hip. Usually, they find mischief all the time because standing still and doing one thing for a long period bores them, and they become restless.

"Yes. You smell better than the pumpkin pie," he mutters, pressing his nose into my hip. Zach places Wyatt on the floor, and he joins his brother from the other side. "Patience promised us to bake chocolate chip cookies afterward to wash away this smell." He glances at me. "Do you think she's done?"

Before I can answer, Emmaline runs out of the kitchen, her pink dress covered in flour, and exclaims, "We're done!"

"Woo-hoo!" the boys reply, jumping off me and then racing to the kitchen to demand their cookies, I guess.

Our daughter pauses several feet away from us and cocks her head to the side. "How are you?" Her eyes dart back and forth between us. "No worries?"

My girl is a sweet empath who senses tension well, so I shift closer to Zach, who wraps his arm around my waist, and wink at her. "Yes, honey. We're just tired."

"Ah! I need to clean up, and then I can show you my video! Aunt Valencia praised my technique today and gave me a few more pointers." So much love coats her voice when she speaks about her favorite ballet teacher, Valencia Scott, who also happens to be married to one of the wealthiest men on the planet, although why is beyond me.

The few times I've met Lachlan due to their business with Zachary, he has been nothing but cold and chilling. Everyone knows he adores his wife and children, even if he acts...strange, but no one can say shit to him for all the power the man possesses.

Valencia has several schools across the globe, so to be personally taught by her is a privilege. She has a mile-long waiting list and usually prefers to give a chance to those less fortunate or who need a scholarship to get into good schools to have a dancing career.

I had to personally ask her to teach Emmaline after she assured me that this was the career she wished to prosper in and was very serious about dance. To my surprise, Valencia agreed under one condition.

Zachary would supply a scholarship for five of her students every single year until Emmaline becomes a prima. My husband found the idea hilarious since no one demanded shit from him. He agreed, though, so here we are.

"She probably sent this video to you as well, right?" Emmaline pulls me back to the present, and I blink, remembering our conversation.

Fishing inside my bag for my phone, I snatch it out and see several notifications. "Yes. We can watch it together once you clean up. How does that sound?"

Her face lights up. "Sweet! I'll be quick." She races up the stairs, her feet slapping soundly on the marble, and I lean on Zach's shoulder while we hear the twins and Patience argue.

"Boys! Melody has to clean the kitchen before we can bake cookies. And this old lady is in need of a break." My heart pangs at the sound of her tired voice. She's in her seventies now, and while Zach offered more help with the kids, she refused.

She vowed to retire and take the year-long cruise Zach promised her once the twins no longer needed her.

"Oh, come on, Patience! You can just sit and let us do everything!"

"We'll have dinner soon. After that, we'll bake so you can enjoy cookies before going to bed. Take it or leave it, boys."

I can just imagine them glaring at each other with the battles of wills going on. Unfortunately for my boys, though, she raised their father as well, so their stubborn nature does little to faze her. I'm not surprised when they groan, and Wyatt says, "Fine!" A beat passes. "Isn't your favorite TV show about to start?"

"Yes!" Ian tries to make his voice deeper. "Where the guy said *I know I'm the father of your child!*"

"Oh yes! Let's find out if he is!"

"One day, Patience is going to quit quietly, and we won't be able to find her," Zach murmurs into my ear, and I grin. "Would you like to rest before dinner?"

It doesn't escape my notice that he doesn't try to bring up the conversation we had in the car, but it's unavoidable.

Although I can see the beginning of my headache from miles away, I refuse. "No. I'll watch Emmaline's video, then work in the greenhouse for a bit."

He designed it specifically for me a few years back when I had this difficult patient that was wrongly diagnosed and couldn't figure out why her original medication wasn't working. I spent so much time inside the house, pacing in my office and room back and forth that Zach had had enough.

He built a greenhouse rather quickly where we grow roses, and I have a special small place there of my own. I can work and enjoy the weather and nature around me while surrounded by beauty and nice scents.

All because I once mentioned that the sight of roses soothes me.

"Okay." He presses a kiss to my temple. "I'll spend some time with the boys. Maybe we can find out together who the father is on that TV show." I laugh, and he glances at his watch. "You have two hours, love."

I nod and head upstairs, although his words ring in the air all the way to our room.

You have two hours.

And while he meant dinner...a part of me knows...

He meant more than that.

I have two hours to open up about what happened today, and I just don't know if I have enough strength to do so.

U nsub

The wooden clock hanging on the wall ticks loudly in the night, the sound reverberating through the space as I sit on the couch, flipping the lighter between my fingers, and finally light it up.

Everything inside me blazes awake when I watch the orange and blue flames merging, the warmth and ruthlessness of fire sending pleasure through me and awakening every hair on my body that screams at me to drop it on the floor and see how easily it can destroy things.

How easily it burns everything to ashes until nothing remains.

Cruel element with absolutely no mercy to those around him, thriving among more pain and consuming things one after another at such rapid speed that all people can do is either run away or face their death with screams.

The intensity matches the one swirling inside me every second, urging me to participate in hideous crimes and soak in darkness so much I'll be invincible to fire.

For how can you destroy a monster?

Nothing can stop it except...

"I need to go to the bathroom." A soft voice speaks up, and I look through the flame at the girl, gently freeing herself from her siblings' hold. They mutter something in their sleep and then curl closer to the wall and press tighter against each other.

Catriona covers them with a blanket and scoots to the cage's door, avoiding my gaze while her cheeks redden, probably from her request. When the fire burns my thumb, I hiss and turn it off.

Nothing has power over the element except water.

A water her crystal-clear blue eyes remind me of. An endless ocean that might swallow you whole if you're not careful enough.

"I told you to go a few hours ago, didn't I?" I ask, annoyance lacing my words. She jerks at my tone, gripping the bar harder until her knuckles turn white. "You should have listened to me instead of pretending to sleep."

She rubs her arms, probably from the frigid air in the apartment since my window is wide open, letting in the wind, the cold causing goose bumps on her bare skin. "I really need to go." If it's possible, her face becomes even redder while she holds back tears and bites on her lower lip. The distress she emits only inspires anger within me.

Because for whatever reason, I despise it along with her fear in such circumstances where she has to beg me for simple necessities.

And it makes me hate her even more.

Throwing the lighter away, I get up, my boots soundless on the carpeted floor, and insert the key on the lock. She still avoids looking directly into my eyes and instead focuses on my chest.

Opening it up, I motion for her to get out. She quickly does, wincing as she straightens up, and her knees dip a little bit before she regains her footing. Her legs must be cramped from sitting in one position for such a long time. "You have five minutes."

She nods, her short hair doing a piss-poor job of covering her flaming cheeks, and I wonder why she cut it off.

Her hair used to be long, almost reaching her ass and falling down in waves, reminding me of the sunset at the beach, bright yet warm almost calling your name to come closer to her and get some heat, even if your soul is dead inside.

And while it still has its beauty, I hate its length.

"Well, fucking move," I bark, uncaring about her siblings, and she practically runs to the small hallway leading to the bathroom. Her hand freezes on the doorknob when I warn, "Don't lock the door."

"I won't do anything in there." Only my chuckle meets her words because *please*. When in dire circumstances, people tend to do stupid shit. While she seems to love her siblings, her recent change in behavior signals her unstable state of mind to me. And when cornered, unstable people tend to turn to self-harm.

If anyone is going to harm Catriona, it's me.

"I don't give a shit. Besides, I've seen you pee your pants. Trust me, I have no intention to walk in on a live show."

At this point, her face almost matches her red hair. "Oh my God," she mutters and shuts the door while I lean on the wall, waiting for her to be done, and frown.

I understand why most serial killers kill their victims immediately after satisfying their sadistic cravings. Keeping them and putting up with all their fucking whining tires me more than the voices in my head constantly pushing me to cause more chaos.

After all, I never knew peace, for this world has been cruel to me. Why should other people?

If I didn't get justice, why should anyone else get it?

The barely audible sob snaps my attention, and I come closer, listening to Catriona cry inside the bathroom before she starts running the water, loud splashes echoing in the room, and her inhales and exhales fill the air.

After a second, she opens the door, and our chests almost bump against each other's. She quickly steps back, and although she still refuses to look at me, I realize she needed a space to cry.

She didn't flush the toilet.

Too proud to cry in front of her captor? Or too concerned to cry in front of her siblings because she needs to be strong for them?

Her actions inspire curiosity in me as human emotions always confuse me. They make no sense to me. The idea to care about someone else rather than be selfish is just...stupid.

When the chips are down, no one will save you. No, they will let you rot in hell and laugh while watching your flesh be teared until nothing remains.

That's why empathy and compassion will be the death of humankind. There will always be true monsters who won't hesitate to use it against these so-called good people.

She wipes her cheeks and passes by me, still staring at the floor as she goes to the room but pauses midway. "Can I have some water?" She cracks the question. Her throat must be really dry because her voice reminds me of nothing of the melodic one she used to have.

When she read stories, it had the ability to lull anyone to sleep, even a soulless creature like me.

"Go to the kitchen."

She follows the order, her bare feet padding on the tile. Despite only the moonlight streaming brightly through the window mixing with the streetlights, I still see how her toes curl into the cold floor, and she shivers. I removed their shoes once they came here so they wouldn't get any stupid ideas.

She grabs a glass and goes to the tap, but I stop her. "Take a bottle from the fridge." This place is such a dump. I don't think this water is safe to drink, and while I don't give many fucks about her health...the last thing I need is for her to get sick and fuck up all my plans.

But even as such thoughts cross my mind, thoughts that should be normal to me...still the idea of her in pain causes rage, confusing me.

Why does this girl inspire so many conflicted emotions within me?

She goes to the fridge but then stops. "Can I have tea instead? It's very cold," she whispers, and I laugh, making her jump with her back facing me.

"I'm sorry, princess. We are no longer in your castle where everyone caters to your wishes." Maybe if she thought about herself for a change, she wouldn't let her siblings hog the blanket. "If you're thirsty, get the bottle or go back to the cage."

She sighs heavily and resumes her walk to the fridge but then darts to the kitchen counter where the knives are located and snags one out, spinning around. But I'm already on her, splaying my palms on the counter from either side of her and trapping her between my hard chest and it.

Her raspy breath fills the space as she presses the knife to my neck, our faces inches apart. Our gazes clash, her blue eyes filled with fear and determination. "I will kill you. Let me go," she orders with trembling hands, the silver barely grazing me. She swallows hard, probably summoning nonexistent courage. "This will be self-defense," she says, convincing herself she'll kill me for the greater good, and it'll somehow justify murder in her eyes.

Ah, naïve little soul.

If only she knew that the justice system doesn't favor the innocent. It favors the most cunning and powerful ones.

I should know. No one gave a fuck about me.

"Do it then," I tell her, and she blinks several times in shock at me.

I inch closer, the blade pressing harder against my neck but still not drawing any blood, and she leans back. "Make sure to go for the carotid artery. One little swipe, and I'll quickly bleed to death." I shift even closer, and our hips bump against each other's. She gasps, and I inhale her scent, the silkiness of her hair teasing my skin and calming something inside me for a brief second. "Do it, Catriona." I address her by her name for the first time, tasting it in my mouth, and a tremor runs through her while she pushes the blade at my neck. "Do it, and you'll be just like me." I whisper the last part, egging her on, and a part of me wishes for her to do it.

To end my suffering once and for all so she can join me in my darkness. I wouldn't be alone in it then.

Because once you're in it...it's so fucking lonely, even if you love it.

She hesitates, her raspy breathing the only thing breaking the silence, and this hesitation tells me everything I need to know.

Her soul isn't capable of violence, even toward those who deserve it, making her a creature who won't ever survive in the darkness.

I place my hand on hers, squeezing it so hard she gasps in pain when the knife pierces through her skin and mine, blood dripping down our palms and mixing. "Stupid, stupid girl. When fate gives you a chance to kill a monster, use it," I say, my lips inches away from her mouth as her eyes form tears, and they slide down her cheeks, somehow diminishing the pleasure spreading through me.

Extinguishing my fire that's been one constant in my life all these years and kept me alive.

Gripping the knife with my other hand, I throw it in the sink and then drag her toward it, turning on the water and putting our hands under it to wash the wounds. They aren't that deep to begin with, so why is she crying?

"Ouch." She hisses, "It hurts."

"Bear it. It was your idea to play with weapons you don't know how to use."

She bristles at this, whisper-shouting at me, still mindful of her siblings, it seems, "Well, I'm sorry that not all of us are a murderer!"

Ignoring her words, a bit too late to show me her character, considering she acted so stupid just earlier, I stop the water and then go to the other counter, still holding her, and take out the first aid kit I bought on a whim when I injured my hand.

Psychologists would have said I have anger issues.

Keeping her in the corner between the fridge and counter, I flip the kit open and snatch antiseptic from it, pouring a generous amount on both of our palms, which earns me yet another hiss. "Can't you be gentle?"

"I'm a psychopath. Gentle is not a word in my vocabulary," I inform her and then spread some ointment on it.

"Yes. You killed my father," she replies, the air hitching in her throat when my thumb presses on her wound, and she bites on her lower lip, staring at me. "I hate you," she adds.

"I don't care." Taking out a bandage, I wrap it around her palm and tie it all together. "Answer my question, though." She freezes when I step closer, and she curls her hand, clearly prepared to fight me.

Like I said, the girl is stupid, which makes my...weird emotions toward her even more confusing since I don't admire the weak.

I admire the strong and resilient, one of the reasons I involved Phoenix King in this case.

She's the definition of these words.

"I don't want to answer your questions," she mutters, trying to free herself, but I give her no wiggle room.

"Are you really sorry he's dead?" Her eyes widen. "Are you, Catriona?"

With this, she pushes me away, and I stumble back, letting her run to the room and get inside the cage, the bars rattling when she closes it.

Maybe she believes this will save her from the ugly truth her psyche doesn't want to face.

She isn't sorry at all.

I walk back there, not bothering to bandage my own hand. This little nick hardly pains me.

When one lives in chains and gets choked on a daily basis, light wounds don't affect them much.

Catriona sits next to her sisters again, shivering at the wind, and tries to block the frigid air from affecting her siblings when she rests her back against the wall, creating an even warmer cocoon around them since she blocks most of the coldness with her body heat.

She momentarily flicks her gaze at me, and holding it, I tug at the back of my sweater and take it off. Then I open the door and throw it at her, where it lands by her feet.

I lock the cage and go back to the couch, kicking my feet up and enjoying the coldness nipping on my T-shirt-covered skin while Catriona gapes at the sweater for several seconds.

Eventually, she picks it up and puts it on, curling next to her siblings, and after a while, she falls asleep.

Yes.

Phoenix King needs to hurry with her investigation and move forward so this madness can finally end.

It's very dangerous to leave a psychopath with a girl who calms down his inner demons.

You see, we get addicted to things easily.

And when those things reject us?

We tend to retaliate in the most tragic ways.

CHAPTER SEVEN

"You can fall in love with your enemy.
But can you forget what he did to you?"
Phoenix

*P*hoenix
    The moonlight shines brightly as I step into the greenhouse. Owls hoot in the distance, mingling with crows squawking, and I breathe the sweet scent of roses into my lungs, welcoming the calmness.

Throwing the stack of folders on the nearby table, I turn on the lamp to bask the greenhouse in a shadowy glow. I remove my sweater, leaving me standing in a light dress and ballerinas since the humidity and heat in here can warm the dead.

Dropping on the chair, I sigh in exasperation and close my eyes, enjoying this one moment of silence while gathering my thoughts and mentally preparing myself to face the facts about this case.

After changing my clothes and spending time with Emmaline studying her videos and listening to her stories that included Anthony, of course, I had just thirty minutes to go over some bullet points in my room with the case before it was time for dinner.

We took our time eating as the kids each shared some outrageous stories about their day. We fully focused on them, so I successfully avoided speaking to my husband for almost three hours. That's a record for us.

Nervousness shook my body in anticipation of tonight, so when the twins asked him to watch them bake, I darted upstairs, scooped up all the information sent to my home, and decided to hide here.

"Really mature, Phoenix," I mutter, huffing and making my locks fly high. Hooking my hair behind my ear, I sigh, reaching for one of the folders focusing on Miranda's marriage with several new details that chill my blood but don't really surprise me much.

Like I said.

Rarely, if ever, do people end their marriages with murder for the heck of it. The signs are always there. Most people just choose to ignore it, hoping it will all sort itself on its own, but it never does.

Because the biggest lie everyone tells themselves is that people change. They do as an exception and never as a rule. As such, whenever we see someone and fall in love with them...we need to accept that this version of them will be the one we'll spend the rest of our life with.

I still when the door opens and see Zachary entering, holding a silver tray in his hands. "What are you doing?" I ask, surprised since he never bothers me here. This is my little sanctuary where I stay alone with my thoughts.

Don't get me wrong, I never forbade him to come and always welcome his presence. It's unusual, though.

"In your quest to run away from our conversation, you didn't drink your evening tea and missed out on your favorite chocolate cake," he teases without much heat in his words. I hunch my shoulders, guilt swiping over me or the exhaustion from the inevitable doom.

He walks toward me, moves the folders to the edge of the table, and places the tray right in the middle with my tea and his coffee. The steam swirls in the air above the mugs, and one huge piece of chocolate cake dripping on the plate makes me lick my lips. "Oh, it looks delicious."

"The cook made it specifically for you. He didn't count on the boys baking cookies. He still glares at the pie," Zach replies dryly, and I laugh, just imagining his expression.

The cook is the sweetest man ever in his sixties; however, he hates anyone but Zach cooking in his kitchen. Maybe because almost everyone makes a mess out of it, and he can't say much to the man who signs his paychecks.

"Well, it's his tradition on Fridays to bake us a cake for the weekend."

I pick up the fork, digging it into the cake and scooping a little before lifting it to my mouth and tasting it. "Mmm." I groan and then roll my eyes when Zach hisses through his teeth, his gaze filling with heat. "Control yourself, Mr. King."

"Hard to do when you make such sounds, darling." He sits on the chair opposite me and wraps his hand around his coffee mug, taking a huge sip. "How is work?"

Shocked by his question, I sip some of my tea and sigh. "Good, I guess? I studied a little bit of the material Noah sent us." His face darkens at the mention of the agent's name, and I see his grab on the mug tightening, which lets me know he's still pissed at him. I can relate a hundred percent, so I'm not even mad he hit him.

I know, I know.

It makes me an awful person, but I don't care. If what we suspect is true, he deserved it because he dumped us in hell without so much as a warning.

"Did anything stand out to you?"

"I don't think Catriona killed her father, let alone tortured him in such a sadistic manner." Dipping my forkful of cake into the dripped chocolate, I eat some more of it before continuing, "All the information on her speaks about some trauma that must have occurred a few months back, but nothing in her childhood indicates a sign of psychopathy."

He ponders on it for a few beats. "Noah mentioned they had several birds over the years that mysteriously died."

I wince at this, hating the idea of anyone harming animals. "Yes.

For all we know, though, the reasons could have been anything. Matt was known for his short temper, which explains why his wife had so many trips to the ER over the years." Zach's brows rise at this while anger crosses his face because he understands my meaning at once. "So I suspect the birds probably didn't survive his temper, not Catriona's." Finishing my cake, I wash it down with tea while reaching for the folder again to flip it open, studying her picture. "There are so many emotions on her face. Plus, she has this aura about her in every single photo that combined with her life story...I don't think she's capable of any violence."

He leans back on his chair, sipping his coffee while he looks to the side and studies the oak tree in the distance. The wind bellows outside, contrasting so much with the quietness and heat inside the greenhouse. "So it leaves Miranda as the murderer and her accomplice on the loose."

My brow furrows at this. "No. I think the unsub is a highly intelligent man who used the family's history to his advantage to commit a crime. And he's such a skilled manipulator that he found a way to control Miranda. Even though she's in prison, he has her terrified out of her mind. That's not a skill everyone possesses." This makes this case a thousand times worse since this unsub, for whatever reason, wants me on the case, so he has some deep motives that probably involve a lot of stuff that will scare me even more.

Simply put, I haven't met or heard about an unsub without a disturbing backstory.

No one is born with bloodthirst. All our characteristics and traits are the result of our environment, and if we choose evilness over goodness...then once upon a time, someone who was supposed to love us failed us in such a way we found no other way but to turn to darkness and forget about humanity.

A scary thought.

I gulp, suddenly starved for fresh air, and quickly take a large sip, welcoming the warm liquid in my throat that momentarily grounds me to the present and away from the thoughts that disturb my mind.

However, I forgot one crucial thing.

My husband is not one to shy away from confrontation—one of the reasons his reputation is legendary in the business world. "Why are you hell-bent on defending her?" My eyes widen in surprise at this. "Is it because she's potentially a victim of abuse?"

"I'm not trying to defend her or her actions. What happened to this family is tragic, but if she's guilty, by no means am I trying to defend her."

"You lean heavily on the theory that someone is controlling her."

"Because the signs point to it." What is he implying here, exactly? "Or would you prefer for her to be guilty so you wouldn't have to worry about my safety?" Despite understanding some of his emotions, I can't keep the bite out of my words, and he must sense it.

His green orbs flash in a warning that I refuse to listen to as a strange yet exciting electric volt travels through me, charging my blood and pushing me toward a break I don't think we can survive unscathed.

He chuckles, and for some reason, the sound of it grates on my nerves and sends trepidation through me. As if we are on the edge of a cliff and will fall once we take a single step farther. "Not at all, darling. I just wonder if you're defending her because the idea of her murdering her husband terrifies you."

"What?"

"Yes. Maybe the idea of a woman forgiving her man and then staying with him for years before something inside her snaps and she decides to kill him terrifies you. As it means the part that hated him all these years won and couldn't be overshadowed with all the love and even having children."

Silence falls between us after this statement as we stare at one another. Anger rises inside me, and I put my mug on the tray with a loud thud, the tea splashing as I get up swiftly, and Zach follows suit.

"It all comes back to the past, doesn't it?" I ask, a bitter laugh escaping me and rocking off the walls. "It all comes back to the past you cannot let go of," I whisper in disbelief. I can't believe the accusation he just threw my way!

"How can I if you refuse to talk about it?"

Is he serious right now?

"Well, I'm sorry if I'm not in the mood to discuss one of the most traumatic experiences of my life!" I shout the last part and spin around, running my fingers through my hair and praying for a calmness that, for whatever reason, doesn't come.

No, instead, I become even more restless and desire to find an outcome to these pent-up emotions inside me that have been brewing for some time now.

However, my frustration doesn't come from what my husband thinks. It's a different thing entirely, and while I did my best to protect him all these years, maybe I shouldn't have.

"You're hiding a part of yourself, and you don't have to. I know it exists, and that's okay." A beat passes after his confession. "I love all of you. Even the part that hates me and wishes she never met me."

Taking a deep breath to stop myself from strangling my clueless husband, I turn again to face him while he watches me grimly. Agony fills his eyes, and it's the only thing softening my anger because, deep down, I know why he cares about it so much.

That's why I never wanted to talk about it because, contrary to what Zach believes, it has nothing to do with me.

And everything to do with him, just not in the way he thinks.

"No part of me hates you."

He perches on the huge table covered in various pots and bags of soil. The moonlight and the lamp above him shine on him, showcasing his emotions and, more importantly, that he doesn't believe the shit I'm saying. "Tell me you didn't remember all the hideous things done to you today." He swallows hard. "All the things I ordered done to you."

I huff in exasperation. "I did. Of course I did! I spent three and a half years in prison from being beaten to starved to exhausted and wishing to die there. All while the world hated me, and everyone turned their backs on me, including Sebastian, who was supposed to stand by me through everything." The muscle in his jaw tics, and his hands clench. I know he hates me for ever mentioning having feelings for any other man, but his possessive nature will have to rein it in since he wanted to have this conversation. "I'm a human! Therapy or not, I was bound to react this way. It's normal, and I hardly deserve an interrogation for it!"

"This is not about that," he snaps, and I'm ready to pull my hair out at his stubbornness. Everything in me begs me not to breach the subject, but I have no other choice.

Otherwise, this will forever haunt us, a bitterness in our otherwise sweet life that will eventually grow into a bigger issue if I allow his emotion to stew.

"You want to know why I refuse to talk to you about it? Why my past is off-limits?" His crossed arms is the only reply as thunder echoes outside, the rain season in full force. Right now, I welcome Mother Nature's mood because it matches my own so perfectly. "It's not because I feel resentment or hate. I put those emotions to rest the minute I decided to be yours and build a life with you. The fact that you think this...it hurts me, Zach. I understand, but it hurts me." I whisper the last part, and he jerks as if I've slapped him while I rub my chest, the ache inside me rivaling that of physical pain. But as I've discovered through the years, your soul has the ability to hurt way more than your body, and isn't that just tragic? "I don't talk about it because you are the one who hates himself for what you'd done to me."

He stills, straightening up as the heavy weight of my confession drops on us. We gaze at one another, my heart beating fast, and I feel the pulse in my throat while nervousness shakes my entire system, too afraid of what he might say to this.

But the truth is out now, and I guess Zachary will have to face the consequences of it.

"You're a man who loves with everything in him. And when someone hurts or threatens the one you love...you retaliate, craving to execute the most hurt on the guilty person for daring to do this to your loved ones." He stays silent, just staring at me, his face unreadable. "That part of you...it's always craving blood because to you...there is no forgiveness or atonement for the things people do to your loved ones. You don't forgive, nor forget." I rub my forehead, the tension easing around me. I inhale a breath, feeling a weird sense of freedom to have all this in the open because his anger and silent demands were playing havoc with my mind. A shadow loomed above me wherever I went. "And the more you love me...the more you hate yourself because these..." I lower down my dress, tapping on one of my faded scars before adjusting the dress back in place. "Will never go away. I will always have reminders of the day that changed everything."

Zach turns away from me, hiding his emotions while he must ponder on the truth that's hard for him to face, and I glance at the stack of files, sighing in resignation.

I don't think I can focus on work anymore. I've already made all the bullet points I need, though, and see this case a bit more clearly. I'm not sure if it will be enough to catch the unsub, but one can only hope.

Despite what anyone might think when it comes to the past, I let go of a lot of things a long time ago. Otherwise, I'd go insane, and while some might still scratch old wounds, it doesn't mean they hurt the same as they used to.

Or have the same effect on me.

Miranda's words today affected me so much because I knew we had this unresolved issue between us, this sore spot no one wanted to speak about, yet I guess as a psychiatrist I should have known better.

Secrets and pain tend to come up sooner or later, and it's better to face the issue head-on than hide your head in the sand.

As life proved to me, this strategy really never works.

Sighing at the prolonged silence, I come closer to Zach and place my hand on his tense back, his muscles flexing under my touch. Thunder shakes the sky again, gracing the night with a flash of lightning that brightens up the space around us and creates a wicked atmosphere that should chill my blood.

Instead, strange heat travels through me, buzzing my insides, and I clear my throat, shaking my head and doing my best to focus on the situation at hand. "I'm going to bed. I think it's for the best right now." My husband tends to stay in his head for a long while when he thinks over things, and I believe my presence makes it ten times worse for him.

I move to the side, ready to walk out, but my gasp echoes in the night when he wraps his arm around my waist and pulls me to him. His hands grip my hips, lifting me and setting me on the table, various pots falling away and dropping to the floor, shattering into tiny pieces.

"Zach!" I hiss as he widens my legs and steps between them, his splayed hands on either side of me, caging me in his embrace. "What are you doing?" My voice might be accusing. However, goose bumps break on my skin along with anticipation when his masculine scent twitches my nose, and his eyes drill their stare in me, his handsome face unreadable.

Instead of answering my question, he fires his own. "How?"

"What how?"

"How did you forgive me?" His hold on me tightens, my gasp rocking between us as he leans so close to me we are a breath away from each other. "How did you forgive me?" His voice lowers to a husky whisper akin to the softest silk that glides over my skin, almost caressing me as it urges me to give in to him and whatever he wants from me. "Tell me."

My heart flips inside my chest. I swallow and sigh. "Because that's how you love."

His fingers dig deeper into my flesh. The pulsing vein on his neck the only indication of his internal battle, it seems. "How do I love, Phoenix?"

Oh God.

"The man who hurt me didn't love me. But he did love someone who he lost, so he lashed out where he thought it was deserved." Something crosses his face, but it's gone so quickly that I don't have the chance to examine it. "It doesn't mean what you did was right. It was wrong, Zach. Over the line," I add, and we both know what I mean here. Knowing where he comes from and excusing it are two different things. "However, that is who you are, and I fell in love with you. And loving you means accepting every part of you, especially the part that shows me your love." Palming his head, I inch closer to him while everything around us goes still.

At this moment, the greenhouse is a live creature that knows we're experiencing a pivotal step in our relationship, and interruptions would not be welcomed.

"I guess it's my atonement to live with the consequences of my actions." His lips brush against mine.

"Yes," I whisper. "But you know what else I know?"

"What?"

"That if I were married to you when the hell happened...you'd never ever leave me alone or believe the lies. You'd always be on my side." He jerks in my hold, his heart speeding up, and I press myself closer to him while his hands travel to my waist, gripping it before he wraps his arms tightly around me. "Your love has no boundaries, which means I will always be under its protection." Thunder booms once again. "For me, it means the world. I was alone and afraid for such a long time, but with you, I'm not."

"I'll destroy anyone who so much as—"

"I know. How can I hate any part of your love then, Zach?" I rest my forehead against his, sliding my hands to his shoulders and clasping them. "That's how I forgive you. Because the Zach who loves me never hurt me and never will. I love you."

"You're mine, darling. Every. Single. Inch of you belongs to me." His hand drifts to my hair, and he fists it hard, tilting my head and exposing my neck to his wandering mouth, creating thousands of prickling sensations all over my body. "And I will kill anyone who dares to harm you." A promise rings in his voice, but I barely focus on it, gasping when he presses his lips against my pulse before sucking on the skin, starting a fire in the pit of my stomach that has the power to consume me.

My fingers curl into his shirt, clenching the cloth and pulling him closer while my thighs flex around him when he moves forward, wishing to keep him with me as long as he continues to bring me pleasure.

When we are together, we burn so brightly that it's a wonder we're still alive.

However, rational sense still rears its head, and I whisper, "The kids, Zach." We've never done anything risqué in the greenhouse since it's completely glass. Despite its location on the secluded part of the property with several trees covering up the view, anyone can still walk in on us at any minute.

If possible, the energy changes rapidly. The tension in the air swirling around us is so prominent I can almost touch it. Zach's fingers curve on my waist as he pulls harder at my hair, making me arch as he licks over the abused flesh, flicking his tongue back and forth and earning himself my loud moan.

Desire travels through me, awakening every hair on my body and sending scorching heat down my spine. My core clenches in anticipation of the joy and love of his touch, which always has pleasure on the receiving end of it. "Zach," I whisper, not doing anything to stop him yet still trying to stay responsible.

We can't be as reckless as we'd been on that first night in the kitchen...

"Ah, my darling," he murmurs over my skin, skimming lower and grazing my collarbone with his teeth. Tickling me and then biting me, he quickly soothes the pain washing over me with another lick. "Do you really think I'd ever put you at risk?" I gasp when he presses the thick bulge covered by his jeans into my core, growing instantly wet just imagining his cock stretching me while driving into me. "No one will see a thing." He slides his lips upward, leaving blazing shivers in his wake and nips on my chin until finally, he reaches my mouth, and our breaths mingle. We stare at one another, the desire in his eyes matching my own while silently promising me all the wicked ways to make me come apart in his arms. "Now, darling," he murmurs, licking over my lips before trapping the lower one between his teeth and pulling at it, the pain mixing with pleasure, sending me into a maddening spiral. "Kiss me like you *fucking* mean it."

He connects our mouths in a hard kiss, his tongue roaming inside and seeking mine. They entwine in a duet, sending heat waves through me just as the rain starts pouring outside, tapping on the roof, which only enhances the lust boiling in my blood.

We groan when he shifts a little, his hard-on digging into me, and I wrap my legs around him as my one hand laces in his hair while the other still keeps its hold on the shirt, too afraid he might change his mind and leave me in this insanity all alone.

My nipples peek through the thin dress, the cloth almost unbearable on my sensitive skin. He swallows my moan when he cups one of them, squeezing it gently while he continues to ravish my mouth, owning it with the licks and flicks of his tongue.

Each stab, each brush, against mine is a claim in itself, invisible imprints that warn anyone else away from me. He caresses my nipple with his thumb, the heat enveloping me whole, and he swallows my moan when he pinches it, his possessive hold hard to miss.

How funny because I've belonged to him since our first kiss.

Every woman should experience the kind of kisses Zachary bestows on me once in a lifetime. As if nothing more important exists for him on this earth, and he'd fight anyone for this privilege. His skilled mouth is an addiction that has the power to send me flying down the abyss where bliss awaits me.

I wrap my legs tighter around him at the thought, snatching my mouth away as we both gulp for oxygen, and our eyes meet.

With a groan, we kiss again, giving in to the passion clawing at me from the inside out. I know his need matches my own because if he doesn't do something, I will come apart in his arms forever, begging for a relief that only he can give me.

Tremors rush from the tip of my hair to my toes as he angles my head for better access and slowly lowers me down on the table until my back touches the warm wood. My lungs plead for air, yet I palm his head, deepening the kiss and welcoming his growl.

His hand grips the top of my dress, lowering it until my bare breasts spring free. My nipples tingle when the air nips on them, making me finally pull back and breathe oxygen into my lungs as his lips drift to my collarbone, rubbing his nose back and forth. A burst of laughter escapes me, then turns into a prolonged moan when he shifts his attention to my breasts.

More goose bumps pop on my skin, and fire spreads inside me when I feel his hot breath on the mounds of my flesh.

He circles my nipples with his tongue, flicking it back and forth and sending shivers down my spine before drawing it in, sucking on it hard, and tangling my fingers in his hair. I keep him still, begging him to give me relief and shifting restlessly on the table at the same time as the need that builds up inside me demands an outcome.

Every instinct in my body screams to end this madness and grant me what's rightfully mine because he belongs to me as much as I belong to him.

And as such, my pleasure should always be his top priority, just like his is mine. "I want you, darling," I whisper, my nails clawing into his nape. He groans, the vibration only adding to the inferno blazing within me, and I whimper.

"What do you need?" he asks gruffly, dragging his teeth upward and then biting my nipples, making me jerk and raise my hips, only for his other hand to keep me still as he licks around it again. "Answer me."

"You. Fucking me hard until nothing but you remains in my head." I feel his muscles tense after my request, and a moan escapes me when his palm drifts to the hem of my dress, hiking it upward. He clenches my bare ass cheek, molding it in his grip.

Lust consumes me as he lavishes my flesh with attention. Thousands of electric volts energize my skin and push me toward the invisible cliff that holds the answers to all my prayers. The man who owns me continues torturing me in the sweetest way. "Zach, please," I whisper, tugging on his hair, but he stays relentless to my pleas. Giving one long suck to my breast, he moves his mouth to the other one, cupping it gently before repeating his actions and driving me further insane. "I need you, darling." I raise my thighs, closing them around him, and gasp when his hard-on rubs on my sodden panties, up and down, playing with all my nerve endings. My core spasms, wishing to feel his hard length inside me. "Zach!"

He finally lets go, his wandering mouth moving down to my stomach, leaving wet imprints on my dress. He straightens up, and his wild look alone has the power to make me come.

Holding my stare, he tugs on his sweater and takes it off, throwing it to the side. My eyes drink in the perfect male specimen, my lips itching to trace his six-pack and mark it with my bite so everyone would know his body is claimed.

What can I say?

His possessive, barbaric tendencies have rubbed off on me as well, but I don't care.

I want the whole world to know we belong to each other. Sometimes, it feels that even our rings and marriage certificate aren't enough. That's how fully entwined our souls are with each other.

Life without him has no meaning, and I wouldn't have it any other way.

How could he think even for a second that a part of me hates him?

I couldn't even if I wanted to because I'm powerless when it comes to this man and fully accept my fate.

Because I know he's powerless too when it comes to me, and the knowledge is an aphrodisiac in itself.

He sucks his breath through his teeth as his gaze swipes over me, my skin tingling at the heat shining brightly in his eyes. "You're a beauty, darling. *My* beauty." He unbuckles his belt and snatches it out with a loud whoosh. The cracking leather adds sensual tension between us, causing my core to spasm. "Look at you all flushed and begging for your man. Are you wet, darling?"

Placing my splayed palms on my stomach, I glide them down until I reach the hem of my dress and slowly lift it, exposing myself to his hungry view. "Yes." Cupping myself, I rub up and down before pressing my heel on my clit and whimper as pleasure rocks through me in waves. "See?" I pull my panties to the side, showing him my center, and tap with my index finger. "Here. I need you here. Fucking me hard," I repeat. Closing my eyes, I imagine it, and my moan echoes in the greenhouse when he covers my hand with his, stilling my movements.

"Darling, your man is here. No one makes you come but me when I'm around." Pushing my palm aside, he hooks his fingers in my waistband and slowly pulls my panties down before throwing them aside. He clicks his tongue. "Darling, you're in bad need of a fucking." He traces his finger from bottom to top, his thumb brushing over my clit, and I whimper when he presses on it hard. Fireworks come undone inside me, and if I could just find the right amount of friction for me to find my bliss. "So wet and so mine." He fists my dress and then drags me upward, trapping my mouth in a hot kiss as he settles his palm on my flesh, pressing his heel hard while his finger thrusts into me, and we groan when my core clenches around him even though it's a poor substitute for his cock.

A scorching heat zips through me. I hook my hand on his neck, shifting closer to him as he dominates my mouth, stabbing his tongue deep and mimicking his actions. He drives me insane with each passing second while the tension rises within me, seeking to burst, yet my whole body weeps from dissatisfaction as he once again withholds my pleasure.

He chuckles when I bite on his tongue, grazing it with my teeth and tangling his fingers in my hair. I arch my back as he ravishes my mouth in even strokes. He adds one more finger inside me, pushing them farther and farther to prepare me for his wide and thick length.

Finally, he starts working his heel and fingers in tandem, and I rock my hips in time with his movements, finding the friction that shoots sensual stabs to my clit, making me see stars, and my whole being buzzes with anticipation.

I cry out in protest when he ends our kiss with a bite on my lower lip, his teeth sinking deep and stinging me. He licks over it. "We're going to fuck hard, darling." The air sticks in my lungs when he thrusts his fingers deep and then withdraws them leisurely and lifts them to my mouth, smearing my lips with my juice and my musky scent twitches my nose only tempting me more. "First, though, I'm going to worship this pussy as it deserves."

I yelp when he sends me flying to lie flat on my back. Shouldering my legs apart, he raises them, and my heels dig into the table's edge.

His breath fans my center, and I gasp when he rubs his cheeks on the inside of my thighs, pure fire consuming me at his touch. His light stubble marks me, and my core clenches at the thought, becoming wetter if possible.

I love when he marks my skin with love bites because they serve as a reminder of his obsession with me.

He sucks on my soft skin, earning my moans. His palms move around my hips, sliding underneath and palming my ass, his fingers digging deep, and I hiss at the contact. He lifts my ass and captures my stare, all while the fire turns everything around us to ashes where nothing but us remains. "Watch, Phoenix," he orders, and that's all the warning I get as he opens his mouth wide and places it on my core. My hips jerk, but his strong hands keep them still as he delivers sensual warmth and heat to my core.

I grab his dark locks and pull at them hard as he enters me with his tongue, swirling between my folds. He pulls back only to dive back again, pushing deeper with each stab and stretching me around his velvet flesh, the waves of heat hitting me all at once. I hate the feel of my skin right now because even my skin feels like a foreign object.

Sweat drips down my back, and I groan when he glides his tongue over my lips one by one. Sucking them both in and biting on them, he awakens all my nerve endings to the point of pain, and I hurt for some relief.

I put my foot on his shoulder, opening myself more for him. He growls against my flesh, the action tickling me and spreading tension all around me. The air becomes so thick you can cut it with a knife, yet I do nothing but let him play with me as he sees fit.

Because the idea of stopping him might just kill me.

His tongue moves back to my center, circling it before dipping in and out over and over again, pushing me closer to my release that's finally on the horizon. Fisting his hair tighter, I grind on his tongue in time with his movements, almost existing in a bubble of his own creation. The pressure grows and grows, urging me to shatter in his arms because only then will I get what I so desire.

"Zach, please," I plead as he moves his tongue upward, licking me from bottom to top, and jerk in his hold when he taps on my clit, scraping his teeth over it and then licking it, sucking on it. His tongue flicks it, sending arrows straight to my lust. My core clenches at the emptiness he quickly fills with his tongue, entering me again to repeat his torture all over.

He places my hips back on the table. I whimper at the warm wood that's almost hurtful on my flushed skin, then groan when he presses his thumb on my clit while his tongue roams inside me, exploring and feasting on me. "Zach, stop this." My nails cut into his nape, and I whimper at the inability to move my hips now, his forearm stilling me in place while he drags his mouth upward, licking me as his two fingers enter me. He thrusts them a few times, then invades me with his tongue again, showing no signs of stopping.

He keeps me on edge, and right when I think I'm going to fall, he pulls me back again and plays with my body once more.

I cannot stand it, the sensations traveling through me in rapid waves announcing my slipping control, and I decide that two can play this game. "I'm in need, darling," I tell him, my voice so husky I don't recognize it for a second. "I don't want to come on your tongue." I clench his hair and forcefully tug on his head until he meets my eyes, his lips glistening with me and causing my core to contract. "Fuck me, darling." Putting my fingers on my center, I open myself up more. "Right here and now."

He chuckles, the sound causing goose bumps, and instead of listening to me, he delivers a long lick to my flesh.

"Zachary, please." I thrash my head from side to side. He continues to drive me insane, moving his tongue around me leisurely. "Please do something!" I cry out in frustration.

"What do you want, darling?"

"You!"

"And who do you belong to?"

I exhale, grinning despite my frustration at the possessive note in his tone. Such a caveman. "You."

He drags his tongue one last time over my folds before wiping his mouth on my bare stomach. Tickling me, he straightens up and unzips his pants. His hard-on springs free, the precum leaking from the tip.

I run my tongue over my lower lip, just imagining his taste, and he chuckles when he notices my lingering stare. "Next time, darling. I'll enjoy putting you on your knees while I fuck this pretty mouth of yours." My groan fills the air, the images he's painting in my head making me hotter and craving to do just that.

Anything as long as he will finally give me what my body craves so much.

My skin is so taut I might burst at any moment, so I extend my hands to him and whisper, "Zach."

"I know, darling." He wraps his hand around his length and pulls me up with his other hand. His fingers lace in my hair, and he guides his cock to my entrance, rubbing me with the tip. "Put your legs around my waist, darling. You're about to be fucked hard." With a sob of relief, I do as he orders and circle his neck, hugging him close.

"Zach." That's all I manage to say as he captures my mouth with his. He thrusts into me swiftly, and we both groan at his length, stretching me wide.

But also...

From relief as we are once again connected in the most primal way.

I can taste myself on him, which only enhances my senses and makes me welcome the stroke of his tongue as he sways back and enters me hard once again, my core burning.

Sex with Zachary is an art form that ignites my blood and opens me up to a pleasure I never knew existed. Each time is different because sometimes he's gentle and slow, savoring every moment.

And sometimes...

Sometimes he's wild in his need and fucks me as he sees fit, owning my body and stamping his claims of ownership all over me.

Tearing my mouth away, I gasp for breath as his lips move to suck on the crook of my neck while his hips continue to drive into me. Each thrust is harder than the previous one, and his hands on my hips grip me so tightly they will leave bruises tomorrow.

Bruises I would love to caress in the morning while echoes of his lovemaking make me shiver.

The pressure inside me grows, his electric touches lighting me up and charging my blood with fire so strong, I can no longer contain it and just want to burn in it until nothing is left.

He speeds up his pace, his drive growing deeper, faster, and harder, pushing me and pushing me until I clamp my thighs around him, crying out when I find my peak.

My core becomes tighter around him as he thrusts into me several more times all while I hug him closer, running my palm over his damp back and letting him use me for his pleasure.

His muscles become rigid, and he tenses, entering me three more times before he groans into my neck, spilling inside me and probably creating a mess.

I don't care, though.

I don't care about anything when I'm in his arms.

Our raspy breaths fill the space as the rain blasts outside while the humidity is almost unbearable, and Zach says, "We should discuss your cases more often." A beat passes. "Consider me a frequent guest at your greenhouse in the future, love."

My laughter is the only answer.

We'll be okay.

After all, our love can survive even a storm.

CHAPTER EIGHT

"They say you need to live a life in such a way so you won't regret a single thing.
I never understood this, finding just the idea delusional.
How can you not regret the awful things? The pain and the tears?
But the older I become, the more I see the wisdom in it.
All our choices bring us to our present, and if we feel deeply loved and love in
return in our present...we don't regret it.
As regret means one thing only.
Wishing things could be different."
Phoenix

Phoenix

Something soft touches the tip of my nose for a brief
second. That's enough to wake me up, but instead of opening my eyes,
I burrow my face deeper into the pillow and sigh at my aching muscles.

My man knows how to exhaust my body in such a way even my
mind rests, my thighs still sensitive and sore from last night's torture.

I roll to my other side, adjusting the blanket on me only for the
bed to shift around me, and something touches my nose again. This
time, though, it presses hard on the tip, and I frown.

Hearing giggles around me, I snap my eyes open only to close them again from the blinding sun streaming through the curtains. "Wake up, Mama!" Ian says, tapping me on the nose again.

Wyatt must sit on my other side because he pats me on my shoulder. "Rise and shine!" he yells.

I hold back my chuckle because, really, waking up by them is never boring. I look at them, blinking several times to adjust my vision, and grin at Ian's beaming face in front of me. "Hi, honey."

"Hi." He leans closer and smacks a kiss on my cheek, and once he's done, Wyatt perches on my shoulder, smacking a kiss as well and winks at me.

Ah, my little ones.

"Daddy said that we need to wake you up," Ian tells me and sits up on his knees, pointing at the bedside clock. "Because you need to be somewhere soon, and you have to eat breakfast before that." My heart grows heavy with this, reality finally breaking into my sanctuary and heaven, pulling me back to the situation at hand with a case that's nothing but a headache.

I have an hour before heading to the prison and hopefully getting much-needed information. I studied the files yesterday after our greenhouse adventure.

Well, as much as I could before Zachary turned into a caveman and possessed my every thought, this time in our room, and wouldn't stop for hours.

Ian lowers his voice to a whisper. "Daddy is cooking it right now, but you didn't hear it from me."

My twins go through this stage where they make everything a big secret that they share with you alone even though no one tells them to keep it as such. We indulge in their little games since they bring no harm and probably create a sense of adventure for them.

Although judging by their character traits, they will grow up to be excellent chameleons and get to know everything they want from people because of their ability to create a sense of trust around them.

That's not here nor there, though.

"Okay. My lips are sealed." I do the zipping motion over my mouth, and they clap their hands. "Let me get up then."

They scoot away on the bed to give me space, and I sit up, grateful

I'm wearing pajamas right now, and take a second for a deep breath. It sticks in my lungs when they both hug me tight from either side, squeezing the life out of me. "Good morning, Mama," they say in unison, and I hug them right back, letting them soak up the embrace because all my kids have one trait in common.

They are huggers, and we never deny them any.

"We didn't come without knocking, Mama," Wyatt adds, frowning. "We didn't rebel." He sighs as if the idea saddens him. "Next time."

Unless they get scared in the middle of the night, they aren't allowed to enter our room without knocking, but generally, Zach sends one of the kids to wake me up in the morning.

After prison, I cannot stand alarm clocks. They always send this desperation through me along with a hopelessness that pollutes my mind. I get pulled back to flashbacks, making getting up a chore because I think I'll have to face some hideous things again.

Once Zach figured it out, he got rid of the alarm clock, and since he always gets up earlier than me, he took care of the problem.

Warmth fills every bone in my body at the thought, and tightening my hold on my children, I wonder how could anyone think I regret this life or one day wake up to just randomly hate everyone for no reason?

I love my family, and I would never do anything to hurt them, which only solidifies my theory that Miranda's either protecting her child or is a puppet in someone's hands.

She loves her girls, and she'd never put them through hell.

The twins lean back and grin at me. "Okay, little ones. Go downstairs, and I'll be there shortly," I whisper, making them nod. "Make sure to put a strawberry syrup on the table. It's my favorite." If Zach is cooking, that means we're having pancakes for breakfast.

"Sure thing, Mama," Ian shouts, and they hop from the bed, their little feet slapping against the marble as they run into the hallway, screaming their lungs out. "Daddy! Mama is awake!"

"Mission accomplished!"

I go into the bathroom, shimmying out of my pajamas, and quickly take a hot shower, welcoming the jets hitting my sore muscles while thinking about the case.

I have a strategy in my head that might be very effective to pull Miranda out of her cocoon and force her to feel emotions. However, the downside of that is...it might backfire, and she could close up altogether.

Although at this point, we don't have much to lose since we have no leads that would clue us in on what the potential unsub might even want with the kids. Those who kill a male figure in the family so violently rarely, if ever, happen to be a child predator as well.

Usually, the father is forced to watch his family's pain, undermining his authority and figuratively castrating him by making him helpless. Now in such cases, yes, the women and children are the targets.

This unsub, though, inspires more questions, and I damn sure need some answers to save the girls before he strikes again to sustain his desires or, worse, leave their dead bodies somewhere.

I turn off the water and grab a towel, drying myself off while stepping on a fluffy rug.

Coming closer to the mirror, I wipe away the fog and gasp as various hickeys mar my skin on my neck and collarbone. There are even some on my stomach.

Zachary staked his claim all over my body once again, using it as a canvas for his possessive nature, and while goose bumps break on my skin from the memories alone, I groan when I think about how I'll have to cover them all up.

Last night my husband needed reassurance that I'm his, and I don't regret a thing as well. I hope he understands with all his being that I love him with everything in me.

Quickly blow-drying my hair and leaving it loose, I go to the room and put on clothes, opting for a woolen dress with a high neck to cover all these love bites.

But also because I cannot stand the cold since prison, I need to be warm. For more than three years, I was constantly freezing, figuratively and literally.

Dumping my keys and phone into my bag along with the case file, I wear my boots and go downstairs as the hallway hums with a mixture of my family's voices from the kitchen and classical music.

"Emmaline, my ears will bleed soon," Ian exclaims dramatically. "Can we listen to something else, please?"

"I can't! I have a performance soon. I have to listen to classical music." She has a point there. She memorizes her steps easier when she listens to the music frequently.

"You can do it in your dancing room. Not here while we eat." Wyatt pitches in, and I hear him sharing a high five with his twin. "This music is boring."

"Take it back! It's not," Emmaline shouts, offended, and she taps her foot on the floor judging by the sound. "Take it back, Wyatt!"

"Children, please. Behave!" Patience chastises them, but of course they don't pay her any attention.

While they have deep respect for their nanny, who used to be Zachary's nanny as well, the competitive and stubborn nature they share with their father always trumps their common sense.

Sometimes I think this will be my children's downfall.

"I won't. It's boring. I said it again," Wyatt shouts and laughs, only for his laughter to turn into a groan as I enter the kitchen and see Emmaline trapping him in the crook of her elbow and holding him still while he tries to free himself.

"Apologize!" she tells him, and he pulls at her arm, rolling his tongue at her while Ian stuffs his mouth with a pancake, chuckling as he watches them.

Patience looks scandalized, I think that's her permanent facial expression ever since the twins were born, though. I glance at my husband, who flips several pancakes on the stove, creating a rather tempting picture.

He's wearing sweatpants and a shirt that showcases all his masculine beauty in its glory and reminds me that these hard muscles were pressed tight against me last night. My cheeks heat, thinking about the nail marks I must have left on his back.

He half turns to me, a wicked smile curving his lips, and he winks at me, sending scorching heat through me. It should be a crime to be this affected by your husband.

However, the kids' fight pulls me back to the present as Emmaline shouts, "Say sorry, Wyatt!"

"No! Your music is boring!"

Okay, enough of this.

Placing my bag on the kitchen counter, I walk to the mug shelf, snag my favorite one, and pour myself hot green tea in it while saying, "I'm going to count to five." The minute the words slip past my lips, my kids freeze, clearly surprised to see me standing here. Emmaline quickly lets him go.

They straighten up, guilty expressions crossing their faces but then stubbornness fills their eyes, and they lift their chins high, sending each other a glare.

"Ha, ha! I'm not the one in trouble,'" Ian exclaims, raising his splayed palm. "High five, Patience." To my astonishment, the nanny slaps his hand, and he goes back to eating his pancake while my two other children just stare at me without blinking.

"Emmaline. Remember our conversation last month?" She nods, biting her lip. "You can listen to your music without headphones in your dancing studio, your room, or when it doesn't bother anyone else around you." I motion to the table where the speaker stands. "The kitchen is not one of those places."

Wyatt opens his mouth to comment but shuts it when I focus on him. "You need to apologize to your sister for being rude." I wait for a beat. "You can voice your opinion without being rude about it. We discussed this."

While my kids are the best of friends, and their fights never last long, their characters, due to the courtesy of their father, make me worry about leaving all these issues unnoticed.

If they don't learn how to deal with their hot-headed nature early on, it will bring a lot of problems in the future, and I'm trying to actively avoid it.

"I'm sorry, Emmaline. Even though your music is boring, I love you and should not have said it."

"It's okay, Wyatt. I'm sorry too, and I love you." They hug each other and then go to their seats, joining Ian since Patience has already filled their plates with food.

Zach turns off the stove and puts the last pancake on the plate next to it. Spinning around to face me, he grabs my elbow and pulls me close to him, wrapping his arm around my waist. "That was excellent parenting, Dr. King."

Rolling my eyes, I lift my face as we share a quick kiss, and then I mutter against his lips, making him laugh, "You're just glad you didn't have to play the bad guy and got to keep your popularity with the kids." For all his ruthless nature, he can never ever punish them or scold them.

It's funny, really.

"You know me so well." He cups my cheek, rubbing his thumb over my skin, and a sigh escapes me. "Everything all right?"

"Yes. Couldn't be better." I puff air. "Except—"

He puts a finger on my lips, silencing whatever else I want to say. "Remember about the rules. Breakfast with the family and then work."

Ah, yes. The rule I came up with so we could enjoy family time without Zachary constantly being on the phone and neglecting the kids. My work usually is never this hectic because I don't try catching criminals on the loose eager for my suffering.

I bite his finger, and he hisses through his teeth while his eyes flash in heat. "You're too cocky, darling."

"I know. I think that's why you love me, right?" I shake my head at him and turn around, marching to the table and sitting opposite the kids. Emmaline occupies the seat between the twins, and they all dip their forks full of pancakes in syrup and then shove them in their mouths, smearing chocolate all over their chins.

The table is heavy with food, from pancakes to berries and fruits and syrups. The kids have their cups filled with tea while Patience sips her hot water for her gallbladder. It's been giving her issues lately. "How do you feel, Patience?"

She winces a bit as she shifts in her chair. "Better than yesterday. Need to schedule a visit to the doctor." She tears a tissue and gives it to Ian. He wipes his mouth before snatching a strawberry and munching on it soundly. "I hope you don't plan on any more kids because I won't be able to watch over them," she mutters from the corner of her mouth. "I've dealt with the infamous King temperament for over forty years. Let me tell you, I'm done."

"No worries. We don't plan on more." I'm also not ready to handle more of the said temperament.

"Today is your lucky day, Patience." Zachary drops next to me, grabbing two plates for us, and I put avocado and pancakes on it along with some strawberries while he helps himself to just a pancake, pouring syrup over it.

"Why is that?"

"Because I'm taking the kids to their grandparents'."

"Woo-hoo!" the twins exclaim and share a high five above Emmaline's head. She rolls her eyes at me but claps her hands as well, excitement written all over her face.

Zachary's father and his stepmother love to have the little ones over several times a month, and usually, they are so spoiled rotten there that dragging them home is a chore.

I look at Zach, who answers my silent question. "Dad called earlier and asked if it was okay to have the kids for the weekend. I figured it's a good idea, all things considered." Swallowing my avocado and washing it away with tea, I nod.

If we have a psycho on the loose who, God forbid, decides to enter our home, our kids are way safer with their grandfather. His house is so protected, a fly won't pass by without someone noticing. He became a bit paranoid in recent years, not that we blame him. "Yes." Plus, the kids won't have to witness my stress over the case or find any disturbing images. Since the clock is ticking, it should all be done by the end of the weekend.

"So you have time for yourself, Patience," Zach tells her, and she smiles, sipping her water as we all eat for several moments. The kids chat animatedly about the upcoming trip and what they will do at their grandparents'.

"We can bake cookies with Grandma!"

"You always want to bake cookies, Ian. Only for you to eat them all and leave nothing for us." Emmaline points at him with her strawberry. "Let's bake a cake."

"I hate baking cakes. No, I hate baking, period. It's boring!" Wyatt replies, dragging his fork over the pancake. "I have a better plan. Game night!"

"No!" Emmaline shouts, horrified, and I barely hold back my laughter while Zach grins. "You will both cheat and then claim victory." Before anyone can protest, she adds, "You are sore losers!"

"We are not," Wyatt defends them. "We just sometimes argue if the game was not played in our favor." Ian nods, fully agreeing with him, and Emmaline sighs heavily. My poor girl, always being outnumbered when it comes to their antics.

"It's the same thing, Wyatt."

"They will make excellent lawyers one day." Zachary sips his coffee and leans closer to me, placing his arm on my chair, surrounding me with his scent and power. "Will put to good use all their natural skills."

"Your natural skills, you mean?"

He gasps, horrified, placing his hand on his chest. "Are you implying they get it from me?"

"Well, they didn't get it from me. You're banned from family game nights for a reason."

He frowns, displeasure dripping from his words. "That's because I won that game fair and square, and no one could handle it."

"Ah, so they do get it from you?"

We share a long stare, then he kisses me as the kids groan loudly and cover their eyes.

Someone rings the doorbell, and we both freeze. I lean back and blink at him in surprise.

No one ever rings the bell. Usually, to get inside the property, the security needs to get the all clear from the home staff.

Zachary glances at Patience, who already has an explanation. "I got a text from Ryan asking to let in a man who wants to see you. He took his ID." Which means he's never come here. "They checked his car and everything else. He said it was urgent, so I gave the all clear. Is that okay?"

By how tense Zachary grows next to me, I know it's not, and he must use all his willpower not to snap at the woman.

We don't go on lockdown or anything, but with the current state of affairs, we are more agitated than usual.

We hear one of the maids open the door, letting someone in, and she informs him, "The family is currently having breakfast. You can wait in the living room and—"

"It's fine," a husky, deep voice replies, and Zachary's eyes flash in recognition. Any tension eases from me. At least it's not the enemy.

Loud tapping fills the space, and in several seconds, a man wearing a suit enters, but I barely pay him any attention when I notice the time on my watch. I kiss my husband once more and murmur, "I have to go."

"Call me once it's done."

"Of course."

I blow a kiss to my little ones, and they do it right back. "Behave at your grandparents'."

"Don't we always, Mama?" they ask innocently, and then giggle when I wiggle my finger at them. Snagging my bag, I muster up a brief glance at the man, who nods at me, and then dash into the hallway.

I hear Emmaline announcing she's done and is going to practice now as Patience tells the boys to clean up, probably giving Zach privacy.

Breathing in fresh air as I step outside, I dial my driver's number, mentally preparing myself to face Miranda and all her secrets.

And hope like hell these secrets will never hurt what I love the most.

My family.

CHAPTER NINE

"Keep your friends close.
And your enemies?
As far away as possible."
Zachary

Zachary
   "Tell me, Rafael. Do you have a death wish?" I ask the fucker the minute the twins leave with Patience. I groan inwardly at the cocky smirk because the kid is trouble in the making. He might think that his brains and talent make him somewhat special, but news flash?

   No one fucking is. That's why everyone craves power for those who have it...rule the world and get whatever they want.

   I gave him a warning in my office yesterday to stay away and instructed my staff as much, blacklisting him, but I didn't think about warning my home security.

   Truth be told, I didn't expect him to be this stupid or bold, depending on how one prefers to look at it. And the worst part about it?

I'm even curious about why he's here because the fucker reminds me of myself at his age.

God bless my father for putting up with all this bullshit from me.

"Hello to you too, *Mr. King*." He emphasizes it, clearly mocking my request to address me like that. Grabbing a chair at the table, he pulls it out and drops onto it while he points at the coffee pot. "I like mine black."

"I must have missed the part where I offered you one," I deadpan, and he laughs while I grab my mug, studying him since I'm sitting on the chair opposite him. "What brings you here?"

"I must say you're very rude to your guests." He picks up a clean fork, digging it into one of the pancakes, and is ready to lift it to his mouth when I slap his hand, and it drops on his lap. "Fuck," he mutters under his breath, tearing a tissue from a box and wiping his pants. "The hell, Mr. King. You're so cheap I can't even eat a pancake?"

Welcome to the real world, Rafael.

"To be considered my guest, you have to be invited." He wipes harder, although the butter will probably stain, and he'll need a new suit. "And unless you're here to apologize for barging into my office and making demands, you aren't allowed to eat my food." I take a sip from my coffee, welcoming the bitter taste on my tongue. "What's it going to be, Wright?"

"I don't apologize. Ever," he replies steely, and my brows shoot up at this. He truly is in a lot of ways like me.

I guess he has sixteen more years to discover that some conviction can be shoved up our asses, but that's a story for another time.

"However, if I were you, I'd be nice to me. After all, I came here." I stay silent, just watching him broodily, and he rolls his eyes while he pushes away all the plates. "Against my better judgment, may I add."

Oh, this is going to be good.

Because if what he says is true, then it means his high moral code urged him to look deeper into the case, and what he might have uncovered doesn't work in favor of his client.

We stare at one another for several beats, and I motion with my hand. "Well? Will you continue to keep the suspense going or finally say what it is about?"

He places a folder between us and slides it to me. "This is the lab result studying your signatures." Frowning, I flip it open and quickly scan through it. "According to it, the signature on the contract is indeed yours."

Sitting up straight, I put my coffee on the table with a loud bang where it splashes a little. "I've never signed this contract."

"You might have. You're a busy man who signs a lot of things. Maybe you didn't read it properly or notice it."

"That's impossible. I always read what I sign."

That was one of the most important rules my father drilled into me from an early age.

Whatever you sign or agree on, you read properly because the consequences of not doing it might be severe. To manage an empire, you always have to know what's going on because if shit hits the fan, it's your face and reputation smeared in the dirt.

Rafael shrugs, snagging a strawberry and popping it in his mouth. "The fact remains that it's your signature, and it will hold power in court." He raises his hand, stopping whatever I want to say. "And while you told me to keep in touch only via Sebastian, I thought you'd prefer to hear it from me." He pops another strawberry, chewing on it soundly. "So I have a new contract for you." He points at the folder, and I flip it to the next page, reading it. "Five hundred million settlement. The deal stays between us, and no information will be leaked to the press. My client is happy, and your reputation remains intact. With one condition."

I barely hold back my laughter, considering this proposition sounds more like an order, but I'm too curious to see what's next to tell him to go to hell. I take a large sip of my coffee and ask, "What is the condition?"

"You fire Howard, and he goes to jail for fabricating the signature and deceiving my client." My brows shoot up at this. "I think it's clear as day that your employee has been going behind your back and fattening his pockets. In fact, if you look closely into his latest activities, he somehow opened up all these bank accounts in Europe." He leans back on his chair, his calculating stare filling his cold green eyes as he elaborates. "This contract is a win-win situation."

The audacity of this man has to be seen to be believed.

Howard is a dead man when it comes to the corporate world anyway. I've already started the process of firing him while Zeke gathers the dirt on the man so we can give all the paperwork to Sebastian and start our own lawsuit against the crimes he's committed.

The man even dared to open up a company under our family name, so he has to be dealt with in the cruelest of ways.

I will show no mercy and won't rest until he ends up on the bottom of the food chain, wanting to see his misery. The only kindness I will show is to his wife and two children, allowing them to keep some of the money and properties, but the rest?

Oh, it will be auctioned off all right.

Especially the gold coin collection he cherishes so much.

Finishing my coffee, I play with the rim of the mug and finally speak up. "Let me get this straight. You want me to pay your client five hundred million and fire one of my employees, publicly humiliating him for committing a crime and wronging your client?" He nods. "Rafael, you see the problem here, right? Why would I pay anything if my signature was fabricated?"

"Because you cannot prove it. If we go to court with this, you will have to pay more. Even the best lawyer in the world can't argue the test results." He motions with his chin at the papers.

I'm starting to think Rafael isn't bright to begin with. This doesn't even make sense. "If we prove Howard fabricated my signature, the court won't side with you."

A sinister smile shapes his mouth, and excitement crosses his face. "Here comes the fun part. What if I told you I have video proof of Howard committing a crime and talking shit about you? The kind of proof that will make your life easier." I ordered Zeke to do as much. Based on my suspicions, I could fire Howard immediately, but to ruin his reputation, I needed proof. My head of security has come up blank so far. "And should the public get it, Howard won't be able to show his nose...anywhere."

"How do you have it?"

"I have my methods." He leans closer and pops his fingers. "My client is just the beginning. You might have more lawsuits heading your way if you don't find a good proof to shut everyone up. Five hundred million is a small price to pay for your peace. We both know it's like pocket change for you."

I study him for several seconds and then look back at the contract, carefully evaluating all the points and thinking about his proposition.

On the grand scale of things, yes. Five hundred million isn't a lot for my company, plus the benefit of sending Howard behind bars and ending any potential lawsuits is tempting.

But a man doesn't put this much effort into a case if he doesn't have personal gain in it, and Wright needs to do more than win this case.

"I come from generational wealth." His brow furrows at this. Clearly, it's not what he expected to hear from me. "We have more money than we will be able to use in thousands of lifetimes."

"Exactly."

"And while it might seem that it makes us entitled assholes, we do, in fact, know the value of money. The Kings don't react well to blackmail."

"No one is blackmailing you, Mr. King." Steel coats his voice with annoyance as he must guess this meeting won't end to his satisfaction. "In fact, I'm trying to save you."

"Oh, you are? And why is that, Rafael?"

"I believe in justice. I'd hate for you to be called a liar when you aren't."

"How generous of you." I decide to fire my own question. "Hard, isn't it? Sacrificing your own integrity due to your boss's wish." He freezes, the muscle twitching on his cheek, but he stays silent. "Whatever you want from him must be truly special."

"It is," he replies to my surprise, and that's when I remember Lauren has a daughter that's around Rafael's age.

Oh, poor kid if that's the reason, because his boss guards her like a hawk, not because he loves her so much.

The fucker is too cold for that.

He saves her beauty and charms to trap the biggest prey and gain even more leverage in the world. Simply put, Rafael isn't good enough and won't be for years to come.

I close the folder and push it back at him. "Thank you for this proposition, but like I said before, I won't pay a dime to atone for something I haven't done. You want to sit on the Howard information and allow your client to sue me, knowing full well what he does is a crime...be my guest. I do warn you, though. When this comes to light, your life will be very difficult." I glance at the wooden clock hanging on the wall. I need to wrap it up before taking the kids to my father's house and inform him about this problem. "I don't want to repeat myself, Rafael. I said it all in my office."

With this, I get up, and he does the same, gathering his file and shaking his head at me. "You're so willing to lose this case just because someone outsmarted you?"

I grin at him. "No. I just don't betray my principles for anyone or anything, even my empire." His eyes flash dangerously. He doesn't appreciate the hint, but who gives a fuck? "Regrets are a heavy weight to live with. Remember that. It's still not too late to change your mind."

"Keep your advice to yourself, Mr. King." He waves his hand in a *don't bother* gesture. "No need to warn me off your property either. Believe me, I won't step a single foot in this house again. Coming here and talking some sense into you was a mistake. You want war, so you shall have it."

He spins around, ready to bolt, but pauses when Emmaline runs inside the kitchen and collides with him.

She sways backward, and he manages to catch her before she falls. "Thank you!" she tells him, and he barely spares her a glance before looking over his shoulder at me and leaving without uttering a single word.

Yes.

Dealing with Rafael Wright will be truly a treat.

Emmaline gapes at him and then shifts her attention to me, and I expect her to chatter about the upcoming trip to her grandparents'. She shocks me, though, when she says, "He's a lawyer, right?"

"Yes. How do you know?" If this guy spied on my kids, I'm going to go fucking ballistic.

Coming to my home was already crossing a line.

"I've seen him before. At Nancy's house." Her classmate who recently moved to New York after her father got a promotion.

The kid was awfully quiet so Emmaline took it upon herself to be her friend and often went to her house where they did homework. This pleased her parents because, according to them, Nancy never had any friends.

"What did he do there?"

"He came once and delivered some bad news to her father. Nancy said after that he drinks a lot." Emmaline frowns, sadness lacing her tone, and I wonder what Nancy's dad could have possibly done.

His reputation in the professional world is stellar, so only God knows what Rafael has on him to drive him to such a state.

Emmaline comes closer and hugs me, concern filling her eyes. "Everything is all right, Daddy, right?"

I smile at her, running my fingers through her hair, and thank the universe for the hundredth time that this little girl is mine because she and the twins are perfect. "Yes, honey. Just a little issue that I will solve." I trap her nose, and she laughs. "Because what do Kings do?"

"Win anything with anyone!"

"Correct. Now, go get your brothers, and let's take you to Grandpa and Grandma's. They can't wait to see you." She squeals in happiness and rushes upstairs while I snatch my phone and text Zeke.

Whatever Rafael has, he needs to find.

Like Emmaline just said.

Kings win anything with anyone.

CHAPTER TEN

"Sometimes to understand the evil done to us, we need to travel back to the past.
Not our own.
But to the past of the monster who teared us apart piece by piece."
Phoenix

Phoenix

"You're back." Miranda greets me as I enter the interrogation room, relief crossing her face before she gives me the indifference again.

I mentally make a note about it because it pushes toward the theory that her children are in danger, and all her actions yesterday were just an act designated for the viewers.

She sports a new black eye, and according to the correctional officer, she got into another fight so she'd remain in isolation. If she continues at this rate, she won't live long.

Some inmates aren't known to be kind and hold weapons that can truly end your life.

A conversation I had with Noah minutes ago pops in my mind.

"We record the interrogations with inmates to study their facial expressions

later for the profile. We won't do it because the unsub probably gets access to it online. He can watch."

I shake my head. "No. Let him see and listen." *He lifts his brow, cocking his head to the side, probably trying to guess what I'm thinking about.* "These recordings are his comfort zone. I will try speaking to him through it. Or to Catriona. Depending on which theory of ours is right."

He grabs my elbow before I can press on the keypad and lowers his voice. "Careful. We don't want to antagonize him." *Pulling my elbow back, I still give him the cold shoulder for all this bullshit, and he sighs in exasperation.* "It won't happen again, Phoenix. This is the last time I'm asking for your help." *He covers his bandaged nose.* "Trust me, Zachary made that crystal clear."

"We both know you're lying."

Hell will freeze over before I trust any of them again. The law doesn't care about your emotions; it only cares about inflicting its rights and making everyone obey them.

That includes agents who want to use you.

"Do you have some news for me?" Miranda's eager voice brings me back to the present. "You found my babies with all the clues I've given you?"

A humorless chuckle leaves me. "You've given me no clues, Miranda. In fact, I think you expressed your opinions. One of them being that you don't care what happens to them, one way or the other."

She bristles in anger and bangs her fist on the table, rattling it a little while her chains slap against it. "I never said that!" She all but yells it.

Unfazed by her attitude because anger is better than indifference, I sit on the chair and drop my folder between us. "Well, according to you, death was a better option than telling me the truth. I can read between the lines. Sometimes what we don't say has more meaning than the things we do end up saying." She opens her mouth, but my raised palm stops whatever she plans to say.

This time around, she can't have the upper hand in the conversation, and besides, I'm better prepared. Yesterday, I was shaken by all the memories. Today, the professional me pushed through the pain and decided to win this case no matter the cost.

I'll catch the unsub.

"Tell me about your husband, Miranda." She blinks several times. "How did he propose to you?"

"How is this helping my daughters?" she asks, and I just stare at her until she exhales heavily. "We had a fashion show in Paris. He bought the ring with the biggest diamond and proposed to me at the after-party while everyone gasped around us and took pictures." Her tone stays even, void of any emotions. She clasps her hands, though, her thumb pressing on her skin and leaving bruises while she looks into the distance. "I was happy he popped the question and we married. The rest is history."

"So you loved him?"

She bites on her lip. "Yes, I did. He was a prince. What was there not to love about him?" She digs her nail deeper into her flesh while taking a deep breath. "I was lucky. Everyone wanted him, and I got him."

Luck is a tricky word, considering her late husband was known to have a temper and go through his trust fund so fast, his father constantly had to add to it. And clean up all his messes.

"You said that you met him when you were eighteen." I open the folder and snatch out the printed document. "This states otherwise. You had a modeling event in Los Angeles, and he was on the same flight with you." I put the paper closer to it, and she glances at it. "You were seventeen then."

She sits up straight, pressing her back to her chair, and shakes her head. "Yes. Lots of people fly on the same plane without meeting each other. We've known of each other but no one formally introduced us."

"Except that's a lie." I take a picture of them both checking into the hotel and show it to her while she freezes. "These were taken by the paparazzi, who thought they had good gossip. It was never made public because your father-in-law paid a hefty sum to the magazine."

Silence falls after my statement while I study her every expression. She winces while looking at the picture as pain along with fear color her eyes before she closes them and rolls her lips.

Then she stops hurting herself, and her hands start to rub against each other, her breathing speeding up, and she swallows hard.

One might think she expresses such emotions toward her memories because her husband is dead, except the pure terror combined with the information lets me know that's not the case.

Not giving her an opportunity to gather herself, I take out another paper. "On the same night, you were admitted to the hospital with internal bleeding. Plus you had several bruises on your body and a twisted ankle. The hotel maid found you in the hallway holding your ripped clothes to your chest."

The air hitches in her throat, and she taps with her foot, swallowing several times before replying. "Everyone knows about this incident. I was attacked on my way to my room after the fashion show."

Oh, yes.

I was doing my residency when it happened, and it was quite the news, especially with how popular she was back in the day. She spent a week in the hospital and then countless magazines asked for interviews where she spoke about it often.

"Your father-in-law was the first one to arrive at the hospital, wasn't he? It was him who the doctor delivered the news to." She stares at me, not even blinking, and only by the vein pulsing rapidly on her neck can I guess her turmoil. "He was also the one who asked to speak to you before the cops could reach you. As he put it"—I flip several pages, finding the right one and reading it out loud—"your state was too fragile at the moment, and he asked for privacy despite the police intending to catch the criminal who had done this to you."

"Why are you wasting our time?" she hisses, fisting her hands once again. "You're here to investigate and get the clues on my daughters but instead you talk about an incident that happened to me ages ago." The tapping becomes more furious while anger practically pours from her. "Maybe you're not as good as they claim."

Ironic, isn't it?

Because her reaction is exactly what gives her away and lets me know we're moving in the right direction.

Break her, Phoenix, and her behavior will allow you to fill in the blanks in this puzzle.

My heart warms at my husband's soothing voice in my head, enveloping me in his protection and love even if he isn't close to me.

If it wasn't for him, I don't think I'd be able to stay this calm during this interview, considering my conclusions and revelations are devastating no matter who the unsub is.

"You wanted me on the case, right?" I fire my own question, and she grits her teeth, still glaring at me. "I'm working in my own way. I can walk away, though, if you dislike my methods. The ball is in your court."

I give her a second to dwell on it before rising from the seat, when she reaches for my hand, but the handcuffs don't allow her much movement, and she winces. "No. Ask your stupid questions if you must." She looks up at me and then casts her gaze down. Without a shadow of a doubt, I know the unsub is spying on us, so she doesn't dare kick me out.

"Your father-in-law was quite the hero that night, wasn't he? He even bought you a house afterward."

She laughs, the bitter sound of it causing disgusting goose bumps to break on my skin. "Yes, practically a saint. Don't forget about the one million he deposited in my account." She clicks her tongue. "Generous is the word you're looking for."

More like a monster but I keep this to myself and instead snatch another paper out. "You had your next runaway show two months later just as you turned eighteen and where Matt proposed. Somewhere between when you met and fell in love, right?"

"I already answered that."

"Yes, except the math doesn't add up."

"Everyone knows he fell in love with me from the first glance. It took him a week."

I grin, although inside I'm fuming. "What's interesting is that Matt had been to all your fashion shows two years prior, always seeking your company, yet you refused him. There were people."

She bites on her lip, bruising it. "I was the most successful model, of course he wanted to meet me. There was just no time."

"Los Angeles was the exception, wasn't it?" She stays silent, so I change the subject. "You guys married within a month, and then seven months later, you had a baby girl. According to the doctor she was a

preemie with perfect health. Didn't even need to stay at the hospital."
I clap my hands. "Go, Catriona."

"Is there a point to all this?" She taps several times. "I assure you I
don't need a rundown of my life. I was there, in case you missed it."

Ignoring her angry hiss, I get to another document. "Several
months after she was born, you were admitted to the hospital once
again. This time because you fell down the stairs. A concussion and a
broken wrist."

"I was taking medications for my headaches, they made me dizzy."

I barely resist the desire to curse out loud at this because it almost
sounds as if she believes it, when in truth…

Focus, Phoenix, focus. Personal emotions don't exist right now.

"Over the years, you've had a lot of such incidents. Broken wrists,
ankles, hands, and once even a nose. Your dizziness became the reason
you left the modeling business behind and became a stay-at-home
mom. Then you had two more daughters."

"Designers didn't want bruised models." Pain laces her tone, and
she traces her finger on the table. "It was for the best. I wanted to
spend my time with the girls." Her tone warms, and she reaches for her
neck only to catch air in her fist.

A reflex, she used to wear a medallion with their pictures on it, but
the police took it away.

"Yes. You adored them. So did your husband. Perfect little angels,
aren't they?" She nods. "Except Catriona. This one has brought trouble
lately, hasn't she?"

I place one photo after another of her oldest daughter in compro-
mising positions.

Smoking outside the school.

Driving the car without a license.

Getting into a fight with a girl who happened to be the principal's
daughter so she was sent on a month-long probation.

"Overnight, your little girl changed from this—" I tap on Catriona's
photo where she grins into the camera, her red hair glistening under
the sunset while she wears a white dress and holds dandelions in her
hands. "To this. Without an explanation. From a perfect A student and
a cheerleader to someone who ignores school altogether and mingles

with the wrong crowd." I tap on another photo where Catriona frowns into the camera. She cut off her long hair to barely reach her shoulders and started wearing dark clothes even during hot days. "I believe she was even caught drinking at a party."

All teenagers change and sometimes rebel. That's a normal stage of them growing up because they taste boundaries and want to separate themselves from their parents. And contrary to what most believe, they are also in the emotional and sometimes physical pain over their new realities.

Not to mention hormones dictating a lot of their moves.

Catriona's case, though?

A teenager doesn't change her entire personality just because she becomes older. This is a trauma response.

"She was never a trouble," she yells at me and covers the photos with her palm. "My girl is sweet, caring, and kind. She just found new friends, and wanted to be like them."

"Interesting theory, except according to everyone, she stopped talking to her best friends and just hung out with all the misfits."

"She's fifteen. She's allowed a little rebellion." She defends her daughter right away, and I look over my shoulder at the glass, giving Noah a silent signal to turn off the recording process. Then I shift my focus back on Miranda again as she continues, "Besides, her grades were still better than anyone else's. My girl is smart."

Leaning back on the chair, I cross my arms while she fidgets with her fingers, pulling the photos closer to her. "Your husband didn't think so, right? He even signed her up for therapy." I pause. "She didn't like the idea so they had a lot of fights. Your staff said as much."

Panic flashes in her eyes, and she sucks a breath through her teeth before replying, her voice trembling slightly. "Matt loved everyone and everything in his life to be perfect. Catriona ruined the image a little bit, and her grandfather wasn't happy. So he tried his best to talk to her, but she wouldn't listen. She wouldn't listen to me either," she finishes on a whisper, exhaling heavily.

Finally, we are moving in the right direction. I prepare to ask the most crucial questions because everything so far has been foreplay in this investigation to make her lose her guard and dig deep into her emotions. "He arranged for her to go to a boarding school."

She freezes and frowns. "What?" She bangs on the table, the smoke almost coming out of her ears. "That son of a bitch wanted to send my baby away?" She shouts something incomprehensible and then bangs on the table even harder. "Bastard!"

It's safe to say that was not the reason she might have killed her husband, then.

"Although he made all the arrangements, the school was never notified of her arrival. He did buy an apartment near the school for her, though." Which I found strange. What's the point of a boarding school if your kid has to live somewhere else?

Besides, how else would he control her?

Her breathing speeds up, her veins pulsing wilder while her eyes become glazed. Fury pours from her, hitting me with its energy as if a thousand waves crashed into me. By how hard she squeezes her fists, I know she's barely holding on to her control. "Bastard. That bastard!" she hisses, anger and hatred lacing the words.

So finally I go for the kill.

"Tell me, Miranda. Did you kill your husband because he abused you all this time?"

She snaps out of her shock and then erupts in a manic laughter till tears slide down her cheeks.

"Oh my God." She splays her palms open on the table. "That's the conclusion you come up with after studying my life? That he abused me." Another round of laughter. "Everyone knew that, and I wasn't the only one. He'd hit the staff too, but then pay them so generously no one ever reported him." She grins, flashing her teeth. "Do you know that once he took a belt and hit me with it one hundred times? I still have scars from the metal buckle. My back was bleeding, and I couldn't leave my room for a month." Chills run down my spine just imagining it. "I shouted for help over and over again. And no one showed. Not one single person dared to interrupt him while he beat the shit out of me."

"So you hated them for it?"

She shrugs. "No. I mean, I stayed with him, right? I guess I deserved it in their eyes."

"No one deserves it."

She dismisses my words with a wave of her hand. "Please, spare me the speeches. I know what people think. *Why won't you leave him? It's so easy.*" She makes a high-pitched tone on the last sentence. "I've heard enough of this bullshit."

"So you didn't kill him because he did all this to you?"

She cocks her head to the side, seeming to gather all her vulnerabilities, and stares at me in her general *don't give a fuck* attitude. "No. I mean, don't get me wrong, he deserved all this, but no. It's almost disappointing that you came up with that conclusion." She sighs dramatically. "Although it's understandable. After all, you married a man who paid inmates to beat you up in this prison."

Everything around me goes still at this. The energy changes from semi angry to full-on furious when she attacks me, and because she makes it personal, I know we are coming closer to the truth.

My heart flips in my chest. However, I control my facial expressions and just lift my brow. "He did," I simply say, not hiding the truth.

Annoyance crosses her face. Clearly, she didn't get the desired effect, so she tries again. "Is this why you came to such a conclusion?"

"What do you mean?"

"Do you sometimes remember what your husband did and want to just kill him for all the pain you experienced?" she asks giddily, leaning in as if wanting to savor my devastation, and I swallow at the assumption.

Her grin slips away at my reply, "No. My husband never hurt me."

She huffs. "You will deny—"

"No. What he did to me in this prison, well, what people did per his order...it was done by a man who hated me. We didn't know each other." She blinks. "He never hurt me afterward. So I don't know what it is like to be with a man who hurts you on a daily basis because my husband has been nothing but loving to me." This is the truth that I wish I could shout from the rooftops. Although I don't have to prove anything to anyone, and while my trauma might echo in my brain from time to time, I know my husband.

He loves me and when he loves...he loves with everything in him, and unfortunately, his vicious hate toward those who threaten or hurt his family is the result of such love.

I have no illusions who I married, and maybe that's one more reason I don't like to discuss the past with Zachary. It pains me to rehash it because then it feels as if I blame him for everything that has happened to me all these years ago when I don't.

His one decision hurt me, yes, when he took Emmaline away from me, but with that particular serial killer hunting after me...looking back on it, I think it was the best decision overall, even if it still sends hurt through me.

Zachary is ruthless, cruel, and far from perfect.

But he has been nothing but perfect to me after I was released from prison, and I love my man.

I clear my throat while Miranda continues to stare at me. "His abuse was not enough to give him a death warrant, then?" She shakes her head. "Okay. Then I have another question." With this, I remove Miranda from the suspect list, leaving Catriona and some other potential unsub.

Miranda could have committed a crime of passion. In that case, she would have just killed him, and that's it. Once the shock had worn off, she'd regret what she had done and would have been afraid for her babies.

Nothing in her biography or actions proves her being capable of all this, let alone keeping away her children. It can even protect the person who should face the consequences of their actions rather than let them suffer.

"It's useless, and you're wasting time. How many hours do you have left anyway?" The furious tapping of the foot comes back, and she pulls at her wrists. "You should be with the agents trying to find my babies with all the clues I've given you."

"We follow the process, Miranda. As we uncover things, we talk them through and uncover more." I rest my elbows on the table's edge, holding her gaze. "Unless there is something you want to tell me? Something that could speed up our investigation."

For a second, regret shows on her face, but she tears her eyes away from me, focusing on the cuticle on her nail, flicking it back and forth. "No. You need to discover it on your own." Her words are barely audible. "Otherwise, the game doesn't count."

The game.

Because psychopaths love to play them and manipulate you the way they see fit, enjoying the process far more than the outcome.

I bet the person watching us gets off on all this, and us cutting off his video now sent him into a hissy fit, not that I care.

Based on all the information so far, he is very methodical and follows rules to a T, so he won't do anything with the kids because of us.

He might, though, if they piss him off, and I have no choice but to be intentionally cruel right now.

"If you haven't killed your husband...do you think your daughter might have?" She raises her eyes back at me. "Because she discovered she was the result of a rape?"

Her screams reverberate through the walls, and I get up swiftly, moving away when she pulls at her restrains, trying to get herself free, and yells, "Don't call her that! Don't you call her that!" She screams some more, thrashing on her seat, and I hear the door open behind me. The correctional officer gets inside, but he stops at my raised hand.

He cannot interfere now. I almost broke her, and while I sympathize with her pain, we have no time.

"Matt raped you, didn't he? You got pregnant and married him. Catriona was never a preemie. She was born right on time, but you all had to hide it because you were underage."

She shakes her head, her saliva flying in different directions while she leans down and covers her ears. "No, no. It was not rape. Don't call her that." She whimpers. "Don't call her that. My baby is not...she is mine!" She shouts at me while tears stream down her cheeks. "It was a mistake. He was drunk, and I didn't stop him. It was my mistake. It wasn't rape."

My heart bleeds as I listen to her right now, hating how all these people convinced her of this to the point where she became a villain in her own story who thinks she deserved it all.

"No one knew except your father-in-law. He had all the power, but he wanted a grandchild. An heir better than the one he had since all Matt did was drink and party. He only wised up after his father threatened to cut him off."

"Catriona is my baby," she repeats, not even acknowledging what I say. "Mine. I wanted her even if at first I hated her." She erupts into more sobs, and I stand still, refusing to come closer. I wish I could comfort her right now.

"Did your father-in-law force you to have her?" I wait a second before my next question. "Forced you to marry Matt?" Zeke found old records where she made an appointment at the clinic but never showed up. I assume she wanted an abortion, but the father-in-law didn't let her.

She shakes her head over and over again, then starts rocking on the chair back and forth. "He said I could be either a daughter-in-law or a whore eager for money and fame because no one would believe me. My career would be over." More rocking. "I had no one, and I was a no one without him. I had to say yes." She grips her hair, pulling at it harshly, and yells, "I had to say yes!"

"I understand."

Her whole life, she has probably hated and judged herself for agreeing to all this. Otherwise, she wouldn't have felt the need to justify it to me.

The first step for her healing is to admit that what happened to her was rape. However, her psyche isn't ready for it right now.

So I approach from another angle. "Catriona. How did she find out about it?"

More whimpers and sobs. "She didn't. She couldn't. We don't talk about this with anyone. It's a secret." She hits herself on the chest before scratching her skin there. "My secret. She can't be tainted by it." Except for the thing about teenagers, they always find a way to find something and know how to hide it well.

Even if Catriona knew the truth, she wouldn't run to her mom to talk about it. But she might have turned all her life around into...whatever she decided to turn into while grieving in her own way.

It would also explain why she started hating her dad and avoided his company at all costs.

"She's a good girl. A good girl." She finally looks at me, and such devastation is reflected in her gaze. "She didn't do it."

"Then who did, Miranda?" I come closer, and the correctional officer moves right along with me but remains behind. "Who killed Matt? Where are your children?" Her lips tremble, and she sobs while inhaling and exhaling deeply, scratching her nails on the table, still rocking back and forth. "He can't see anything." If Catriona had nothing to do with the death, then the unsub is one hundred percent a man. Women generally shy away from being this violent in their crimes, avoiding blood. "Tell me, Miranda."

She opens her mouth, cracks a sound, but then shuts it and shakes her head. "He'll hurt them. He'll hurt them." She starts shouting over and over again, thrashing uncontrollably, and the correctional officer quickly subdues her while the tears fall and fall from her eyes.

Spinning around, I march outside, where Noah waits for me, and grab my coat. "She's innocent. Or actually, scratch that. She's a victim."

"I know." He rubs his chin. "We need to dig deeper into Matt's environment. Torture in his own house means it was personal. So he must have wronged the unsub in the past."

Yeah, I agree. Except there is just something about this case that doesn't seem right. Why take the kids and force Miranda into this role? Personal crimes usually are designed in such a way that it would hurt the ones they are killing.

Is it because Matt loved the kids but despised his wife? That's why he didn't do anything to Miranda besides leaving instructions on how to act?

Which reminds me. "Have you noticed any change once you turned the video off?"

"No."

I pick up my phone, seeing a message flash on the display, and the bile rises in my throat when I read it.

> Don't ever do it again. Play by the rules if you want me to play by them too.

The warning is loud and clear.

And as fear sinks into me, sliding through my veins and sending chills down my spine, I do the only logical thing in this situation.

I call my husband.

Because whenever shit hits the fan...he's the only one who can protect me.

CHAPTER ELEVEN

"Atonement needs to be earned.
And anyone telling you otherwise is a liar."
Zachary

Zachary
Furious doesn't even begin to describe me when I enter the restaurant, where several heads swirl in my direction and nod at me in greeting.

Classical music blasts from the speakers in this luxurious space that my wife loves so much because it's the first place I took her, and somehow, it became special to us both.

It has beige furniture scattered all around the perimeter of the rectangular space on the roof of the building. Pink vases holding tulips sit atop the round tables surrounded by four chairs.

A glass covering serves as the roof, allowing for streams of sunshine to brighten up the place, making it almost glow and giving it a sophisticated look from an earlier century when such designs graced every luxurious house.

The waitstaff wears black-and-white uniforms. Their soundless leather shoes don't disturb the customers with their constant clicks on the parquet as they run around delivering the orders.

The enclosed space creates an even greater sense of urgency because people's desire to get in are even greater if they feel special and important by snagging a table.

Within years, the demand for it only grew and, as a result, getting an invitation became almost impossible unless you knew someone important or were someone important.

Luckily for me, my abundant wealth means I always have a special table reserved for me.

My woman will never stand in line or be denied the opportunity to eat wherever the fuck she wants, whenever the fuck she wants.

From the right corner, the view opens up to the city panorama, showcasing the magnificence and beauty of it all. Being so high up, we almost seem to be floating in the air.

"Mr. King! Happy to see you again." Betty, our usual server, rushes to me and smiles. "Dr. King is waiting for you."

Pleasure rushes me whenever I hear anyone addressing my wife by the title.

While I'm proud of all her accomplishments, the fact that I managed to pull all the strings and come up with bullshit excuses to change the name from Hale to King on her degree certificate...puts me on another level of obsessed and possessive.

The idea of everyone calling my wife Dr. Hale just sent rage all through me, and I had the deep desire to go and punch Sebastian every single time. Bad enough her ex-husband still stays in our lives, and we even work together, but for her to carry his name in any form?

Un-fucking-acceptable.

"Would you like your usual?" Betty asks and, at my nod, taps something on the tablet, ready to escort me to my table.

"No need. Thank you, Betty."

With this, I stroll toward the round table closer to the panorama where the crystal chandelier shines brightly, casting colorful lights on the guests. I see my wife sitting and reading something, her forehead creasing as she rubs her thumb over her wedding and engagement rings.

Her dark locks fall down her spine in beautiful waves while the gray woolen dress hugs her body so tightly, showcasing all the delectable curves to everyone who dares to look.

Pleasure glides over me, my eyes drinking in her beauty and wishing to kidnap her from here and lock her in our room again, ravishing her body until nothing but thoughts of me remain.

It should be concerning how much I want my wife after all these years. The thoughts of her consume me, and that's why the idea of that fucker messaging her snaps something inside me.

I wish to find the piece of shit and subject him to such torture he wouldn't even think about my wife, let alone give her orders.

She looks up, and joy and relief fill her brown orbs when she notices me. "Zachary," she whispers and gets up as I reach her and hug her, allowing her to soak me in so that hopefully all restlessness can go away. She might hide it well. However, my wife is vulnerable. And it's my job to ensure she feels safe and loved. "I thought you hit traffic and would be late?" she asks, leaning back and gripping the lapels of my jacket.

My mouth lifts in a half smile. "Darling, a little traffic wouldn't have stopped me from having lunch with my wife." She rolls her eyes at my confident tone, tension easing out from her. "I decided to walk."

"How romantic of you, Mr. King."

"For you, Dr. King? I'll do anything." I kiss her hard and then tilt her chin. "Are you okay?"

She sighs, giving me another kiss before replying. "Yeah. Just frustrated and annoyed."

"You and me both."

Someone clears his throat next to us, and I look to my left, where Noah sits on the chair, pointing at his nose. "This hurts. So you're paying for my lunch today." He digs his fork into his steak as he cuts it into several pieces, and the beast in me roars in approval seeing the bandage on his nose.

Totally deserved it, and no regrets from me.

"Fine. I'm still not sorry, though."

"Yeah, I figured. I'm going to have a dessert as well." Like I give a shit.

I help Phoenix sit down while I drop on the chair beside her, opposite the man. "Have to say, Noah. This isn't what I had in mind when I wanted to have lunch with my wife."

"Zach," Phoenix says, mortified as she lifts her tea mug to her mouth and takes a tentative sip. "Be nice."

"That's not going to happen, darling, and you know it."

Betty chooses this moment to come with my order, placing my coffee in front of me. "The steak will be ready in twenty minutes, Mr. King."

"Thank you." She picks up used napkins and darts off to another table while I drill my gaze on Noah who chews a bit too fucking loudly for my liking. "Based on what my wife told me, we are now a hundred percent sure the fucker is a man?"

"Ninety percent," Noah corrects, swallowing. "We leave a ten percent chance it might be a psycho woman who Matt wronged in the past, and she has this desire to nurture his children to shield them from his family."

Phoenix puts her mug on the saucer with a loud bang and shakes her head, focusing on the papers inside a folder again. "I disagree. Female serial killers are rare, and besides, they seldom showcase this much violence."

Noah fishes inside his pocket and gives his phone to Phoenix. "Check the photo gallery." And goes back to chewing, seriously. The man can't afford a good steak or what?

My wife clicks on the gallery and scrolls through it before tapping on the image, and a photo of Matt flashes back at me in all his bloody glory. "Fuck," I mutter, my appetite gone completely, and I grab my coffee to wash the bitterness from my mouth.

I've seen a lot of stuff back in the day when Phoenix and I were on the hunt to catch a person who turned our lives into hell. However, the killings back then were never this bloody.

"The unsub just massacred the body," I say while Phoenix flicks her fingers, getting more detailed pictures zoomed on the particular organs and torture devices.

Finally, she reaches a picture where the knife is stabbed into the heart while blood soaks the entire body, or rather what's left of it because it just reminds me of the raw meat. As if a butcher had removed all the skin and was ready to chop the meat piece by piece.

Yeah, it was a bad idea to order a steak.

Noah points with his knife at this photo. "A heart. Usually, female unsubs pay attention to it. Sort of alluding to them loving a person and them breaking their heart so they break theirs."

"The heart was a final piece, though. All the torture and gore speak of a revenge and desire to inflict as much pain as possible on the victim. The final stab feels almost like—"

"A gesture," I finish for her, leaning closer and studying the photos better. Indeed, while the majority of the wounds are precise, cruel, and downright psychotic...the last one is gentle but serves almost as a final note on a finished masterpiece. "Can this be his signature?"

Noah wipes his mouth and drops the napkin on his plate, then gives it to the passing server. "We ran it in our databases, and there haven't been any serial killers with similar *modus operandi*." A beat passes as he ponders on it. "To be honest, the unsub tried everything on the victim sans the gun. The crime is so messy, it's impossible to connect it to any previous crimes since this particular murder has all the elements."

Phoenix goes back to the beginning and scrolls through them once again, staying silent as she studies the details, and then her brow furrows while she goes back again, zooming on the very first picture where Matt lays on his back, his veins cut open.

Noah and I share a look, so I ask her, "What is it, darling?"

"All the wounds...they are hideous, yes, but also...curious?" She scrolls some more. "It's as if he's learning the human anatomy for the first time and explores what happens when you cut someone open." She puts the phone in the middle, tapping on the image and then zooming in on his stomach, where all his intestines are out in the open. "Autopsy revealed that he died from the final stab to the heart, right?"

"Yes."

"So roughly for twenty-four hours, the unsub tortured and learned the body while the victim stayed alive. But if we take into consideration the severity of his wounds, it's impossible."

"Fuck," Noah mutters, grabbing his drink and taking a sip. "This is going to be a problem. But it fits the profile."

"What are you implying, darling?"

"He must have drugged Matt first and delivered a blow to his head to get advantage. Then he probably roped the guy and kept him in the same place while cutting him open and watching how everything works in the human body. His main source of pleasure came from exploring." She sighs. "And when he got his fill, he killed him and forced Miranda to play his next game."

"So he took the girls as hostages and framed Miranda in a way. Although in his twisted head, he probably didn't see it as a crime." Noah supplies this theory, and I don't miss how Phoenix doesn't agree with it outright and instead shifts her focus to the paperwork, scanning through it.

Musing on everything she has said so far and all the other information, I slowly start to align the blocks in my head, and I groan inwardly because this is worse than I originally thought. "A teenager. He's a teenager, isn't he?"

Noah decides to answer my question. "Yes. When the desire to learn and explore overshadows anything else, usually unsubs are young and reckless."

"How young?" Before he can reply, I fire another question. "Who are we talking about here? A born psychopath who tortured animals in the past and then, when it was not enough, moved to humans, and Matt was the unfortunate victim?" Although all things considered, good riddance and the fucker may rot in hell. "And the girls are, what? His new study boards?" As much as it pains me to say it, I've seen the pictures, and having a daughter myself, the idea that someone might hurt her terrifies me beyond measure.

The unsub made it personal to me, though, so the head has to be cold at all times, and I can't win this if I don't have all the facts.

"My guess is from sixteen to eighteen max. He has to be strong enough to handle Matt. Everything else is up for debate. I don't think he hurt animals, though."

"How would you know that?"

"The unsubs who hurt animals don't explore with humans as much when they get their hands on them. I think this guy never ever hurt anyone in such a way. And it's good, but it's also bad." He finishes grimly, drumming his fingers.

Yeah, bad because if he is the serial killer who tasted blood for the first time, the temptation to touch the girls and subject them to their father's fate might be too strong.

A seasoned murderer could wait to chase the high and play the game, but teenagers don't have as much control over their desires and actions like adults do.

"Still, I don't understand why he targeted my wife and created this plan. If Matt was some random dude—"

Phoenix finally speaks up. "I don't think he was random." We glance at her. "On the way here, I was going over the case in my head, confused with Miranda and all this. Especially Catriona." She licks her lips. "And then it dawned on me. She looks exactly like her mother at her age sans the hair."

Deafening silence falls after her statement, cold along with anger polluting my cells while my fist clenches, and if Matt were alive right now, I'd rip the fucker to shreds. How could a man do this to anyone, let alone to his child?

I don't doubt my wife's assumption, though, because all the signs point to that.

"I'll be honest here. If it weren't for the girls, I wouldn't be this eager to catch the unsub. The more information we uncover, the more grateful I am that Matt is dead," Noah says, putting some sugar into his coffee while Betty brings his chocolate cake, Phoenix's carrot one, and places my steak too. The delicious smell penetrates my nose and makes my stomach rumble, despite the circumstances. Grilled vegetables surround the well-done steak still pouring steam while several sauces on the side finish the composition.

We wait till she leaves before continuing, "You think he made a pass at this daughter?"

Phoenix digs her fork into her cake, shrugging. "I don't know, but I think yes. After he raped Miranda, his father took a tight hold on his finances and behavior. He visited a brothel, and we know that thanks to Zeke." Noah doesn't even bat an eye that I had my head of security on this man, and that's hilarious. Usually, they guard all this classified information like hawks, but I guess all this goes out of the window when they reach dead ends. "Men who lust after the underage don't just change their preferences. However, Catriona growing up might have triggered stuff, and he started to see her in a new light."

"That would explain the change of appearance. She wanted to be less desirable for him," I conclude, picking up the silverware and cutting my food. "You mentioned boarding school, right? What if he just wanted her far away from home? And this way, no one would stop him?"

Phoenix's fork pauses midway to her mouth at this, and she drops it back on the plate, her brow furrowing. "I didn't think about it."

"It worked for him once. I highly doubt he thought his daughter would tell anyone." Noah says, "Still, it gives us no insight into the unsub." He grabs his phone. "I'm going to message the update to the detective on the case. He might investigate further. It's not like we can do anything else but brainstorm."

Right, profilers don't go into the field and actually catch criminals, and thank God for that. The last thing I need is for Phoenix to be involved in such bullshit.

My wife sighs, picking up her fork and munching on her cake while thinking, and silence falls for several minutes as we all eat while I wonder if this will be our life now.

Handling cases with Phoenix about psychopaths and their motives. I would have loved to stop it, but I know better than to do that.

Because my wife has a compassionate nature that wishes to help everyone around her even if it hurts her. That's why we make such a good match.

I'll never let her put herself in danger for the greater good as it doesn't exist, and anyone claiming otherwise is a fool.

We're all selfish one way or the other.

"Oh my God," Phoenix exclaims, startling us both, and I stop chewing. "I can't believe I missed this."

Quickly swallowing and wiping my mouth with a napkin, I ask, "What is it, darling?"

"Catriona. It all comes down to Catriona." She must read the confusion on my face as she elaborates, "I read some short summary on her biography. She dreams about becoming a heart surgeon and helping people. Her grandmother, who she adores, had a heart attack a few years back and ever since then she wanted to be a doctor."

"Still lost, love."

"She volunteered at the shelter for abused children and women. Their family business runs an organization that helps these people to have temporary housing while they figure out their stuff or social workers. Not really sure on this."

Wrapping my hand around my coffee mug, I lift it up and say before drinking it, "The Kings have such shelters over the country as well. They can stay however long they need." It was started by my mother more than forty years ago, and we continued the tradition. "We grant scholarships too."

"Yes. But this family operates differently. The children leave the shelters at eighteen because they can work and legally become adults." How the hell is that supposed to be helpful to a person? "Anyway, Catriona never stopped volunteering there, even when she 'changed.' Religiously, she went there twice a week." She flips the papers. "Before she used to go there with her father."

"I see where you're going with this," Noah says and quickly types something on his phone. "You think the kid met her there and got obsessed? He removed the obstacle in his way and the other two girls are just collateral damage?" He slaps his hand on the table. "Then we have even less time to find the little ones. If they're alive, that is."

What the fuck?

This escalated from a murder done by a moody teenager to some grand scheme done for love and passion by an obsessed psycho. "Then why does he need us?" I start to sound like a parrot at this point, zero fucks given, though.

I want to know why the little shit got us involved in this case and what's his agenda, I don't believe for a second he's this naïve.

Naïve first-timers don't have such plans and don't go after as powerful families as mine.

They ignore my question. "No, Noah. It's not that." Phoenix rubs her hands and exhales a heavy breath. "The unsub must have witnessed something to make him realize that Matt made advances on Catriona."

"Yes. She got his attention."

"No! She triggered his trauma." She runs her fingers through her hair. "However, as long as she came to the shelter, he controlled his urges. But a week ago, Matt announced to the staff there that she would be leaving the country." She taps on the paper. "They also have computers in there and I doubt they supervise every single kid."

All my business degrees and life experienced didn't prepare me for the constant riddles these jobs require, which is hilarious, considering I married a psychiatrist and didn't expect to play profilers. "Where are you going with this, darling? Because isn't that exactly what Noah said? The kid got obsessed."

However, judging by Noah's face, he no longer believes in his own theory.

"The unsub sees himself as Catriona and in this tries to protect her from the unfortunate fate he had to suffer."

My head swings to Noah when he says, "He probably grew up in an abusive household where he was sexually assaulted. Frequently. Among other things."

"I don't get it. If that's the case, wouldn't everyone there trigger his trauma? What makes Catriona so special?"

Phoenix snatches the Catriona's family photo from the file. "This. The perfect family from the outside and rotten from the inside." A beat passes. "He probably grew up in a socially acceptable good family. Where his mother failed to protect him."

"From his father?"

She shakes her head. "It could be any male figure who ran her house. Father, grandfather, uncle, and so on."

"This explains why he framed Miranda and forced her to play a game."

I look at Noah. "Because in his eyes, she didn't protect her daughter?"

THE LAND WHERE SINNERS LOVE

"Yes. And that's why he took away the girls."

"I think he didn't have the chance to kill his abuser, so Matt was a substitute for him. It could have been anyone." Phoenix palms her head. "That's the reason he got me involved in this case."

Finally an answer to that! "Why?"

"My story is very popular. The injustice done to an innocent person. In his eyes, we're one and the same. He wanted for the world to know that the family was rotten and they deserved everything they got."

"Miranda loves her daughters."

"And that's her only saving grace in his eyes. We're dealing with a really traumatized teenager."

"This just got worse. I'm going to call my tech team to get us a list of all the boys who attended that shelter and who might have recently left, correlating with Catriona's visits. Our clock just got down by a day." He curses under his breath and gets up, already holding his phone to his ear and walking away somewhere quiet to talk.

Half turning in my seat, I place my hand above Phoenix's and pull her closer to me until we are inches apart, and I can practically feel the nervousness pouring from her. "Why did it get worse, darling?"

She closes her eyes and rests her forehead against mine before our gazes clash. "Because his greatest desire is to end his suffering. He sees death as the only solution to that problem." My hold on her tightens. "He didn't give us three days to find them, Zach. He gave us three days to uncover the truth and then make an example out of all of them."

I hug my wife close to me as fear slowly envelops me whole at the implication and how gone in his head the kid is.

He wants us to find them all right.

He just wants us to find them all dead, so the story will get the most coverage and make the people face the harsh truth.

Even perfect families hide the most hideous secrets.

. . .

Unsub

Patience is a virtue for some.

For me, it means nothing but stalling as patience never brought me anything good.

Phoenix King broke the rules.

The time has come for me to do the same.

Seventy-two hours was a generous offer I should have never made.

Because the madness slowly consuming my brain whispers one thing only, to avenge for what was done to me.

CHAPTER TWELVE

"Not all villains are the same.
However, they do have one thing in common.
They were denied love, and in this, hate filled their soul.
Leaving nothing but hollowness in its wake."
Phoenix

*P*hoenix

I jerk awake when the car stops abruptly, blinking in surprise and trying to understand my surroundings. Zach puts his hand on my thigh and squeezes it, bringing up goose bumps on my skin, and I smile, thinking about how this man affects me after all this time. With one single touch, everything in me comes alive. It's a crime to be this affected by a man, but it's so hard to care when I'm hopelessly in love with him. "Wake up, darling."

Patting his hand, I raise my arms and stretch inside the car. "We're home? That was quick."

I grab the handle, and my brow furrows when the modern, luxurious building comes into my view through the window in the center of the city, judging by our surroundings.

People leisurely walk around here wearing designer clothes and carrying expensive bags that are hard to find even with all the wealth and power. Shimmering lights illuminate everything around us, bringing attention to the exclusiveness of the place.

Two doormen wearing black suits stand by the revolving door, and one of them races toward us the minute they spot our car while the other takes out his phone to call someone. Judging by how he keeps his stare on us, this phone call must be about us.

Probably to check if our room is ready. This hotel is one of the most expensive ones in the world, and it's loved by so many wealthy people because of how attuned they are to their clients.

You can get whatever you want, you just have to pay generously, and Zach has countless times when he took me out on romantic dinners, or we just needed time for ourselves, which is hard to do with kids around, even in our mansion.

Confused, I ask, "What are we doing here?" Just in time for the doorman to open my door and smile brightly at me.

"Welcome back, Dr. King." He extends his gloved hand at me, helping me out of the car, and I'm too stunned to react. My brows rise in question when Zach goes around the car, throwing his keys at the guy. "Mr. King. Nice to see you again."

"Likewise, John. We won't need the car until tomorrow morning."

He nods. "Are there any bags we need to take upstairs?" I guess he remembers the last time we spent our anniversary weekend in a hotel room for three days straight without interruption before heading to Greece for a week.

"No." Zach grabs my hand, lacing his fingers with mine, and pulls me toward the swirling door while cars honk in the distance along with headlights almost blinding us in the night with dark clouds fully blanketing the sky. Not a single star is in sight, and I sigh because our room has the best views. Too bad I won't be able to admire the stars tonight. "Come on, darling."

"You haven't answered my question!" I hiss at him, drinking in the beauty around me when we enter the lobby, where classical jazz music instantly greets us along with a rose and lavender scents floating in the air, creating an inviting atmosphere.

The golden marble glistens under the crystal chandelier, casting colorful squares on all the guests sitting on the various couches with tea, coffee, and snacks on the nearby table. All while speaking in hushed whispers.

Some are by the reception desk, talking about something and signing their paperwork, and one of the receptionists notices us, plastering a smile on her face. She picks up her tablet, speedily walking to us. "Hello, Mr. King. Your room is ready for you." She gives Zach the keycard and shifts her focus to me. "Dr. King, we already put your favorite champagne and chocolate there. I hope you'll enjoy your stay."

"Thank you, Alice," I tell her, and she beams at me as Zach drags me toward the silver elevators. Pressing on the button, one of them opens. "So we're spending the night?" As we enter the elevator, I throw another question his way, and he presses our floor.

He leans on the wall and wraps his hand around my waist, making me rest my palms on his chest while he winks at me. "I figured with the kids at my dad's, we can spend some quality time together." I lift my brow, and he exhales, rolling his eyes dramatically. "Fine. You guessed my plan. I wanted to ravish you here," he whispers, sending warmth through me, and I laugh, happiness sinking into my cells and calming my nerves despite the case becoming so complicated.

It's one thing wanting to catch an unsub and quite another finding a teenager who still has all his life ahead of him and probably snapped because there was no one around to contain his anger.

And what if...

"Darling, look at me." Zachary rubs my forehead with his thumb, smoothing the lines between my brows, and I meet his stare. "The minute we enter our room, you will leave all the worries behind." He puts his index finger on my lips when I want to protest. "You'll turn off your phone and let it be. Noah can handle the situation and search for whoever the hell that is. Tonight, just focus on us, okay?" He kisses me on the nose at my nod because I understand.

Despite the case hurting my heart, it's not personal, and nor should it ever be. I can't help them all, so I have to prioritize myself and my family.

Stepping back from him when the elevator dings our arrival, I say,

"You just want to have me all to yourself for that wicked mind of yours."

He gasps in outrage and shakes his head. "Oh no. Was I that obvious?" My laughter echoes in the hallway as we go to our room located several feet away, and Zach swipes the card, the lock clicking, and lets us both in.

Beige and white dominate the color scheme of this hotel room, reminding me more of an apartment consisting of a living room with a couch and two chairs, standing opposite a huge TV hanging on the wall. A bar in the right corner contains various bottles and snacks.

The small table in front of the couch has the champagne Alice mentioned earlier in the ice bucket, while different flavors of chocolate occupy several bowls along with a fruit platter.

A balcony door that's usually open is closed now due to the colder weather and rain season.

If you walk through the living room farther to the left, you will see a door leading to another room with a king-sized bed and a bathroom with the shower and bath.

It costs a fortune to spend the night here, and this room has been reserved for the Kings forever, although Zachary never used it before marrying me.

So it became our little safe place. No wonder he doesn't want me to bring up anything tonight here.

Zach grips my coat, snapping me from my thoughts and bringing me back to the present as he slides it from my shoulders and takes it off. He puts it on the nearby chair, removing his own, and I run my gaze over his jeans and sweater along with a five-o'clock shadow that gives him a rather wild and hot look, instantly igniting my blood. "Looking hella fine, Mr. King." He chuckles at my compliment, and I slip off my boots, curling my stocking-covered toes on the carpeted floor that feels like silk underneath me, gently caressing my skin. "It's too bad we can't enjoy the starry night."

I pick up the wet wipe box near the food and take one out, cleaning my hands before reaching for a white chocolate and popping it into my mouth, groaning at the taste. "Their chocolate is the best." I glance at Zach, who hisses through his teeth, and roll my eyes. "You have a one-track mind."

"When it comes to you? Always, my darling." He strolls closer, grabbing the champagne and pouring it into the two glasses before giving one to me. "Let's toast to—" He raises his glass to me

"To love?" I suggest sweetly since we are being all cute here, and he grins, clinking my glass and the sound rings in the air. Sipping it a little bit, I welcome the taste in my mouth and twirl my glass. "Good stuff. How come we never have it at home?" I narrow my eyes on him. "Is it because you prefer whiskey?"

Zach has a whiskey collection at home dating back to a century ago, and it's a ritual when he drinks it. I think I've seen him share it only with Lachlan on a rare occasion he came to our house.

Maybe because he brought him a limited edition bottle to add to his collection. Otherwise, he jokes he'll leave it in his will for the boys, and I don't find that very funny.

Knowing them, they will either demolish or sell it to the highest bidder.

"What would be the fun in coming here if we didn't try something new?" He picks up a dark chocolate, the only chocolate he likes because he doesn't have a sweet tooth which makes us both so different when it comes to food. "I was thinking about something."

"What?"

"We haven't traveled in a while. How about a little trip to Italy? Sometime next month?" I don't miss how he doesn't voice our current situation, doing his best to avoid the subject. "It's beautiful this time of the year."

"Ah, Italy. I would love to go back to Florence. We haven't been there since our honeymoon." Which was magical, except puking every damn morning because I was pregnant with the twins.

"My thoughts exactly. Should we take the kids this time?"

When we married, we decided that we would always take one vacation together and one with the kids. Mostly, though, we traveled alone for a couple of days due to Zach's job and the kids stayed at home busy with school and other activities. There was no point in dragging them around and subjecting them to all the jet lags, even if the Kings owned their private plane.

"I think they'll have a lot of fun there. Although..." I laugh under my breath, nibbling on a strawberry as Zach sends me a questioning glance. "I'm afraid the twins will destroy something in a museum and even the King's money won't be enough to save us from trouble."

"Oh, yes. They're *my* sons."

"Try sounding less proud."

He shrugs. "Why would I? We're either going to be the parents of brilliant men who make some worldwide careers or famous con artists. Either way, they will be excellent at what they do." I slap his chest and he chuckles, sipping his drink. "Oh, come on. Emmaline is an angel but our boys will be sinners. No doubt about it."

"That's true. We have a little prima on our hands." My daughter will succeed in her career because she is very driven for success like her father and brothers.

One might say I'm the most chilled in the family, which is funny, considering I'm also very passionate about my profession.

"Do you want to watch a movie?" Zach motions with his head to the TV. "Some black-and-white classic that always makes you cry."

Ah, my possessive man.

He truly brought me here to make me feel better and settle my mind. Usually, he'd be on me right away.

Once, he fucked me against the entrance door and had to cover my mouth with his hand so no one would hear my whimpers and moans.

The memories send a hot flush through me, and heat blazes at the pit of my stomach, urging me to do something wicked that would drive my man insane.

Traditions should never be broken, especially when they entail our mutual pleasure.

Putting the glass back on the table, I ask Zach, "You know the saying great minds think alike, right?" He nods, although instead of looking at me, his gaze falls on my fingers gently drifting from my collarbone to my narrow waist. "I think husband and wife think alike."

"Yeah?"

"Yep." I step back a little from him and hike my dress upward, opening myself to his view. He swallows hard when he sees my black stockings. I remove my dress, throwing it on the couch.

His face darkens as I run my hands over my black lacy bra and panties that match in style with my stockings. "I felt a little naughty in the morning and decided to wear this lingerie you gifted me the other day."

He takes in his fill, his green eyes caressing me with their blazing heat as he scans me from head to toe, desire etched on his features.

Opening my arms wide, I slowly twirl around and then place my hands on my hips with a loud slap. "What do you think? Do you approve?" I run my fingers through my hair, flipping them back and fully exposing myself to him.

He finishes his glass with one gulp and puts it on the table. I'm surprised it doesn't break from the force. Then he reaches for the back of his sweater, taking it off.

He throws it away and crooks his finger at me. "Come here, darling. Let me show my full appreciation to this body." He unbuckles his belt, but the shake of my head stops him. "No?"

I love my husband's dominant nature, but he's been running the show long enough, and the time has come for me to play a little.

If I give him the reins right now, he'll just torture and seduce me over and over again during the night, but I want to have my fun too.

Sauntering toward him, I sway my hips with each step. I place my splayed palm on his bare chest, his muscles flexing under my touch, and my skin burns from the contact, sending fire through my veins. "Remember what you said last night?" I murmur, raking my nails over his six-pack and earning myself a hiss while rising on my tiptoes and pushing my lips against his. He lifts his brow in a silent question, so I repeat it for him. *"Next time, darling. I'll enjoy putting you on your knees while I fuck this pretty mouth of yours."* He stills after my whispered words, the energy changing around us all at once, soaking in lust and passion so strong the air hitches in my lungs and prickling sensations travel down my spine.

A gasp escapes me when he threads his fingers through my hair and clenches it hard, dragging me closer to him and trapping my moan in his mouth when he slams it on mine, entwining us in a deep and hot kiss, awakening every nerve in my body.

The kiss wipes away time, world, and anything else, leaving us alone in our created cocoon filled with love. Need consumes us both, urging us to give in and dissolve in the pleasure that's possible for us to only find in each other's arms.

He tips my head back, deepening the kiss, his tongue stabbing and playing with mine, and each lick tells a story on its own.

Because it's like branding me all over again and claiming me as his own, announcing to the entire world that I belong to him so no one better even dare to hurt me.

By how tightly he holds me, his body so rigid, I know he barely controls his impulse to throw me on the nearest flat surface and fuck me so hard nothing in my head but him remains.

So past and present won't disturb the peace we have.

Countless goose bumps break on my skin as the need grows stronger within me, his toe-curling kiss seducing me to give in to the temptation and let him do to me whatever he wants.

To use me as his personal pleasure toy, subjecting me to his wicked ways while guessing my every forbidden wish.

We separate for a second, gulping for air, and stare at one another. He licks over my lips, pulling them apart agonizingly slow and delving his tongue inside me once again, locking us in a soft, gentle, yet hot kiss, inspiring shivers all over me.

Moaning, I claw at his stomach, and he groans, angling his head a little and driving me insane with the swirls of his tongue.

I could spend a lifetime just kissing my man and require no other pleasure because even with a kiss alone, he has the ability to show me his love and bring me joy.

For he shows me I'm the center of his universe, and though he might be ruthless, cruel, and sometimes cunning in order to get what he wants...I'm sheltered from that part of him.

He can only use this part of him to protect me or warn all other men away from me.

And in this, I'm not afraid of the darkness surrounding him, but instead adore it just as the rest of him.

He tears his mouth away from mine, both of us breathing heavily, and a sinister smile shapes his lips. "Get on your knees, darling." He rubs my lips with his thumb, a wicked glint flashing in his eyes and intensifying the fire rapidly spreading inside me. "I'm about to fuck this pretty mouth."

Thousands of tickling sensations rush over me in waves, the heated fog enveloping me whole while my body becomes so hot I'm surprised I'm not bursting from the desire gliding through my veins and urging me to listen to his command.

Winking at him, though, I lean closer and place my mouth on the underside of his chin, my lips drifting to his collarbone and biting on his hard muscles, earning myself a groan while his fingers tighten in my hair.

I love the taste of his salty flawless skin as his body reminds me of a statue for how perfect it is.

Shifting lower, I graze his six-pack with my teeth, moving to his stomach, slowly lowering on my knees until I reach the base of his cock, the sight of his hard and thick length making my core clench and drip, soaking my panties while lust consumes me.

Rolling my tongue out, I trace the pulsing purple vein, and he groans above me, his fingers digging into my scalp, and suck on the tip, moaning when I taste his precum.

Leaning forward and placing my hands on his hips, I take his cock deeper while he hisses, my lips gliding over the sensitive skin.

Zach tilts my head back, the prickles of pain from his hold making me moan and sending vibrations through his length, and he hisses, pressing with his other hand on my chin. "Wider, darling. Suck it like you mean it." Scorching heat travels down my spine, my stomach dipping at the command, and his husky voice alone shoots arrows of desire straight to my clit.

Relaxing my throat and opening my mouth wider, I slide my palm from his hip to the base of his cock, enclosing it in a tight grip. I take him deeper into my mouth and his green eyes darken, desire filling them while his breathing changes. "Good girl." His praise burns me, and stroking him in time with my mouth earns me another guttural groan. He palms my head and holds me still as he rocks his hips forward. His cock drives deeper and deeper, making me choke a little around his length. He grins, slowly pulling away to give me room to breathe as I run my tongue over him and lap up on the precum dripping from the tip. "My good girl." His muscles dip when I scrape my teeth over him, gliding to the base and inhaling his masculine scent before going back to the tip, showing him love and affection with each brush of my tongue.

One of my favorite things is having him at my mercy where he can't control himself, chasing his high. The knowledge alone that I have such power over this magnificent man makes me dizzy as happiness penetrates my every bone.

I take him in my mouth again, caressing him with my lips, and my tongue connects with his pulsing flesh.

The sight of him using me for his own pleasure zaps electricity all over me, charging me with thousands of volts and pushing me closer to the edge. I can't help myself because the need for friction drives me insane.

My hand drifts to my panties, slipping inside, and I whimper with relief when the heel of my palm pushes on my clit, the pleasure so close I can feel it nipping on my skin and pulling me toward the invisible cliff where only passion awaits me.

My core clenches around my finger, sucking it in, and I hate and love it at the same time. It gives me a temporary reprieve from the maddening need enveloping me whole as my man rocks forward again.

But I hate it because it doesn't bring me relief and instead serves as gasoline to the already burning fire demanding one thing.

Pleasure.

If he doesn't do something soon, I will shatter into tiny little pieces.

Zachary

"Phoenix." I pull at her head, making her moan as she swallows me deeper and fucking drives me insane as I barely hold myself from coming right in her mouth.

My cum dripping down her throat is a beautiful sight to behold—however, not tonight.

Tonight, I need to come inside my wife and remind myself that no matter the danger outside, she's mine and with me, which means no one and nothing can hurt her because first they'd have to go through me.

And I'm a King.

Whatever I want, I get, and fuck what anyone else thinks about it.

I let her play for a few more seconds, her hand squeezing my balls, and I tighten my hold on her, finally forcefully pushing my dick out of her mouth, and she lets go with a loud pop. "Darling." She looks at me, her plump lips red, and she leans closer, scooping the precum with the tip of her tongue and moaning. Her skin is flushed while her other hand rubs up and down her probably drenched pussy inside her panties, and this just won't do.

When my woman is in need, I provide.

Always.

"You're done."

She must hear the steel in my voice because she slowly gets up, her breast and stomach brushing over my dick and smearing my cum on her, leaving wet spots on her body, which only makes me hotter.

Because everyone knows she's mine and she's a claimed territory, I don't really give a fuck that it makes me sound like a chauvinistic asshole either.

I don't share my woman, ever. She belongs to me.

Her beauty will always attract men who would want to soak up her goodness and passion. That's why she should always wear my marks of ownership on her, so they know the repercussions of approaching my wife.

Lacing my fingers in her hair, I put my free hand above hers, pressing it hard on her clit, and she gasps, her pussy soaking and begging for me. "My darling, you're in deep need of your husband's dick, aren't you?" She sways toward me, her nipples peeking through her see-through lace. I take out her hand and lift her wet fingers to my mouth, sucking them clean, groaning at her sweet taste. However, it's not enough. I need to taste her straight from the source so nothing but her scent will surround me.

She whimpers when I lock us in a deep kiss, sharing our combined tastes, my hand drifting to her hip and squeezing it tightly. She gasps, our mouths separating for a fraction of a second when I hike her up, her legs wrapping around my waist and my cock digging into her pussy.

She palms my head, seeking my mouth again, and this time, the kiss grows heated and blazing as I walk us to the room, grabbing champagne on the way. The cold bottle connects with her flesh, making her shiver all while I bruise her with my raw kisses. The desire for her consumes me so much I can barely see straight.

Her curves, her scent, the mewling sounds she makes that I greedily swallow are designed to drive me to the edge and turn me insane.

Phoenix has the ability to make a madman out of me, and I'll gladly face such fate as long as she loves and needs me because her love is a gift.

With each of my moves, my dick pushes into her. She snatches her mouth away, and arches back, exposing her neck to my hungry onslaught. "Zach."

Ah, my name whispered on her lips coated in craving and anticipation is a pleasure in itself.

I suck on her neck, drawing the skin, and her thighs clamp around me, her fingers lacing in my hair and pushing me closer.

Moonlight streaming from the huge window lights up the room when I enter, casting a magical glow around us and inviting us to indulge in sin and forbidden temptations behind these walls without anyone knowing or judging us for it.

Biting on her shoulder and then soothing the sting with my tongue, I pull at her hair, and she leans back, her eyes watching me. She's a sight to behold with desire filling her gaze.

My woman.

But more importantly.

My wife.

Her arms circle my neck, and she hugs me, her breath tickling my ear when she speaks to me, her lips brushing against my skin and causing lust to shoot through my system. My balls grow heavy while my dick becomes harder if that's fucking possible, my hips thrusting forward into her wetness, separated from full penetration by the thin lace. "I want you, Zach." She gasps at the contact, clenching her thighs and shifting a little, seeking friction, but that won't do.

My wife will come tonight, all right, but it won't be from dry humping my dick.

Her squeal echoes in the room when I send her flying on the bed, where she bounces a few times and then huffs in frustration when she flips her hair back, sitting up. "That was mean."

Snatching out my belt with a loud whoosh, I reply, "Don't feel particularly kind right now, darling."

She bites on her lower lip when I remove my shoes and then take off my pants. Kicking them away, I stand naked in front of her and palm my hard-on, dragging my hand from the base to tip and wiping the precum with my thumb.

Phoenix moans, shifting restlessly on the bed and turned on out of her mind.

"Show me your pussy, darling," I order, and she leans back on her splayed palms while widening her thighs and placing her feet on the mattress. She cups herself, slowly twisting her panties to the side, opening her glistening dripping folds. "My darling, you're soaked." I click my tongue, and she gasps when her fingers connect with her bare skin, moving up and down. "You poor thing. What do you want?" I ask her, gripping the base of my cock, and her gaze falls on it. "My dick fucking you so hard we shake the bed?" Her eyes darken, and she nods. Pushing her fingers inside her, she squeezes her thighs, pleasure crossing her face. I think if I wanted to, I could get her off with my voice and instructions alone, painting carnal images in her head.

My dick is as hard as fucking steel, listening to her raspy breath and the wet sounds her pussy makes. "Zach," she moans, throwing her head back, her dark locks caressing the black sheets underneath her. I resist the urge to flip her on her hands and knees, fisting her hair and claiming her from behind until she can't think straight.

Tonight, I want to be more patient.

Phoenix presses the heel of her palm on her clit while pushing her fingers in, and I order, "Deeper, darling." She whimpers, doing just that as I step closer and take a large sip from the champagne, welcoming the burning sensations in my throat matching the desire setting ablaze everything inside me. "How does it feel? Good?"

"Yes," she replies, rocking her hips slightly forward in time with her double movements, but then she shakes her head. "No," she adds with frustration, practically sobbing the word.

"What is it, darling?" I ask, stepping closer to the bed until my knees bump against it. "Are your fingers a poor substitute for this?" I palm my cock, and she nods. "Then come here." I crook my finger at her and she practically jumps on me, standing up on her knees and wrapping her arms around my neck, seducing me with her addicting kisses.

I place my free hand on her stomach. It dips under my touch, and I slide it upward, still holding her mouth prisoner. The kiss grows raw and hot as she whimpers with each lick of my tongue.

Finally, my hand reaches her throat, circling it, and she stills. I squeeze it harder than usual, pulling her away from me, and then loosen the hold slightly, letting her take a breath before imprisoning her in my hold again. "Zach," she whispers, her eyes filled with need so strong it almost makes me come undone.

Almost because I have other plans for now, and no one should rush me when it comes to pleasuring my wife, even Phoenix.

Trapping her lower lip between my teeth, I tug on it while feeling her pulse under my thumb and squeeze her neck again, her plump lips opening at the action. Sucking on her lip, I soothe the abused flesh.

I catch her mouth in one more dominating and brutal kiss, and then without any warning, I push her on her back. She lands with a loud pant, her hair splayed all around her while I get on the bed, shouldering her thighs apart to make room for myself.

Looming above her, I raise the champagne bottle, and she frowns only to squeal when I pour it all over her body, the bubbly liquid sliding down her skin and soaking the bed underneath us, the scent floating in the air and mixing with ours. "Zach," she gasps in outrage, but it quickly turns into a loud moan when I place my mouth on her collarbone, licking it off her skin. She shivers, arching her back as my lips glide lower to her breasts.

Biting on the mounds and then sucking on her skin hard, for sure leaving marks for me to admire later as they speak to my possessive soul, I wait till she threads her fingers in my hair before swiping my tongue over her nipple. "Please," she whispers. Cupping her breast, I lift it to my mouth and suck on the flesh. The taste of her skin along with champagne sends flashes through, and my dick becomes rock hard, digging into the mattress.

Phoenix jerks her hips upward, her thighs edging wider as she pulls me toward her, seeking my cock, but with a chuckle, I slide my mouth to her other breast, repeating my actions.

Lavishing it with attention, I drink in champagne from her body as she whimpers underneath me, goose bumps breaking on her skin, and her breathing grows heavier with each lick.

Clamping her thighs around me, she begs, "Zach, please. Fuck me now."

Giving her nipple one last nibble and a kiss, I resume my journey on her body. Moving downward to her taut stomach, I trace my tongue over her skin until I reach her belly button.

Nipping on her flesh, I grin when her stomach dips under my touch, and her scent twitches my nose, sending all the blood rushing to my dick that physically hurts from not claiming her.

Torturing her is torturing myself, but I won't fuck her until I taste her pussy that drips for me so sweetly.

Settling between her thighs, I run my hands over her stockings, loving their silky texture, and breathe in her scent. She groans, twisting her head on the bed. "No, no. You'll make me come, Zach." Although she protests, she still opens herself for me and whimpers when I slide my palms under her ass and lift her to my hungry mouth. "Darling," she wails, intensifying the need to satisfy my woman, pumping my blood with lust so strong I can barely see straight.

"Zachary." The sound of my full name sounds incredibly fucking hot on her lips, and she grips my hair, offering herself to me. "Please fuck me with your tongue." She whimpers, and that's all the invitation I need.

Placing my mouth wide on her pussy, I thrust my tongue deep into her, earning myself a moan, and her hold on me tightens while her taste hits me.

There is just nothing like her in this world, and I plunge deeper, my fingers digging into her ass cheeks, driving into her over and over again all while she grinds on my tongue, clearly finding the friction her pussy needed.

She puts the heel of her foot on my shoulder, her pink flesh spreading wider, and my tongue slips farther as she tugs on my hair. "Oh God," she mutters, raising her hips in time with my movements, only to sob in frustration when I slowly pull out of her. Dragging my tongue up and down her soaked flesh, I suck on her lower lips one by one before biting on them, and she cries out. "Zach, please. I'm aching," she begs, and I skim up her pussy to her clit, tapping on it lightly and catching it with my teeth. She pulls my hair so hard it's a wonder she doesn't rip it out. "Not like this, Zach."

Ignoring her plea, I suck on her clit as she whimpers. I lower her hips on the bed, putting my hands on the inside of her thighs and pushing them wide, baring her flesh to me completely. Her scent drives me insane, my cum leaking on the mattress, not that I give a fuck.

Brushing my thumb over her clit and then pinching it, I slide my tongue down, roaming between her silky walls before entering her once again. Her pussy clenches around me and spasms a few times as her breath hitches.

Frustration and annoyance along with desire coat her voice when she shouts, "Zach, give me what is mine!" Her demand shreds the last bit of my self-control, and I thrust my two fingers into her as I drag my tongue upward, drinking her juices.

"And what's yours, my darling?"

Our gazes clash, and she raises her chin stubbornly. "You are." She pulls at my hair, tearing my mouth away from her. "I'm yours, so give me the pleasure I deserve."

Chuckling at her command, I nibble on her clit as my fingers stretch her and prepare her for my thick cock. "What do you want, darling?"

"You."

"And who am I?"

"My husband."

"That's right." Giving her pussy one long lick and a gentle kiss, I move upward, rubbing my face on her stomach and leaving wet imprints on her that mingle with the champagne.

Dragging my mouth, I pepper small kisses on her flesh until finally, I put my hands on either side of her, hovering above her. She raises her thighs, locking me in a tight grip.

She circles her arms around me, her nails clawing at my nape as she presses us closer, and her eyes darken when I rub the tip of my cock over her wet folds. "Please," she whispers, covering her mouth with mine. I swallow her scream when I enter her with one swift thrust.

Her pussy stretches around my length, and we both groan when she clenches around me, sucking me in deeper as an inferno threatens to erupt all around me and burn us alive before we can drown in the pleasure of our creation.

Locking us in a bruising yet gentle kiss and entwining us in a heated embrace, I pull my hips back only to slam into her again, rattling the bed. She moans, flexing her legs around me. She digs her heels into the base of my spine, her hands hugging me closer, and she tears her mouth away, gulping for breath as she arches her neck, offering herself to me.

Skimming my lips on her neck, I lightly bite on the skin and continue to drive into her hard over and over again. Each time, my strokes become deeper, enjoying the mewling sounds coming from her throat or how she rakes her nails over my back.

I'll have marks to show off tomorrow, and the beast inside me roars because wearing them will be a privilege and a pride.

Mine and only mine.

Lacing her fingers in my hair, she pulls me closer until our mouths are inches apart and gasps when I thrust extra deep, her pussy clamping around me, the tightness driving me crazy with want.

It should be forbidden for a woman to be this wanted as she holds so much power over me, yet I'll gladly give her all the weapons if it means she'll stay with me.

Because without her, there is no me.

Her lips brush against mine when she whispers, shredding my heart to pieces, "I love you, Zach." She moans at the next hard thrust. "I love you."

Instead of answering her, I capture her in another kiss while speeding up my pace. The urgency in me can't be ignored any longer.

How can I when she says these words to me and looks at me as if no other man exists in this world?

With each jerk of my hips, her pussy clamps around me tighter and tighter until she finally comes apart in my arms, snatching her mouth away and crying out, the sound echoing through the space.

She falls on the pillow, watching me intently as I sit up a little bit and grab her ass cheeks, clenching them in my hands. Then I start to fuck her really hard, and she palms her breasts, squeezing them.

One.

Two.

Three more thrusts and I can no longer ignore the tingling sensations down my spine. My balls grow heavy, and finally biting her shoulder, I ram into her one last time and spill inside her while she continues to spasm around my length.

Breathing heavily, I fall on her, our bodies soaked in sweat and champagne while she hugs me close. We share this moment, content to just lie together as the wind blows outside.

"We need to clean up," she whispers into my ear, and I grin, completely exhausted, but I still manage to lift myself, catching her gaze. "A bath sounds nice." She wiggles her finger at me and yawns. "No funny business, though." She notices my intense stare at her and cocks her head to the side. "What?"

With adoration filling my every bone and warmth that managed to defrost even my frozen heart, I tell her, "I love you too, Phoenix."

She hugs me once again, and this time for a long while, no one says anything.

After all, this is our little heaven.

We'll have enough time to go back to reality.

But tonight, nothing matters but us.

· · ·

*U*nsub

The owls hoot in the distance as I get out of my van, inhaling the frigid air in my lungs, and my boots step on a harsh ground.

Dark clouds gather above me, covering up the thousands of stars lighting up the night while the moonlight still finds a way to shine brightly on the forest with its countless brown trees located far, far away from the city.

Because wild animals reside in it and always look for flesh to feast on. Otherwise, it wouldn't have been the perfect hunting ground.

A shudder rushes through me at the thought of killing an animal. Although if one threatened my safety...I would never hesitate.

In the wilderness, there is only one rule.

Either eat or be eaten, the strongest one always survives.

Everyone else preaches about choices, taking the higher ground, and all other bullshit they love to talk about?

Nonsense. They've just never been in a place where they had to make a hard choice.

Crows caw soundly, occupying the trees before flying high up in the air while thunder shakes the sky, scaring them away, and a smile shapes my mouth.

She used to say they're the sign of an upcoming disaster and avoided them at all costs. In fact, whenever one flew around her, she'd go back into the house and hide there.

Hilarious considering she married a monster and still allowed him to do the unthinkable.

Anger sparks up inside me, sliding through my veins and polluting my mind while the familiar voices scream in my head, and I cover my ears. Biting my lower lip, I rock back and forth, refusing to listen to them.

Not yet.

They have to come here and see for themselves what their law allows to happen while they all live in a happy bubble.

The banging inside the van snags my attention, and I growl in annoyance. The little shits cannot follow instructions to save their lives. Catriona probably convinced them to make a noise in hopes of stopping me on the way here. What a stupid girl she truly is.

Because if she looked hard enough...she'd understand I have more money than anyone else. I just prefer to play the part of a poor serial killer searching for his next fix.

Simply put, no one would ever suspect me of shit, let alone my car.

Puffing air, I walk to the end of the car and open it, instantly letting the light in. The girls press their backs to the wall and watch me, devastation written all over their faces that it's me. "I told you all to be quiet." The little ones tremble and start to cry but quickly cover their mouths while Catriona glares at me.

If she wants to succeed with her intimidation tactics, she needs to do more than glare at her opponents. Silly girl indeed.

But a beautiful one.

I take a moment to study her red hair falling down her shoulders in waves. My fingers itch to touch them and run my fingers through them like I did the last time.

For just a moment—a single, tiny moment—it calmed something inside me, almost...almost made it bearable to live on this earth.

And then she had to grab a knife and prove to me once and for all that people are vicious creatures who will use any opportunity to hurt you as they do not see goodness.

Only vices because all of us in one way or another are rotten from the inside.

Earlier rage hits me in waves, and I remove the safety from my gun, pointing it at them. The little ones scream while Catriona comes forward, blocking my view of them, acting as a human shield. "Get out of the car."

"Where are we?"

I bang with my fist on the car, and they scream some more. "I said get the fuck out." I cock my head to the side, noticing how Catriona's eyes dart between the gun and me while she shakes her head, disgust written all over her. Somehow, that just serves as gasoline to the fire already burning in me for more than a decade.

She's judging me without knowing my story, and I hate her for it. This hate pushes me to lean forward and grab her hand, pulling her toward me. The air hitches in her throat when I press the gun to her temple.

Our faces are inches apart, we share a breath, and I slowly slide the gun to her cheek, chin, and finally the wildly beating pulse that calls my name like never before. Just the memory of the blood trickling down her palm rushes pleasure through my entire system and a craving to lick it off her. "Hate what you see, princess?"

To keep her balance, she places her splayed palm on my chest, right above my heart. An organ that pumps blood and has no other purpose because emotions will never live in there.

As emotions cause nothing but damage and agony.

I expect her to shy away from me or beg me to let her go, but to my dismay and surprise as it only grows the little fascination in me, she raises her chin high and replies, after exhaling heavily, "Do you think I should love you for pointing a gun at my siblings?" She practically shouts the last part and then rolls her lips, her fingers curling on my chest and fisting my sweater. "Why are you doing this?"

Gliding the tip of the gun up and down her flesh, I grin at the raspy breath slipping past her lips, awakening an odd thrill in me. "Because I can, princess." With this, I push her away and she lands on her ass, wincing while her sisters surround her again. "Now unless all of you want to be dead, do as I say." I wink at her. "Trust me, I'll kill you last so you can mourn your little siblings first."

We share a long stare and then finally she rubs her sisters' backs with her trembling hands and softens her tone for them. "It's okay, girls. Let's just do what he says, and he won't hurt us." Judging by their faces, they don't believe her.

As they should.

Death awaits us at the end of this journey, but not yet, so I guess there is some merit to her words?

Catriona gets down first, ignoring my outreached hand to help her out, and grits her teeth at my chuckle. She helps her siblings next. "Where are we?" she asks, gripping their shoulders and still shielding them from me, standing closer to me while they all gape at the one-level wooden cabin in front of us that has seen better days.

"Scream, boy. Scream as much as you want. No one would hear you." I cry

out in pain when he fists my hair and squeezes my neck while his heavy panting echoes in my ear. "No one."

My hand rises high in the air of its own accord, and I fire several bullets at the sky. Catriona covers the girls, and they all scream in fear. I close my eyes, soaking in their sounds to temporarily block the despicable voice in my head that becomes louder and louder the closer we come to my personal hell.

A place where my innocence, my childhood, and everything human died, and instead, I turned into a monster, vicious and hungry for only one thing.

Vengeance.

"Please," I beg, pulling at my pants while he drags me down again, and I land on my knees. "Please don't hurt me."

"Shut up, boy. Shut up."

Fury boils inside me, erupting into a volcano, and I continue to fire bullets, uncaring about my surroundings as the scenery changes for me.

Instead of the old cabin with rusty wood and broken steps, I see a perfectly put hunting cabin where he pushes me inside, promising me a great weekend of fishing.

And the seven-year-old me grins widely, excited for what's to come while munching on my nuts.

The last food I'd have that weekend as the monster hurt me repeatedly for the next two days, withholding anything from me.

Bang. Bang. Bang.

"What are you doing? Are you insane?" Catriona yells in my face, grabbing me by my elbow and finally snapping me out of my haze. The little ones are on the ground, hiding away. "Get a grip, you psycho!" she orders me, and to my astonishment, my first desire is not to hurt her or kill her because no one talks to me like that anymore.

No, it's curiosity.

Because once again, the voice got absolutely silent and the memories disappeared so fast. No one and nothing has had this kind of effect on them.

She steps back, noticing my change of mood, and quickly goes to her sisters, who instantly hug her while the wind whooshes over us, blowing their hair backward, and Catriona shivers, wearing nothing but my sweater while her sisters have jackets on.

She managed to take those when I kidnapped them but didn't think about her own comfort, and somehow, this makes me so angry I want to strangle her once again.

My desires when it comes to this girl are confusing as fuck, but thankfully, we wouldn't have to tolerate each other for long.

After all, it will all end soon.

"Get inside the cabin. Now!" My tone must leave no room for argument as she drags her siblings toward it quickly, and I follow them when thunder shakes the sky once again, lightning brightening up everything around us before it becomes darker again.

They hop above the broken step, the wood creaking under their shoes, and Catriona twists the handle, entering inside. They all start to cough, and I wave my hand in front of my nose from all the dust rising up in the air. "This house is so dirty," Peggy whispers, and as they walk in farther, I turn on the light. They blink at the scene that opens up before us.

The simple cabin consists of one couch, two chairs, and a rug along with a small kitchen without gas or running water. It's all fully covered with white sheets, on which the dust has become so thick you can scoop it if you so wish.

Spiderwebs hang on every corner of the floor and ceiling, while the rotten combined with disgusting smell wafts the air, making it next to impossible to breathe, so I open one of the windows and let in the fresh air. "Kids, go sit on that chair." I point at the small stool near the fireplace that's semi clean and ironically has no spiders running around it.

Peggy wiggles her nose and looks at Catriona, who gives her an encouraging smile. "Go on." They do as she says, and I shift my focus to their older sister. "Remove all the sheets and grab the broom for the webs." She huffs in exasperation, crossing her arms and growing too fucking confident for my liking. I shake the gun in my hand, and she glances down, although I don't miss how she grits her teeth. "Clean it up."

"I'm not your maid!"

"You'll be whatever the hell I want, princess." When I aim the gun at her siblings, she rushes to the broom and picks it up, already removing some webs.

"I'm going to chop some wood for the fireplace, and then I'll be back. Don't try anything stupid," I warn them all, and they nod. "No one will hear your cries here." With this, I spin on my heel and shut the door while heading to my van. Picking up an axe, I go farther into the forest to get what I need.

The little boy who still exists within me hates me with a passion for uttering the same words the monster used to whisper to me and urges me to let them all go before insanity consumes me.

However, the grown-up me, the one who knows human nature better than anyone as I dedicated the last decade of my life to studying it, knows it's useless.

If I let them go...they will just suffer more, and the result would be the same.

Now, my plan?

It will put an end to all our suffering and set us all free.

Especially me.

Free from the memories.

Free from the voices.

Free from the smells permanently attached to my nose.

But most importantly...

Free from myself, the hideous monster I'm turning into who won't need a reason to hurt and attack.

And I'd rather die than be like *him*.

CHAPTER THIRTEEN

"To understand a villain, you need to see his past.
A past that's so painful it might make you question how he survived it in the
first place.
But understanding him is not enough.
To truly destroy him, you need to find his hidden scar.
The one that still bleeds and hurts.
Because only that part makes him human."
Phoenix

Phoenix

"This is a dream," I say, yawning soundly and stretching my arms wide as I sit up on the bed, and the blanket slides down my form. "I feel like I'm on cloud nine when lying on these pillows." My brow furrows when I don't see my husband anywhere, and swinging my legs to the side, I curl my toes into the plushy carpet. Every muscle in my body sends a pleasurable ache through my entire system.

A smile shapes on my mouth when I lean down and snag Zach's sweater. Breathing in his scent and rubbing my cheek over it, I think about last night and how the chaos constantly swirling around us in the last two days have settled.

It's a terrible state to be in when you feel like you cannot say things you want to a person who means the most to you because of some danger lurking above us.

Sighing, I put on his sweater while looking around for my husband. "Zachary?" He chooses this moment to emerge from the bathroom, the steam following him as his wet dark hair drips on the floor and he wraps a towel around his hips, the droplets of water glistening on his toned skin under the bright sunlight streaming through the huge window. "Be still my heart," I gasp, covering my mouth and running my gaze up and down his muscled form. "Are you trying to seduce me?" I step closer to him and drop my voice to a whisper. "In daylight?" I sound almost scandalized and then burst out laughing when he pulls me to him, wrapping his arms around me. "Zachary, you're wet!"

"And you love it, darling." He captures my mouth in a heated kiss, his tongue pushing deep and tangling with mine. He swallows my moans, sending tingling sensations sweeping over me and scorching heat into every cell in my body.

My hands circle his neck. I rise on my tiptoes and tilt my head a little bit, allowing him to deepen the kiss while the desire stirs in the pit of my stomach. His masculine scent envelops me whole, urging me to ravish my husband right here and now.

Just as the thought enters my mind, though, a loud knock echoes, and Zach forcefully takes his mouth away to my loud protest and confused blink. "Breakfast," he informs me. Giving me a loud smack on the mouth, he steps away, heading to the door while I cross my arms.

"It should be illegal to tempt your wife when you know you invited company."

"Darling, we both know if I hadn't ordered breakfast, you'd kill me." The man has a point.

If there is one thing I love and never skip, it's breakfast. Maybe because growing up in the foster care system, that was the only decent meal we ever had, so it kind of stuck with me.

Zach grabs the handle and then half turns to me. "Go to the bathroom, love, we don't want anyone to see you."

I lift my brow. "But everyone can see you?" I tease him although there is no real heat in it. He's never given me a reason to feel jealous. That being said, I'm veery territorial when it comes to my husband, and I think that's his possessiveness rubbing off on me.

The man still cannot stand Sebastian near me, and always stays around when I interact with my ex-husband. However, to be fair, that has more to do with his protective instinct as well. He knows that my ex-husband isn't my favorite company in the world.

Some wounds just never heal, and I'm okay with that. Forgiving Sebastian and actually liking him again...yeah, no.

There is no coming back from a betrayal like that, plain and simple.

I enter the bathroom just as I hear a server come in, greeting Zachary. "Good morning, Mr. King."

Quickly hanging the sweater on the nearby hook, I step into the shower and groan when the hot water hits my muscles, letting it wash away all my worries. Although that's when reality finally interrupts my blissful reprieve from the madness around me.

Because my thoughts go back to the boy who currently holds three girls hostage.

I purposely blocked away any thoughts about them while being with Zachary. However, I can no longer do that, and all the information we uncovered yesterday plays in my mind over and over again.

Without knowing much, it's hard to make any statements about his sanity, but he let Miranda get away alive, so there is still hope.

Maybe if we get there on time, he will have a chance...

"Stop," I mutter to myself, finishing my shower in record time and drying off with a towel. "You cannot save them all."

One of the hardest things a person has to face in this profession, or while dealing with serial killers, is learning about their past. We uncover all this information about their childhoods where, in most cases, they were treated so badly it's a wonder any of them survived long enough to do their hideous crimes. We wish we could have saved them and feel this overwhelming compassion toward them, wanting to cure them and gripping the hope that their sanity and the little child living inside them can still be saved.

It's an illusion, though, because once a person commits a cold-blooded murder, there is no going back, and it's always a choice.

Thousands of people grow up with the different kinds of abuse; however, they find the strength to move past it and live their best life or battle their demons on a daily basis. So turning to violence is never an answer or an excuse.

Shaking my head, I grab the robe and put it on, tying the belt on my waist before opening the bathroom and asking, "Is it safe to go?"

"Yes."

Rolling my eyes at his approving tone, I walk barefoot to the small table heavy with all the delicious food on it.

Two plates with eggs, avocado, and cucumber along with caviar are served opposite each other. A coffee mug next to Zachary's and a green mint tea, judging by the smell, next to mine while toasted breads are between us.

Several macarons along with croissants and butter are there as well, and strawberries.

My mouth waters, and my stomach rumbles, which makes Zach chuckle. "Like I said, I know better than anyone when it comes to my wife and food." He pulls the chair out for me, and I sit down, picking up the fork and digging it into my eggs, taking a full fork of it.

My groan rings in the air. "Oh my God."

He sips his coffee. "Yeah, nice, right? We should sneak out here more often. The food alone is worth it." I notice both our phones on the table as well and reach out for mine. "Don't," he warns while I pause mid-chew. "Let's eat in peace and then we can go back to the real world and catch the little fucker who apparently we can't even hate 'cause he's a kid."

And they call my husband cold-hearted. Even he is capable of feeling compassion toward a boy who arguably deserves no mercy.

We eat in silence for several more moments, and I grab the croissant, dipping it into the butter when Zach's phone rings and his father's picture flashes on the display. "That's a bit early for him," I say, and instantly, worry washes over me. "Is everything okay with the kids?"

He slides open his screen, and I hear the twins say in unison, "Daddy!" My husband grins and winks at me. I should have known that our sons would be the ones to call.

There is just simply not a dull moment in sight when it comes to them.

"Hello, boys. Why are you calling me from Grandpa's phone?"

"We stole it. Right from under his nose. Literally," Ian informs him proudly.

"He fell asleep with his newspaper, so we sneaked into his office, and *voila*!" Wyatt adds, "His phone has no games, though."

"Oh, you don't say?" Zach asks, drinking his coffee, and I can just imagine them nodding.

"Yep. Boring. We kept it overnight, and he still hasn't noticed! We decided to call you."

"Because that's more fun?"

"Yes!" Ian says, and then whispers, "Don't tell Mama!"

I get up, munching on my pastry, and stand right behind Zach, resting my elbows on his shoulders while both of the boys groan. "Too late, darlings. Mama already knows."

They look at each other, their dark curls swaying with the action before their emerald eyes focus back on me, and they flash me their toothless smiles. "Hi, Mama! You're so pretty!"

"Why did you steal your grandpa's phone?" I stay on the subject, digging my elbow harder on Zach's shoulder knowing full well he won't be able to hold back his laughter for long.

The man is proud of whatever antics these two pull, and while it's all cute and sweet now, I don't need my sons growing up into trouble with a capital T. Although sometimes I think no amount of me being stern with them will help the matter.

"Because it's fun, Mama." I can practically hear the unspoken *duh* from Wyatt. "And before you ask about Emmaline, she's dancing already. We all had breakfast. The cook gave us lectures while Grandma made us waffles." He pats his tummy. "They were delicious."

"Grandpa promised that he'll take us to the zoo later." He leans closer to the phone and breathes so loudly, Zach lowers the volume. "He might buy us a pony after." Not sure how a pony is connected to the zoo, but alas.

After growing up with very little, it still astonishes me how easily Kings can do and buy whatever the hell they want, and the patriarch of the family spoils all his grandkids rotten. Then again, what's the point of having so much money if you don't spend it on the things you love? "Do you think he'll still do it after he discovers you guys stole his phone?"

They blink rapidly, then frown, and right now, they look so much like Zach that I hide my face behind his head so they won't see me smile. "Oh, Mama, you're right. We need to get the phone back!"

"And delete the call history! So he won't know it was us," Ian points out.

"Let's help him find it." They look at us and blow us kisses. "Bye, Mama. Bye, Daddy."

"Bye, my darlings." That's all I get the chance to say before they disconnect the phone call, and I exhale a heavy breath. "They're your sons." I drop back on my chair, dipping my croissant in the butter again, and polish it off quickly before reaching for my tea. "In everything."

"Yet they were yours when they won that award."

"Well, of course." I tap my head. "They got my brains and your looks. Which makes them perfect."

"Ah, I see. And they got their vices from me as well, I assume?"

"Of course." I repeat, and we share a long stare before we laugh, and I drink my tea, welcoming the hot liquid gliding down my throat. "I need to turn on my phone." He doesn't say anything, just digs his fork into the strawberries and eats it while I grab my phone. Several messages pop up one after another once it's on.

Some from work, some from the kids along with Zach's stepmother giving us updates on the little ones, and there is even one from Valencia. She thinks Emmaline can already perform in a play this month, but we need to up the training if we agree to it.

I push these things for later, though, as all my attention goes to Noah's messages that chill my blood and increase my anxiety.

> My team did internal search inside the organization, and there have been ten boys admitted to it in the past five years who fit the profile. I'll update it once we narrow it down.

We nailed it down to five among this list. The other five either didn't fit age-wise or had no sexual abuse in the past after further investigation. I already contacted everyone, and we should get their addresses soon. The detective on the case will get warrants for searches and check it out. We might catch him quicker than we anticipated.

I would really appreciate it if you didn't turn your phone off.

Among these five, two have nine-to-five jobs and an alibi for the night of the murder. The other one is dead. He overdosed last month. The list is narrowed down to two. They both fit it with some minor differences. The detective already got a warrant and will bring these two in for a chat. Either way, our job is done here. The only thing he asks of you is to help him see which one it is.

Sending you their information and call me once you turn your phone back on.

"The job is done?" I hadn't even realized Zachary loomed behind me, reading everything right along with me. "The little fucker messaged you and created this plan, and he thinks what? The detective will catch him now?"

"Well, as a profiler and a psychiatrist, we can't do anything else. If they catch him, it's the police's job to break him so he tells them about the kids." Even as I say it all out loud, though, it rubs me the wrong way.

Isn't this too easy? And besides...my evaluation wasn't wrong. If he planned to kill them all, would he wait in some place that they have on the record?

He's exceptionally smart. Psychopaths love cat-and-mouse games.

"I see your head swirling. What is it?"

"I don't think they found him. It's just—"

"Too easy for him."

I nod just as Noah calls me, and I pick it up, putting it on speaker-phone. "Phoenix. What in the hell took you—"

"Careful, Agent."

He groans at my husband's voice. "Now's not the time. We have a problem."

"You didn't find him, huh?" Zachary asks grimly, wrapping his hand around my shoulders and pressing me toward him from the back. "You failed once again."

"Them. We didn't find them. No one has lived in their apartments for a long time, and we can't locate them. However, we got a message from our unsub. Right into the databases." My heart freezes, and on instinct, I place my palm on Zach's arm and squeeze it. "The clock. He gave us five hours to find him before he burns them all." He waits a bit. "He sent a recording of the girls screaming and begging him to stop as proof that they're still alive."

"Oh my God. How long ago was that?"

"Almost four hours. We can't trace it, and we have no idea where to find them." I hear what he refuses to say out loud, though.

They can't find them because the unsub planned everything in such a way that I would be the one to find a clue. He's playing a game with me, and the system is merely a pawn to get his message across.

"Zach, bring me the laptop, please." The hotel always makes one available for us in case we need to do business meetings here.

He goes toward the desk and then pushes all the food away, danger-ously close to the edge of the table, not that any of us cares. "I'll study their biographies now, and hopefully, we can find a hint. He's in town, so he must be close."

"I hope so, Phoenix. We have one hour and fifteen minutes."

"I'll call you once I have something."

Hanging up, I quickly log into my email and download the informa-tion while Zachary steps away, knowing full well that I cannot have anyone in my space when I study my patients.

In this case, though, an unsub.

Pulling up both biographies, I scan the information simultaneously.

Both of these boys grew up in middle-class families in good neighborhoods. And both at the age of six years old had their lives irrevocably changed when they lost both of their parents in a car accident.

That's where the similarities end, though, and the differences begin.

One of them, Alan, got taken in by his grandparents, who were considered the sweetest people on the street, and everyone loved them. They even hosted weekly barbecues. Alan's mother, their only daughter, was a successful lawyer, so she had started a trust fund in his name that he could access after turning eighteen.

I make a mental note on it because the unsub needs resources to do what he does.

The cops were never called on them. However, Alan was seen with bruises on his body that he constantly got due to his accidents. Only after he turned thirteen and the grandfather killed his grandmother in a rage did everyone know about the family abuse that involved sexual abuse as well.

Alan never spoke about it, though, and just nodded, never outright admitting what was done to him. That's how he ended up in a shelter, refusing to stay at the home or go into the foster system. He ran away so many times that I guess they just gave up.

He left once he turned eighteen and got access to his money, wasting it on whatever he saw fit.

A psychologist who interacted with him after the abuse noted that he displayed no emotions whatsoever and just stared into the distance, and even his grandmother's bloody face didn't warm him up.

In fact, there was this coldness about him that no one could shake. Which might be one of the reasons he never formed long-lasting friendships.

Since I know my husband so well, I'm not surprised to see him hold my phone and probably read these reports on it to catch up with me when I look up. "He fits the profile. Some girls even commented that he always offered to accompany them when it was dark."

"A protective instinct?" He ponders on it. "That would explain his attachment to Catriona."

"Maybe. But..."

"What is it?"

"According to the police, his grandmother was abused for years but never reported it. She made some minor trips to the hospital, but once again, no one ever suspected the grandfather. However, she loved her grandson and even asked a lot of times for him to stay at his friend's house."

"She protected him."

"Yes. I don't think he was sexually abused." They just assumed it because the grandmother was raped before her husband killed her. Alan acted so feral and thrashed in their hold, they never got to examine him, which I find weird as hell. And by the time they did, it was too late, and the signs were gone. They went by his single nod of agreement. "I think he was a punching bag."

"He started with him, and then moved his rage to the grandmother." He wraps his hand around his mug and lifts it up to his mouth. "Are you sure the unsub was sexually abused? He might just hate men who hurt women. Matt would fit that description."

"I don't think I'm wrong."

"Okay, then focus on the second guy."

Pinching the bridge of my nose, I do as he says and read the details on Rhys.

After his parents died, his only living relative was his father's sister. She was thirty years old and hated the idea of raising a kid, but they all lived in a small town, so her reputation was valuable to her.

She took him in and, according to the neighbors, yelled at him a lot, and he was often seen playing alone in the garden.

Compared to Alan, though, his parents weren't wealthy so nothing was left for him. His aunt could barely afford her lifestyle, let alone adding on a kid to it. Despite that, he was always fed and clothed well, so at least she was decent enough to provide him this much.

It all changed when she found herself a new man, a wealthy man in his forties whom she met at work. They married within two weeks, and he whisked them away to New York. He bought them a new house where they lived for the next six years.

A perfect family man who adored his wife, spoiled her, and accepted her nephew as his own son. He even called him his boy and loved to show Rhys around due to his smart brain.

Like me, the kid skipped several grades, and his teacher pushed him further in his accomplishments while his uncle happily paid for it all.

"The family name rings a bell." Zachary snaps his fingers several times. "Yeah. He was a genius accountant. Not wealthy by our standards, but he was wildly respected. He died five years ago after shooting his wife dead. He left all his fortune to her nephew." After he mentions that, I remember some local news coverage of that but very briefly since that's when I gave birth to the boys. "A lot of people wanted to take him in, but he always snuck out to go to a shelter. They thought he had a trauma of losing both of his parents, so he stayed there." Zach reads the last line on his report. "The boy had several old bruises on his body, and that's it. He gave no information. Also, he rarely if ever spoke and just preferred to read in the library." Zach stills. "A place where Catriona usually read stories to the little children."

I click his photo and shiver at the complete hollowness in his gray eyes ascended by his high cheekbones and tan skin. His hair falls down to his shoulders, while his lower lip seems permanently bruised from him biting on it. He wears a black turtleneck sweater, and without a shadow of a doubt, I know this is our unsub.

"It's him. It must be him."

Panic slowly glides up inside me, and Zach quickly grabs my shoulders, digging his fingers deep, and our gazes clash. "Deep breaths." I inhale and exhale, my heart breaking for the little boy he must have been as echoes of pain still can be visible on his face. "We still have almost an hour to catch him."

There is little information about his life, except the fact that he always helped out someone if they needed assistance with the computers. "Zach, he got access to his fortune four months ago. He gave it all away to charity sans one million dollars. He even sold all the properties." I frown, turning my attention back to the screen. "Except a wooden cabin. They frequently went there with his uncle; he was a hunter. Rhys once mention in a school homework paper that the cabin taught him patience and focus." My stomach drops, and I jump up. "That's where he took them."

"Are you sure?"

"Yes." He's already calling Noah while I run to put on my clothes, not caring in the least that I shouldn't go there because deep down I know.

He needs me there to finish the composition, to tell me his story before he does what he wishes the most.

To end it where it all began.

In his abuser's cabin to truly expose him once and for all.

God help us all.

$\mathcal{U}$ nsub-Rhys

"Why are you doing this?" Catriona asks, sobbing while she sits on the floor along with her siblings. A tight rope ties them all together while I spray gasoline all over the cabin. "Please don't kill us," she begs me while her sisters just stay quiet. I think they've learned to keep their mouths shut at this point.

Or I just scared them enough.

Last night, I came back to a semi-clean cabin where the girls all sat on the couch, wrapped in a blanket, while I started the fire and warmed up this fucking hell.

They had one bathroom break, and they fell asleep, all while the oldest one stared at me, silently pleading with me to spare their lives, and somehow that angered me so much.

How dare she ask me that?

She is the one who awakened this desire to kill that stayed controlled and dormant all these years. I even believed I could live in this fucking society with the voices until I saw it.

Her flinching at her father, her avoidance of him, and finally how he promised to teach her obedience once he flies her abroad.

I couldn't stand it, the pain and suffering in her eyes, and I couldn't let him do it. The images of my abuser merged with Matt, and all I could hear in my head was *kill him*.

Kill him. Kill him. Kill him.

I stalked them. I watched them, and finally, I attacked them.

All because of a girl with hurting blue eyes who begged for salvation in a world that offers none.

"I promise you, Catriona. Whatever I have in mind won't be painful." A horrified gasp slips past her lips, and her sisters burrow their faces deep into her. "I'm not that cruel."

And I'm not.

Contrary to what everyone thinks about me, my kidnapping them and inviting Phoenix was my gift to society that failed time and time again.

Before insanity consumes me and transforms me into a serial killer who doesn't know or control his mind, I'll leave this earth.

However, every life and death should have a meaning.

And mine will have it.

CHAPTER FOURTEEN

"One decision.
Sometimes just one decision can change the trajectory of our lives.
For the better or for the worse, though...only time would tell."
Phoenix

Phoenix

"Faster, Zach. Faster!" I tell him as he presses on the gas pedal, increasing the speed and tightening his hold on the steering wheel when he gets on the narrow asphalt road leading to the cabin deep in the woods. "We have twenty minutes!" I almost yell, running my fingers through my hair while wondering if the detective made it on time.

After we called Noah and he informed the police, we quickly jumped into the car because the cabin was forty minutes away, and all this time, I've been going insane with worry for the little ones.

"His aunt frequently traveled to Europe, leaving him alone for long periods of time with this man," I say, resting my head on the window and watching the ever-changing scenery while the wind whooshes soundly, swaying the trees around us from side to side. "She must have known." Nothing but resentment coats my voice toward this woman who used her nephew in her own agenda. After reading his file again, I realized he met her on the children's playground.

On the playground, that monster spotted his victim and did everything in his power to get his hands on Rhys, who he hurt repeatedly for years.

"She got what she wanted from him and didn't care about the boy," Zach replies grimly, and takes a harsh turn to the left. "Won't be surprised to find out the boy shot her." He waits a beat. "Right before he shot his abuser and then staged the whole thing to look like a crime of passion." A hollow chuckle echoes in the car, and I look at my husband. His face is set in stone while anger seeps into his every word. "Can't even blame him."

I place my hand on his arm. The idea of someone willingly hurting a child is beyond our comprehension, and that's the true tragedy of this situation.

Rhys is a victim who had no choice but to become a monster to free himself from hell. Except the darkness sucked up all his soul, and he turned to violence and stays merciless to goodness.

It feeds only on evilness, and if no one stops him now...he will grow more violent each day. It's a wonder Rhys kept the girls alive for so long, which tells me that I was wrong.

He doesn't want to kill them. He just needed our attention and only wanted to kill himself.

Because the desires inside him grow, and he won't be able to control them.

"When we get there, you stay in the car."

Zach's voice snaps me out of my thoughts, and I frown. "What? No!"

"Yes! He's still dangerous, and he'll try to use you as leverage. You let the cops handle this one."

"Absolutely not!" Doesn't he understand? "He wants me there, and if we don't play by his rules, he might hurt the girls!"

"You're my priority. You have a family!" He practically shouts the last part, and I freeze at this as the cabin finally shows on the horizon along with blue and red lights brightening up the space, mixing with the sunlight since several police cars are already there. "It won't be like the last time, Phoenix."

Sighing inwardly at this, I wait for him to reach the cabin and park the car slightly farther away so we won't block the ambulance, then finally turn to my husband. "He won't hurt me, Zach. He's just a kid."

"A murderer." He palms my head, holding my stare while his thumbs caress my cheeks. "He's a murderer and a manipulator, and I won't let another psycho hurt you. One was enough."

And while I understand that my request goes against any protective instinct inside him, it's something I have to do. I'm not a cop and don't think I live in some kind of action movie where I'm the hero who saves the day.

But when a serial killer got you involved in the case right away, you're an important piece of the puzzle, and you have to play by the rules. "You have to trust me, Zach. It's not like the last time. I'm not the object of his rage."

"You don't know that," he replies stubbornly as I see the detective walking toward us, his jaw ticking, and my time is running out. "What if he plans for both of you to die?"

"It's not going to be—"

The detective knocks on our window, and reluctantly, Zach lets me go, and we get out of the car. Zach shakes his hand, and then he extends it to me. "Dr. King. Thank you for coming and giving us the lead. I wish the circumstances were different."

"Don't we all," Zach mutters, and I cover my nose when the smell of gasoline penetrates my nostrils, almost making me gag. "What is this smell?" he asks, clearly reading my mind.

"Rhys sprayed gasoline all over the place and has the girls kept hostage inside. He refuses to talk to anyone, but Dr. King."

Zach tenses next to me, and his voice turns harsh. "So you just, what? Wait for my wife to do your job?"

I expect the detective to take offense to what he said, but he just crosses his arms. "I understand your frustration, Mr. King, but I have three terrified girls inside, and a lunatic who can set them all on fire with a drop of a match. If he sprayed gasoline on them, we won't be able to save them." He shifts his focus to me. "We called in the firefighters, but doing anything else besides talking him into surrendering is not an option." A second passes. "That's our best chance."

Silence falls on us, and I glance at my husband, who grits his teeth and a muscle on his cheek twitches while he clenches his fists. "Zach?" I ask, waiting for his reply because I won't do this without his support.

As I've discovered in this marriage, we do all the things together if we want to have a happy one.

"If there is any danger to you, you will run away. Do you understand?" He finally speaks and throws his question at me. "You don't think about the kid and the girls. Your priority is you."

"Okay." This much I can promise him.

"Great. Let's put a vest on you."

Lacing my fingers with Zachary's, I pull him toward the cops who surveil the situation. I can't see anything happening inside the house because something blocks the window. Rhys must have done it to keep anyone from shooting him.

The detective gives me the vest, and Zachary quickly helps me put it on. Once done, he grabs my neck and presses his lips to mine. He whispers to me as he leans back, "Be careful, darling."

"Always."

With this, the detective steps closer and instructs me, "You can talk to him. Our main goal is for him to get out and give up at least one of the hostages."

The way he says that makes me think he doubts this will happen, and Rhys will instead invite me in. "Okay." Taking a deep breath, I walk farther until I'm standing several feet away from the entrance with everyone else a good distance behind me. "Rhys!" I call, pushing back all emotions and thoughts about his dangerous situation to focus only on the goal.

To save all these kids, including the murderer, from death.

"You wanted to talk, so here I am."

The door to the cabin opens with a loud creak, sending shivers down my spine as I see nothing there besides old wooden furniture.

Not a single sound comes out either.

Looking over my shoulder, I see Zachary taking a step toward me while he looks around the property. I didn't expect Rhys to follow instructions, so entering the cabin that might light up at any moment is hardly wise.

I see my husband nod at me. Whatever he has in mind provides me with an extra layer of protection, so after exhaling heavily and wiping my sweaty palms on my vest, I slowly go inside, the wood screeching under my shoes.

Finally, I reach the doorjamb and despite my heart beating like crazy in my chest, I step over the threshold and take three steps before the door shuts soundly behind me, making me jump. "Welcome, Dr. King." A raspy voice greets me as Rhys comes into view from the right, holding a gun in his hand, and I swallow. "You came with five minutes to spare. I'm impressed." The scent of gasoline is even stronger here. It's a wonder they didn't faint from it since the floor is practically soaked with it.

I open my mouth to reply, but the words get stuck in my throat when I see the girls roped together. Catriona sits holding her sisters while biting on her lips so much that there are traces of blood. Her eyes plead with me to do anything to save her. I notice her clothes are intact, and she doesn't seem to have any other bruises, which hopefully means he wasn't violent with them.

However, that's not what chills my blood and has fear enveloping me whole. It's her siblings lying motionlessly next to her. "Oh my God," I whisper.

No. No. No.

We couldn't have been this late and...

"Relax, Dr. King. They're sleeping." My gaze darts to Rhys, who leans on the fireplace, rubbing his jaw with the gun. "I gave them some pills. They don't need to hear all this. Their ears are too innocent, and I don't want to be the one who breaks it to them that monsters do exist in this world."

Gathering all my willpower into my fist, I straighten up. "I think that ship sailed when you killed their father and kidnapped them."

Something akin to annoyance flashes on his face, but he quickly covers it with indifference and grins, although it doesn't reach his hollow eyes. "Well, the actual murder didn't happen in front of them. But I do agree about the kidnapping." He hisses a breath through his teeth. "One might argue, though, that what I did hardly counts as monstrous." The grin slips as anger etches on his features. "Nothing compared to what I had experienced on a daily basis."

"So is this your revenge?" I ask, and his brow furrows. "Killing the girls because they had a happier childhood than you did?"

He picks up the match near the fireplace and throws them up in the air as he still holds the gun. "Having that piece of shit for a father is hardly better." Catriona gasps, and he winks at her while everything inside me stills when he says, "Hate to break it to you, princess. Your dad almost raped you, so I'm not sure why the fuck you're this surprised."

Tears form in her eyes, and I wish I could hug this girl and get her out of here, shielding her from the harsh truth. "Rhys." I say only his name, and when our gazes clash, he must read my silent request to shut his mouth when it comes to this family because he shrugs. I guess this is as good as I'll get.

The last thing I need is Catriona finding out what her father has done from him. The girl might never recover from all these traumas. "So why did you take them?"

"Because otherwise I wouldn't have your attention." He taps on his chest. "No one would have known my truth." He motions with his gun to the girls. "They're valuable assets, let's call them that. And their mother was too willing to play a game to save them." He clicks his tongue. "She gave up almost too easily for me."

I bet Miranda's love for her children confused him, and somehow, he decided to punish her for it, sending her to prison. "And what is your truth?"

Instead of answering my question, he says, "I was seven years old when he brought me here for the first time. We were supposed to spend the weekend bonding before his marriage to my aunt." Such coldness laces his tone that I resist the urge to rub my arms. "He hurt me over and over again, enjoying my screams. And then we went home as if nothing happened." He speaks in a trance, gazing into the distance. "The only thing I could think of on the way home was telling my aunt what he had done to me so she could protect me. And that's what I did." His laughter reverberates through the space, and my stomach drops. "She slapped me in the face and called me an ungrateful bastard who makes up lies." His voice drops to a whisper. "She didn't believe me."

For a second, I see him as a dark-haired little boy who sought protection with someone he trusted, even if she didn't love him. And instead of healing him, she just fed him to a monster. "I'm so sorry about that."

"Such is life. No matter if you're a man, woman, or a child...no one will believe you if it means they have to sacrifice their comfort for the truth. One must be open to the consequences of the truth before accepting it." He chuckles. "I had evidence too. The teeth marks. She stayed blind to them and married him shortly after."

"Is this when you started to hate her?"

"No. I mean, I never loved her because, let's face it, she was a bitch. I just thought she was dumb, and then as we lived together, and he'd come to me at night several times a month, she proved my point." The bile rises in my throat at the picture he's describing, my hands itching to kill his abuser myself while he speaks about it in this monotone as if we're discussing the weather.

From the corner of my eye, I see Catriona gaping at him in shock as pity fills her gaze, which is dangerous.

The last thing we need is one of the victims developing a Stockholm syndrome, considering they are so close in age.

That's why I ask next, breaking any illusion of a good person when it comes to him. Because a crime done to him as a child doesn't excuse his current violence. "And when you couldn't take it anymore...you killed them both?"

"No. The thought crossed my mind, but no. I discovered my love for studies, and it helped. I even solved hard mathematical equations in my head when he came to me at night. Taught me that sometimes we can be far, far away mentally even while our body is brutally violated."

Catriona is crying at this point while hugging her sisters close. "I'm so sorry, Rhys." Poor thing, I'm used to hearing such stuff in my profession, and it still shakes me.

I can just imagine what she feels.

He shakes the matchbox. "Remember, princess, I light this up, and everyone is dead." She freezes, and he winks. "Don't feel sorry. I despise pity." He looks back at me. "Anyhow, he really killed her. Actually, they killed each other." Per the police report, he killed his wife and then had a heart attack because he couldn't handle it. Rhys neither admitted nor denied it as he had a strong alibi.

He was at school, so no one even questioned him much. "How is that possible?"

"When I turned twelve, he lost interest in me. I grew taller and started football. Basically, he loved pretty little boys, and I wasn't one anymore." Shivers of disgust travel through me in waves at this. "So he decided to leave my aunt for some other single mom. She didn't take it well." He squeezes the matchbox so hard, it crumples in his fist. "That's when she told him she had a camera in my room and recorded everything." The manic laughter returns. "The bitch knew all along. She simply didn't give a fuck."

Oh God.

This is worse than I initially thought. The damage this knowledge has done to his psyche changes my perspective, although it still leaves me curious why he kept Miranda alive.

Somehow, in his mind, she didn't act as a substitute to his aunt. "She tried to blackmail him?" That's the only logical conclusion.

"Yes. She told him she'd send the hard drive to the police, and everyone would know what he did." He clicks his tongue. "Like I said, the bitch was dumb. If she did it, she'd get rid of him and have all his fortune. She just wasn't that bright, so he shot her."

"Weren't you at school? How do you know all this?"

"I was home, watched the son of a bitch choke and beg for help as he clutched his chest." He hisses. "It lasted just a few seconds, but I enjoyed his agony. Then I went back to school and snuck into the library, securing an alibi. With *law,* one might never know." I don't miss how he puts an emphasis on the law. "The rest is history."

I ponder his explanation for several moments while Catriona wipes her tears. "There is police everywhere right now. You brought us here. Because you want to burn down this cabin and for people to listen to your story."

"Yes." He taps on the floor with his foot. "If I'm going to hell, I'm taking this place with me."

It's hard for me to understand what he specifically wants from me since he's already got all the attention he wanted, so I turn the conversation to the situation at hand. "Let the girls go, Rhys. You don't want to do this. You aren't like him."

Rage crosses his face as he grows rigid, and a sadistic smile curves his mouth. "Yes. I'm not like him. But he still made me into a monster." He presses the tip of the gun to his temple. "The kind of monster who hears whispers in his head urging him to kill. To see blood. To watch the organs in all their glory. That's the kind of monster I became."

And that's when I understand he doesn't intend to leave alive tonight, so I have to do my best to save the girls before he does something stupid like drop a match on the floor and then shoots himself.

"Let the girls go, please."

Before he can answer, my husband's voice booms in the space, wrapping the cocoon of protection around me but at the same time sending panic all over me. "Rhys."

"I wondered how long it would take him to speak to me." Rhys chuckles.

"Let the girls go and take me instead. I'm worth more, and my death would make a hell of a headline."

Is he insane?

"No!" I scream at him. Rhys hates men, and in his current state, who knows what he will do to Zach. He cannot enter here! "Stay away!" I can't believe he's doing this.

"A King. In my grasp." Rhys rubs his chin again. "Should I do it, Dr. King? Bring your husband here?"

The idea of endangering Zach doesn't sit well with me, so I snap. "Stop it, Rhys. Let the girls go and do what you want to do."

"If you say so, Dr. King." With this he clears his throat and shouts, "I'll let the little ones go in exchange for Zachary King." I want to dart toward him, but he points his gun at me. "Nuh-uh, Dr. King. Careful." Then he motions to Catriona. "Untie them. Only you can take them outside. Catriona," he barks at her, startling her. "You stay fucking put or else." He doesn't finish his warning, but she nods, relief written all over her at the prospect of saving her siblings.

I go to the girls, untying the rope as the girls remain asleep.

I pick up the youngest and go to the door where Zachary stands, ready to take her to the police. I just glare at him for coming, and he glares right back. I guess I should have expected it anyway.

Shaking my head, I go after Kayla, huffing a little while picking her up as she's older and then barely drag her to Zach. He follows the same moves before entering and shutting the door. "You didn't stay outside. I'm astonished."

Zach pushes me behind him. Catriona runs to me, and I hug her close, rubbing her trembling body. "I'm a man of my word, Rhys."

"Funny. I've never met a man who was." He cocks his head to the side. "I admire you, though." Zach stays silent at this admission, so Rhys continues, "You protect your family no matter what. Even if it turns you into a monster." He glances back and forth between us, probably alluding to our past. "Miscarriage of justice," he says out of the blue, and we both frown. "That's what your case was called, right? They wrongly convicted you."

A bit lost why he brings it up, I nod. "Yes."

"The law failed you. What is it called when it fails the likes of me?" He shakes the matches again, still pointing a gun at me, and I can practically feel Zach calculating how he can disarm him without harming anyone else. "You got your freedom, reputation, everything. But where is the justice for the likes of me?" He yells the question. "He died so easily. So, so easily after hurting me for years. Where is my justice, Dr. King?"

"I don't know," I reply honestly, and he blinks in surprise. "What I do know, though, is one thing. Justice brings us peace on some level. It clears our name and punishes those who are supposed to be punished." His lips curl at this. "However, it doesn't heal us. It doesn't make us forget or soothe the fire living in us from the scars inflicted by those who hurt us." I tighten my hold on the girl when she presses closer to me. "You have a story you want to share with the world. A story that sheds light on what happened to you, what happens to countless people."

"A story you will share with the world," he tells me. "Everyone believes you. Because everyone feels guilty when it comes to you."

I shake my head. "No. Because when all this is done, do you know what they will say? Matt was killed by an eighteen-year-old man who murdered him and then stole his children. Luckily, the police got there in time."

"No. You will tell them why it happened. Why I wanted to kill him. You will tell them how the law failed me."

Except it wasn't the law that failed him; it was the people in his life who should have loved him instead of treating him as a bargaining chip or an outlet for their hideous desires.

But admitting that would bring too much pain, and it's easier to direct his rage at the law. His damaged psyche somehow made me a symbol of injustice done right, and now he expects me to tell his truth, which is still very confusing. "It wouldn't matter, Rhys. It's a far better story for the press when you give people someone to hate. Even the truth about Matt and what happened wouldn't matter. You'd still be a monster who broke the law and stepped over the line." A beat passes, and I add, "Someone who, instead of overcoming his pain and living a life like thousands and thousands of people do, turned to the dark side."

A muscle in his jaw twitches at this, and he grips the gun harsher before pressing it under his chin. I dart to him only to be stopped by Zach's arm. "You think I'm stupid enough to play your psychological games?" He laughs. "If I stay alive, I'll spend my time in prison. No fucking way." He bites on his lip. "He died so easily. He would have been tortured in prison in the most horrible way. And he got away with it!" he screams. "And you think I'll spend my time there? Fuck. That. Shit."

"If you stay alive, you can share your story. And that's what matters, right? For the world to know who the real monster is?" I play on his delusions, swaying him to our side because, despite all this, I'm a doctor.

And doctors do their best to save lives.

"You still don't understand, do you?" He glides the gun up and down his Adam's apple. "No matter what, I'm a monster with no redeeming qualities. I do not seek atonement. I seek justice. I want for people to know that their indifference made me who I am. Get out," he orders, pointing the gun at us once again. "Get the fuck out, all of you, unless you want to die with me. The reason I wanted Dr. King was so that you could see how fucking lucky you are. Justice was kind to you even if it was late." The air hitches in my throat at this as a sad smile pulls at his lips. "But above that, you're strong. If you were like me, you would have never married your husband and have the life that you have." He places a splayed palm on his chest over his heart. "It's because you have a soul. I do not. They took it from me."

"Rhys—"

"Get out, all of you. Now!" He looks at Zach. "Now, Zach, unless you want me to kill your wife." With this, he removes the safety with a loud click and points the gun at my forehead. "I will count to three."

"There are other ways, Rhys," my husband says but grips my elbow, pushing me toward the door. "You can try to get justice by speaking your truth in court."

"No. Because as your wife said, no one will give a fuck. One." He counts, and panic sneaks into every cell in my body as I move Catriona with me yet still look at Rhys.

"Did you survive to die now? Do you really want to give him such satisfaction?" Zach asks, stepping closer to him, and I roll my lips to keep from stopping him because any wrong move now might result in all of us dying. "The son of a bitch stole your childhood. He gets to steal your life too?"

Rhys's hand shakes, and he orders, "Shut up!"

"No, he doesn't steal it. You want to give it to him on a silver platter. The monster who controls you even from his grave."

"I said shut up!" Rhys pulls at his hair, and I see a struggle that must go on inside him because despite what he claims, he still has a soul deep down.

A soul that doesn't wish to hurt anyone innocent in his book.

And I know Zach sees it too, but as much as it breaks my heart to watch all this, I'm not willing to sacrifice our lives for his.

"Two," Rhys mutters, wiping his mouth. "Get out, all of you."

Before we could do this, though, Catriona gets free from my hold and runs to him only to halt her movements when he aims the gun at her. "Please, Rhys. Don't do this. Listen to them."

Zachary and I share a look at this while Rhys just stares at her with an unreadable expression on his features. Several seconds pass that feel like hours when finally he lowers the gun. The detective chooses this moment to barge inside and quickly heads to Rhys as he drops the gun. "Rhys..." He starts reading his rights to him as he secures handcuffs on his wrists, and we all quickly get out, breathing the fresh air into our lungs.

"Come here, honey." I drag Catriona toward the medics who've already checked her siblings and turn around to see the detective taking Rhys to the nearby car while Zachary follows them.

However, as he steps down on the last step, Zach calls, "Rhys!"

He stops the detective right along with him, half turning to him in question.

I hear firefighter sirens echoing in the space, announcing their close arrival as Zach lights the match and holds it in front of him.

Rhys's gaze flickers to it, and then Zachary throws it at the house. It lights up instantly, the orange and blue flames consuming the old structure and destroying it bit by bit. "For fuck's sake, King," the detective mutters, but my whole attention is on Rhys.

Or rather how the fire reflects in his cold eyes, and for the first time, I see something more than hollowness in them.

Because they are filled with relief.

As the cabin where all his nightmares started is no more.

CHAPTER FIFTEEN

"Funny thing about forgiveness?
We either freely give it and move on without expecting any closure in order to
heal ourselves...
Or hold on to the hurt that destroys us to the point of insanity."
Phoenix

*P*hoenix

"Are you sure about this?" Noah asks as we stand in the room, watching Miranda lean down and nervously bite on her nails while she waits for me, worry etched on all her features. She taps her foot on the floor.

Thankfully, there are no new bruises on her skin, and according to the police officer, she has been on her best behavior for the past twenty-four hours and even slept through the whole night without a single incident.

She also kept asking about her children, but no one gave her any answers.

"You don't have to do this, you know."

The agent is right, of course. I've already done way more than I should for this case and overstepped so many lines.

He could deliver the news to Miranda himself while I stay with my family and soak up all their love, grateful for the second chance my life has granted me and know all this hell is behind me.

However...

I think this is the right thing to do.

"I hope we won't work on another case again, Noah." I half turn to him as we look at each other. "Don't involve me in another criminal case. I've had enough of them." I love my profession, and I'll do my best to help people around the world, but the criminal ones...I can't. It takes too much of my soul since they always make it so damn personal. "You owe me this much."

He nods and extends his hand to me, and we share a shake. "It's always a pleasure to work with you, Phoenix."

"Can't say the same, Noah." And then I wink at him, chuckling. "Sorry."

A rare grin flashes on his mouth, bringing attention to his white teeth. "At least you're honest."

"It's a silver lining, although, to some, honesty is not a virtue." I pat his arm and take a deep breath, grab my phone, and press on the keypad. The door slides open, and Miranda's eyes instantly go to me.

"Phoenix." She gets up swiftly only to groan when the cuffs pull her back, and she glares at me, rubbing her wrist with her fingers. "You're finally here." She glances at the clock. "It's been seventy-two hours. Did you find them?" She licks her lips. "Did you find my girls?"

I stay silent and instead walk to the chair, sitting on it while she continues to fire off her questions. "Where are the girls? Why aren't you saying anything? I'm not the one who killed Matt!" she adds hastily, swallowing harshly, and her voice drops to a barely audible whisper filled with so much agony that it pulls at the strings of my soul. "Are my girls...dead?" She bites her lower lip so harshly, she draws blood and then yells, "Say something!"

"I wish you had shown this much enthusiasm during our other sessions. Maybe everything would have been different."

She stills at this, her nails digging into the table. "I had no choice. He murdered Matt and took the girls, leaving me instructions. If I didn't act crazy and say all the stupid things I did, he'd kill my girls."

She presses her splayed palms against each other. "I've seen firsthand the violence he was capable of. I couldn't subject my girls to it."

In truth, if she had been honest from the beginning, it would have been easier to locate Rhys because, despite what he claimed, he didn't have absolute power or ears everywhere. We could have created our own game, and the police would have trapped him sooner before it escalated. The girls will have nightmares for life.

The thing about psychopaths, though, is they smell their perfect victims very well and after years of the abuse Miranda experienced, she was an easy target to manipulate because that's what people around her have done for years.

Used her love for her children as leverage to do whatever the hell they wanted to her.

I slide my phone open, clicking on a video, and place it between us.

In a second, all three girls come to view and shout, "Hi, Mommy!" Miranda blinks in surprise, picking up the phone and gripping it so hard her knuckles turn white. She leans as close as she can toward the phone where Catriona speaks, hugging her siblings tight who all smile at her. "We just wanted to tell you that we love you, and everything is good. We're safe and going to stay with Grandma." Tears form in Miranda's eyes. "She said she'll hire the best lawyer for you, Mom. They say we can't visit you for now."

"But we really want to," Kayla pitches in while Peggy nods in agreement.

Catriona shuffles their hair and continues, "Take care of yourself for us. We love you and can't wait to see you again. Please don't worry about us anymore."

"Yes. We love you!" the younger ones scream, and then all of them blow her a kiss before the video ends.

Miranda's tears drop on the display one by one while she caresses it with her thumbs. She puts it away, closing her eyes while sobs rack her, and she exhales heavy breaths.

As a mother, I understand her. After all this bullshit was done, the first thing I did was run home and hug all my babies, kissing them.

"Thank you." She looks at me again and reaches for my hands, putting hers above mine, and I allow the contact because she won't act violently now. "Thank you." The tears continue to come, and she croaks through her clogged throat, "What happens now?"

"Like the girls said, your mother-in-law promised to hire the best lawyer to get you out of here, but there will be certain conditions." She frowns at this. "You will hash it out with the district attorney, but they should get you out of here." Considering how complicated the case is with certain decisions done behind the scenes, I prefer to keep my mouth shut when it comes to it, and let the other people explain it to her.

As long as they get her out of here, though, who cares, right? The woman committed no crime and should be freed from this place.

"And until then, my girls will stay at their grandparents'?" I don't miss the trepidation in her voice.

"Rhys, the boy who murdered your husband, uncovered some of the illegal activities your father-in-law did. So right now, he's under investigation and won't be staying at home. And I think your mother-in-law plans to divorce him." Her eyes widen, and she sucks in a breath. "That's the only thing I can tell you for now. Your girls are safe, and no one will hurt them." I pat her hands. "You can breathe freely now, Miranda. It's over. And all this"—I swirl my finger in the air— "will be over soon too."

Although it won't truly be over for years to come when it comes to her internal scars.

"Thank you. I was awful. I'm sorry about that. I didn't mean all those things I said about you and your husband." Sincerity rings in her tone, and I nod. In a way, though, this case was healing for me as well, so I guess it was meant to be. "I don't even know what to do now." A humorless chuckle escapes her. "Besides hugging my girls."

"You're thirty-three years old. You have your whole life ahead of you to figure it out. Without Matt and his father looming behind you like a shadow." With this, I get up and grab my phone. "Once you're free, you can always find me in my clinic. We can start therapy if you wish." She sighs, rubbing her hands together while mustering up a smile. "Best of luck, Miranda. I hope you'll finally find peace. And thank God all this ended well."

"Because you didn't give up," she says and laughs. "You still love people, don't you? Even after your past, you have this love for strangers that pushes you to do the right thing."

"Yes."

"Why?" she asks, confusion lacing her tone as she straightens up. "I don't get it. Shouldn't you be selfish? Your husband is a billionaire. Why waste time on all this and feel compassion even to those who don't deserve it?"

Isn't this the question people love to ask me?

And I think up until now I never had a response to it. But after experiencing this situation that put a lot of things into perspective, I finally have an answer.

"My favorite teacher used to say that my brilliant mind was a gift that I should use wisely. And I did. When I decided to get into a profession that heals people. The only way I know how to share my gift and use it for good is by going all in with all my emotions." A grin shapes my mouth. "That's why Zachary is perfect for me. He will never allow my gift to hurt me. Even empathy needs boundaries."

She nods after a second, and I turn around, heading to the door but pause when she calls my name. "Yes?" I look over my shoulder.

She takes a deep breath before exhaling loudly, a stubborn expression crossing her face, and she says with her trembling voice the words that make my heart contract inside my chest. "All these years ago, Matt raped me. He raped me, and it wasn't my fault."

Since she awaits some kind of reaction from me, I reply, "Yes."

Just one word yet it means so much to her because she scrunches her eyes, breathing heavily, and snaps them open again. "I just wanted to say it out loud for the first time to you."

Miranda finally made her first step to healing, and I'm glad.

Without saying anything else, I walk away from the room and just wave at the guys as I pass them by, snagging my coat and going down the hallways, heading to the exit.

The blast of frigid air greets me the minute I step over the gates and flaps my coat backward.

I lift my face to the sun and smile.

Once, a long time ago, I heard someone say that freedom is something you feel in your heart. If you don't feel it inside you, even if it seems that nothing stops you from living a life of your dreams, you will feel trapped.

Today, I believe these words.

Because this place no longer has a hold on the pieces of my heart, and nightmares don't flash in my head.

I'm free.

CHAPTER SIXTEEN

"Choose wisely to whom you display your empathy.
Sometimes you're not helping them.
Instead, you play your part in their twisted game designed to get them what they
want.
A game they control and win by default."
Zachary

Z **achary**
   "Where are we?" Rhys asks, flipping the lighter through his fingers while I drive the car on the narrow road leading to the forest. Most leaves turn golden, falling rapidly on the ground while thunder shakes the sky and wind whooshes soundly, lightning flashes forcing the birds to fly up in the air.

I can't wait for the rain season to be over because I'm done with this weather.

"Isn't it obvious?" I fire my own question, and he grins, although it doesn't reach his eyes. He runs his finger over his lips, resting his head on the window again, zoning out completely.

As I've discovered in the past couple of days after the disastrous confrontation that almost led to tragedy, the kid speaks whenever he wishes to and can check out of the conversations at once, giving you nothing but silence that oddly isn't welcomed or comforting with a psychopath.

Gripping the steering wheel tighter, I turn it to the right, getting deeper into the secluded park on the outskirts of the city, away from strangers' prying eyes, which gives us enough privacy to do what I have in mind.

A plan that was a pain in the ass to come up with, but a man would do anything to make his woman happy, even summon all his connections to get himself a favor from a man who gives none of those.

It's a wonder he didn't tell me to fuck off when I explained the situation to him. I think the only reason he restrained himself was due to the video call and his daughter playing in the background, but if looks could kill...I'd be dead.

"This reminds me of a horror movie," Rhys says, clearly in the mood to talk again while thunder booms in the air once more, bringing attention to the gathering dark clouds casting shadows in the morning. The little shit rolls his window down, extending his hand and inhaling deeply. "Are you gonna kill me and then bury me six feet under so your wife can be happy?" A beat passes. "This way, she won't know what you did, and you can go back to your happy life with your perfect children and fences." Bitterness laces his tone although it's missing the hate and boredom, which is progress for Rhys.

I roll my eyes at this suggestion, and a chuckle slips past my lips. "If I wanted you dead, I'd kill you when you threatened my wife." I look at him, and our gazes clash, "I'm surprised myself you're still breathing, kid, so I wouldn't push your luck." I warn him in advance, so he won't act difficult. My empathy toward a teenager with his past only runs for so long.

My wife has a heart of gold, but me?

I'm no saint and can turn to darkness whenever I need to, and if this kid ever shows up to disturb my family's peace?

Yeah, he's gonna be dead because I don't give second chances to psychopathic killers.

He shrugs. "Whatever." He flips the lighter again, and turns it on, the orange and blue flames mixing and swaying under the wind. "So why are we here?" He lifts the lighter closer to his chin and hisses when the flames touch his skin before grinning. "Is this where the FBI keeps the likes of me? Since I'm to be their bitch."

Once everything was done, Noah arrived at the police station, where he showed his badge to the detective, and it was enough for him to take charge. As an agent, he has more authority to do whatever the hell he wants.

According to him, Rhys's abilities when it comes to cyber hacking attracted a lot of attention long before he made his move and killed Matt. While his talent brought a headache to the authorities because he did some questionable shit for fun when it came to major organizations, they knew better than anyone that such skills are valuable and rare to come across.

Noah offered him a deal. Either he took a job as an FBI hacker and his crimes would go away—be their bitch, as Rhys put it—or he could refuse and go rot in prison for life.

In other words, from now on, Rhys has no choice but to work for the government. They own his ass.

To my surprise, the kid agreed easily, which made us all pause due to his character, not an ounce of resistance. Since he's signed all the papers, the FBI assigned Noah to oversee everything that has to do with him. He has to go through training and learning, but he has his freedom with the condition to be evaluated by profilers every month to watch his mental state.

Noah called me and informed me about this because he felt like he owed me one. They decided to put Matt's death on someone else and clear Miranda's name so she can live a happy and free life.

Which brings me to now.

Rhys's attitude didn't give me reprieve at night, and I knew, I just knew he'd have the desire to kill again. No therapy would help him as the hunter has already tasted blood and would crave more. The powers that be probably needed him on some urgent case and didn't expect him to stay sane for long, so they have no long-lasting plans for this kid.

Such is life and the game, though, so it doesn't surprise me much.

And that's when I came to a decision that will probably change his life, but at least it will save countless innocent people who might face Rhys's wrath.

My wife might be an empathic creature, but I'm not, and as such, I will do whatever's necessary to remove the evil from her.

The only reason I'm doing this is...because I feel for the boy he once was. At least one person deserves to give the kid a chance.

He continues, unbothered by my silence while I press on the gas pedal, speeding up and driving closer to the cliff. "I'm surprised Noah allowed you to take me. He was supposed to show me my headquarters for the time being." He flips the lighter once again, and at this point, I wonder if he has a sentimental attachment to the thing. He always has it around.

"You'll still go to the headquarters."

Only a different kind.

And the fact that I managed to make Noah agree deserves an award in itself, although he gave me only two days for all these intro- ductions before his boss found out.

Two days is more than enough for what I have planned, and then Rhys can go study whatever. Because they will figure it out from there.

We drive some more and finally reach the cliff where a black car waits for us. The engine runs, and I park my vehicle several feet away, our bumpers facing each other. The clouds almost block the sun, adding to the dangerous atmosphere.

"Who is that?" Rhys asks curiously, unfastening his seat belt and leaning forward to get a closer look. "Probably someone rich." He taps on his knee. "Does your friend need a favor? Is this my first job? And it has to be done in secret?"

Without bothering to reply, I hold back my laughter because the idea of this particular man needing a teenager to hack a system is hilarious.

Especially if you take into consideration his power and resources.

I get out, my coat flapping backward when the wind hits me with full force, and I inhale the frigid air into my lungs as the car door opens.

First, I see a polished leather shoe stepping on the ground before the man emerges from the vehicle, and standing up straight, his full attention is on me.

He wears a tailored three-piece suit that fits him like a glove. The aura of dominance and power he emanates changes the energy around us into almost something despicable, urging you to think carefully about what you speak and do in his company, for he has no patience.

Whoever crosses him faces the direst consequences, though he hides his monstrous nature well. With my connections and our semi-good relationship, I know more things about him than most.

A billionaire and brilliant businessman who runs the underground brotherhood designed to send mayhem wherever they go.

Lachlan Scott.

The underground king of New York or, as I'd like to call him, an asshole who could have been my friend had we not both loved power so much. Our similar net worths make it impossible to stay in each other's company longer than needed.

His blond hair glistens when the lightning flashes in the sky while his crystal-clear blue eyes stay hollow and alert, their emptiness serving as a warning.

"Zachary."

"Lachlan." I salute his driver, Jeremiah, who nods at me.

He hooks his thumbs into his pant pockets and walks toward me. "I was surprised to get your call. A King never asks for favors." Amusement coats his tone although dangerous notes ring in it. "Especially when he knows these favors endanger others."

"I wouldn't have asked if it endangered you in any form." My daughter goes to his wife's dancing school, not to mention interacts with his daughter. We might not be close, but it's impossible for us not to have ties in some way. "The kid is harmless." A burst of laughter slips past his lips, although it lacks any humor, so I add, "To you at least. Now, to everyone else—"

He interrupts me before I can elaborate, clearly not giving a shit about my point of view, not that I blame him. I'd probably tell him to fuck off too had I been in his position.

"He's not a kid. He's a man who's already tasted blood. He craves it," he states, and I stay silent. "I read the file you sent me. He might

have fooled your wife and the profilers, but he's a narcissist manipulator who is almost impossible to control."

Anger sparks inside me, and I fire back. "Careful, very careful, how
you speak about my wife, Lachlan."

Another blast of wind hits us both, whooshing over us, and we
move to the side to avoid it while little rain droplets start falling on the
ground. "Precisely why I involved you in this case. If we leave him as
he is, he will commit a real crime."

Lachlan takes out a cigarette from his pocket and lights it up. "He's
already committed a crime, Zach." I grit my teeth because he's right.
Matt deserved no mercy for all the shit he has done. However, a
murder is a murder, no matter how you spin it. And in this case, it
wasn't even self-defense.

"There is still hope for them. He's like all your students. You gave
them a chance." I press on the issue at hand because this is really a
high horse he's sitting on, considering he gathers all these lost souls on
the verge of insanity and turns their sadistic tendencies into something
better.

They are still monsters, but they just channel their desire to kill
into something else.

He exhales the smoke all around me, shaking his head. "My
students come to me after they've killed someone, yes. However, their
murders are hectic and done out of rage and self-defense." He motions
with his head to my car where Rhys sits, just staring at us both,
listening to us. "Him, though? He created a plan, barged into the
house, and threatened a woman and her children. He tortured a man
for days in front of his whole family."

"I'm aware."

"No, you're not. I'm a monster, so I know how we operate. He
experienced such a high. Nothing else will ever measure up to it, so
he'll chase it again and again, expending his victim list and never really
finding it because nothing affects us like our first kill. A hunter without
rules for hunting becomes a threat to society as he doesn't care about
anyone or anything but himself."

Fed up with this bullshit and his attitude, I drop all pretense of
playing nice and cross my arms. "So what do you propose? Sit on our

thumbs and wait till he commits another crime?" He rolls his eyes at my tone. "Because I don't give a fuck about your speeches. Will you help me or not?" One of the reasons we rarely do business together— we are both ruthless and impatient during negotiations, so we can't deal with each other's moods.

"We have to clean up a mess you created." He points at me and then at the kid. "He's going to be a problem. He's an adult, so it might be too late to shape him into a serial killer who fits my brotherhood."

"And here I thought being a murderer was enough to join your secret club. Live and learn."

He ignores my comeback and instead snaps his fingers. "Rhys, come here," he orders, and I see the kid bristle at the command. Anger flashes on his face, and his upper lip curls.

"He doesn't react well to commands from men."

"He'll learn. Otherwise, I'll just have to kill him." His voice stays even as he issues the threat, and for the first time, I wonder if I did the right thing by coming here.

Before I can dwell on this much, though, Rhys flips him off and leans back in the seat, closing his eyes.

Oh, the little shit flashed his teeth to the wrong person.

His behavior just proves once again that Rhys is insane and needs to learn control. Working for the feds only enhanced his superior complex since he will have access to all their resources.

The energy swiftly transforms into something more charged as the lightning brightens the sky, the rain intensifying around us, and Lachlan says, "I guess we'll have to teach him a lesson sooner than later." With this, he throws away his cigarette and goes to the car.

Rhys's brows rise at this, and he blinks when Lachlan opens the door and grips his neck, forcing him out of the vehicle. "The fuck?" he exclaims, only for it to transform into an agonizing scream when Lachlan wraps his hand around his middle finger, and the cracking sound echoes in the air. "You broke my finger!" he yells. Lachlan gives no shit, though, and instead pushes him on the ground, where Rhys lands with a loud smack on his face, sending the dirt flying in different directions while his clothes become soaked with soil and rain. "You bastard!" He shouts this time, placing his splayed palms on the ground and trying to get up, only to fall on his stomach once again when Lachlan kicks him, muttering something in the ground. "Zach!" Rhys calls my name, expecting me to interfere and help him.

Hilarious, if you ask me. I wouldn't have brought him here if I thought Lachlan would be nice to him, and besides, the little fucker caused grief to my family and held a gun to my wife's head.

I have no mercy, and he deserves the punishment.

Like I always said.

Compassion exists in my vocabulary only because of my wife, and only when she asks me for something. The rest of the world has no such luck.

"Sorry, kid. You brought it on yourself." And in more ways than one.

I lean on the car's bumper, watching how Lachlan presses with his shoe on his shoulder and rolls him on his back while the kid breathes heavily, spitting away the dirt and clenching his fist with the injured finger. "Who the fuck are you?" he spits, trying to wiggle free, only to groan when Lachlan puts his shoes on his chest and stills his movements.

If he as much as wiggles, he can cut off his oxygen supply, and for the first time in his life, I don't think Rhys wants to fuck with his luck, judging by how he blinks at Lachlan, awaiting whatever he'll do next. "You flip me a finger ever again, and I'll cut it off permanently." Rhys's eyes widen at this. "When I issue a command, you follow it from now on. Is that understood?"

His tone leaves no room for argument, but the cocky kid who got away with all his shit doesn't take a clue.

"Fuck you, man!" Rhys yells and huffs when Lachlan presses a bit harder, making him wince. "What do you want from me?" He turns his head to me, accusation along with anger written all over his face. "Did you bring me here to punish me?" For a moment in time, very briefly, I don't see an eighteen-year-old man who has already crossed the law many times and has taken a life...but a scared little boy who knows no other way to connect with the world than to use violence.

And the father in me wants to stop all this and maybe try to talk some sense into him.

Sometimes, though, pity is the worst poison we could give to people as it feeds their vices and dark cravings destined to bring nothing but chaos and pain to those around them.

"Look at me," Lachlan orders Rhys, and the kid listens. "Your life is now in my hands. If I so wish, you'll be dead, and no one will ever find your body."

"The feds—"

"I'm not afraid of the feds." Rhys's mouth drops at this as he stares at Lachlan. "If you follow the rules, your cravings will be sustained in ways you can't imagine." Thunder rocks the sky, the rain at this point soaking us. "Break them and lose your head, and you'll die. In the most agonizing way."

Rhys swallows hard. Even I can feel Lachlan's dominant nature that shows the kid in all its glory that for every evil in this world...

There is a bigger one that has the power to destroy it.

He acted out with Noah and me because he considered us relatively safe since he has done research on us. Lachlan, though, is a whole different beast. Rhys knows nothing about him, and cruelty is his second name.

You have to be an idiot not to catch the vibes and keep your mouth shut if you want to survive, and kids like Rhys know better than anyone how to survive in this unfair world.

"Is that understood?" Lachlan repeats his question, and after a long pause, Rhys nods. Although it's reluctant, and defiance flashes in his eyes, letting me know this argument is far from over.

Poor kid.

Lachlan will wipe the floor with him whenever he goes against his orders again, a nice teacher he is not.

He leans down, grabs his shirt, and pulls him upward so Rhys has no choice but to get up on his shaky legs. For all his deeds and past, the kid has zero stamina.

He cradles his injured finger, and the muscle on his cheek twitches when Lachlan barks, "Get in the car. Now."

Rhys glances at me, seeking support, and glares at me when I say, "Good luck, kid. Trust me, this is for the best." Believe it or not, I'm giving him the best chance to live a life and not become a creature who made him the way he is in the first place.

"You can shove your sorry up your—" Lachlan pushes him to the car, not letting him finish his sentence, and finally moves toward the car where Jeremiah already waits for him.

Once they are both inside the vehicle, I extend my hand to Lachlan. "Thank you. I really appreciate you doing it for us despite your reservations." We share a strong handshake. "Phoenix is attached to the boy."

"She shouldn't work on criminal cases. She won't save them all. Empathy is a virtue that's unfortunately not valued in our world. People love to use it." He clicks his tongue. "And what can be used can always be transformed into a weapon."

"Finally, we agree on something, Lachlan." Not that it helps me much.

My wife will do whatever the hell she pleases, and my job is to protect and cherish her always so no monsters will consume her soul.

Her beautiful soul that loves a villain like me, my atonement and reward all in one.

He lets go. "This is just the beginning. He'll be trouble even after the training." He strolls to his car after giving me this cryptic reply, and I go to mine, his words swirling in my head.

Before getting into my vehicle, I call, "Lachlan." He looks over his shoulder at me. "What do you mean by that?"

He half turns to me. "Men like me don't fall in love. We obsess to the point of madness until we get what we want. And once we do? We never let go." A beat passes and my brow furrows, trying to make sense of this statement.

Lachlan loves being a philosophical asshole who says some shit and leaves you to figure it out on your own, but I have no patience for this shit today. "So?"

"He wanted to shoot himself to save people from the monster eating at him from the inside that was urging him to kill, right?" I nod. "When did he drop the gun, Zach?"

"When Catriona asked him." The minute I say it out loud, realization hits me, and I close my eyes.

"Exactly. Once all this is done." He swirls his finger in the air. "He'll come after her, willing or not. And even I won't be able to stop him. She's his obsession now, Zach. As long as they both shall live, she won't ever be free from him." With this, he gives me one final long look, gets into his car, and drives off, leaving me standing in the rain while his statement rings over and over in my ears.

The girl plans to be a surgeon who saves lives one day, which explains why she begged him not to kill himself, but to a boy who knew no love...this might as well have been a love declaration in his eyes.

Lachlan is right, after all.

Their story is far from over.

CHAPTER SEVENTEEN

"Everyone craves power.
What a funny concept.
Because the greatest power in the world is love."
Phoenix

*P*hoenix

Loud knocks rock off the walls, and I burrow my face deeper into my pillow, grinning when I hear the twins shout, "Good morning, Mama! Can we come in?" I sometimes think they share a soul because the amount of time they talk in unison astonishes even me.

"Our sons are awake," I mutter to Zach, shifting closer to him and putting my hand on his chest, only to frown when it lands on an empty spot.

I open my eyes and blink in surprise when I don't see my husband anywhere as the sunlight shines brightly all around our room. "Zach?" I croak through my dry throat and sit up in bed. Glancing at the clock, I notice it's almost noon.

I must have been really exhausted last night to sleep in this late. This explains Zach's absence. The man cannot stay in bed after sunrise for long unless we have sex.

A shiver rushes down my spine at the pleasurable memories, but I shake my head from the lustful haze, still wondering why he isn't the one to wake me up. Usually, he doesn't have work at this hour, but with this stupid lawsuit Rafael Wright has against him, he spends most of his time in his office with Sebastian as they work the case.

Grabbing the nearby bottle of water, I flick it open and take a sip as the boys ask again, "Can we come in, Mama?"

"Just a second, my darlings." I put the water back on the nightstand and swing my legs to the side, curling them at the cold marble as I reach for my robe.

Slipping into it and tying the belt, I go to the door and let the boys in. "Hi, Mama!" they say, hugging me from both sides. I run my fingers through their hair, grinning at them.

"Hi, boys. Shouldn't you be at school?"

They lean back and flash me their toothless smiles. "No. Daddy said today is a holiday."

"He did?"

Their dark curls sway when they nod, and the tapping of the shoes echoes in the hallway followed by Emmaline running inside as well, wearing one of her tutus. "Hey! You were supposed to wait for me." She glares at her brothers, who shrug.

"You were taking too long."

"Dancing." Ian sighs. "We got bored."

She places her hands on her hips. "I need to practice! I have a show soon!"

They roll their eyes. "You always have a show," Wyatt points out.

Knowing that this back-and-forth can go on for hours—the kiddos love each other, but the boys have this deep love of ruffling their sister's feathers—I turn the conversation back to the situation at hand. "What kind of holiday is it today?"

They share a look, and the boys go to stand on either side of Emmaline as they all straighten up. My daughter clears her throat and announces, "We're here as messengers."

"Messengers," I repeat, amusement lacing my tone. I cross my arms, ready to hear it. My children sometimes have the weirdest ideas, and since we don't forbid them to engage in them, we end up in hilarious situations. Zach is a sucker when it comes to kids, so I'm not even surprised they convinced him to stay home and come up with yet another holiday on the calendar that allows them to skip school. "And what might that message be?"

Emmaline fishes inside her skirt pocket and takes out a white envelope with my name on it, extending her hand to me. "Daddy told us to give it to you."

"Did he now?" I mutter. Flipping it up and ripping the seal on it, I snatch out the note inside.

> *My darling,*
> *Come to me. I might have a surprise for you.*
> *Follow the signs, and I'll be waiting.*
> *Yours,*
> *Zachary*

Excitement builds inside me at his cryptic note because if he got all the kids involved, it means his surprise must be one of a kind. And among the madness we've had this past couple of days, I can't wait to see if it will finally bring back our usual dynamic.

Where my husband always has something up his sleeve that brings me joy.

I look at the kids again, and this time, Ian speaks up, "We have instructions, Mommy."

"And what are they?"

"First, you have to take a shower and wear this dress." Emmaline points to the right, and I glance at the chair several feet away, where a black garment bag lies that I haven't noticed before. "Then we will tell you the rest."

Putting the note on the nearby table, I go to the garment bag and unzip it, my eyes widening at the purple woolen long pencil dress that must have cost a fortune judging by the designer tag. "It's pretty, isn't it, Mama?" Wyatt asks. "We picked it out together."

"Together."

"Yes! Daddy showed us a catalog and let us choose. We love the purple color!" Emmaline says, and I chuckle because isn't that the truth? The boys even demanded their whole room be decorated in all shades of purple. Not sure when their obsession with it started. "Come on, Mama. Hurry! We're on time."

We even have a schedule for this whole thing?

"All right, kiddos." I motion with my head to the door. "Did you all have breakfast?" They all nod. "Okay. I'll see you downstairs, then."

The boys squeal with excitement, running away, but Emmaline stays behind, fumbling with her fingers. She opens her mouth, only to close it shortly after without uttering a single word with a heavy sigh. "What is it, honey?"

"Lying is bad, right, Mama?"

I still at this, uneasiness rushing through me because such a question coming from your child is never a good sign. "Yes, that's right."

"Even if it's done to help someone?" She glances down, drawing a circle with her pointe-covered foot. "Is it bad then too? I mean...if a lie saves your friend, does it make you a bad person for lying?"

Okay, now I'm worried. I know better than to show my kid that, so instead of shouting and demanding answers, I decide to tread the subject carefully. "It depends. A lie is a lie no matter how you look at it, but if your friend is in danger, then you can lie." She bites on her lip. "That being said, if a lie hurt someone else but saves your friends, it's still wrong."

Her crestfallen expression tells me everything I need to know, and I grab her shoulders. "What happened, honey? When did you lie?" On the grand scale of things, I'm more worried about the turmoil she's experiencing right now than about the lie.

She's a nine-year-old who has three close friends and one of them has a crush on her. How bad of a lie could it have been anyway?

"I just said something I shouldn't have to someone, and I'm afraid it might bring trouble."

Palming her face, I smile at her. "Then you should make sure that they know how sorry you are. Okay?" She nods, and I lean closer, pressing my lips against her forehead.

"Thank you, Mama." Emmaline hugs me tight, and I make a mental note to check back with her on it in a couple of days. My girl prefers to ponder on things before acting on her decisions. "I love you."

"I love you too, honey."

She strolls to the hallway, and after closing the door, I take a shower in record time and then spend half an hour drying my hair, letting my heavy locks cascade down my back before putting on my dress that fits like a glove. My high-heeled boots finish the composition of my autumn look.

Giving myself just a touch of mascara and blush, I check my reflection in the mirror, and excitement practically pours from me.

Grabbing my purse and phone, I rush downstairs, where the kids wait for me, along with Patience. "No, you can't do it," she argues with Ian who lifts his brow as he throws a ball up in the air and catches it easily.

"Why not?"

"Because I said so."

"Oh, come on, Patience."

Deciding not to even get into what my sons want from their nanny now, who probably due to her age alone stays strong and never lets them push her into something she doesn't want to do, I slip into my coat that one of the maids already has ready. "Thank you," I tell her and then look at my kids who blink at me. "Well, what are we going to do next?"

The twins shrug. "We don't know." Ian pushes on the handle, rising on his tiptoes, and huffing heavily, he opens the door. "The car is waiting for you. Daddy said we are all getting ice creams for it!"

"He didn't say that, young boy," Patience hisses, but my son just winks at her before grinning at me. "We're still negotiating this part, Mama."

I just laugh despite Patience's glare and kiss my sons before hugging my daughter. "All of you be on your best behavior."

"Take pictures! I'm curious what is the surprise," Wyatt shouts, and I nod at them as I step out of the house and descend the stairs to the waiting car.

Our driver, Jim, smiles at me as I get into the vehicle and then in record time reaches his seat, starting the car. "Where are we going?" I

THE LAND WHERE SINNERS LOVE

finally ask, sitting up more comfortably in my seat while Jim drives the car to the gates. "Or is it a surprise as well?"

He catches my eyes in the rearview mirror and grins, the wrinkles around his eyes deepening. "No, ma'am."

Since he stays silent after this admission, I nudge him. "Well?"

And when he utters the name of a place, I freeze on the spot as he takes me somewhere I haven't been for more than twenty years.

A beautiful, magical place that brings back so many memories.

Along with regrets because it always plagued me with what-ifs.

"I'm taking you to the Empire State Building, ma'am."

Zachary

The sun shines brightly as the frigid wind hits my face, dancing around my form and causing my coat to billow backward, slipping coldness into every cell in my body as I blow hot air into my hands, trying to warm them.

I stand near the balcony railing at the Empire State Building viewing platform, where one of the most mesmerizing views on the planet opens up to me.

Up this high, New York showcases itself in all its gorgeous glory with its tall buildings and thousands of cars driving in busy traffic while people pass in a blur.

What seems like thousands of lights brighten up the sidewalk, and I can still taste the pastry I bought on the way here because the street food is to die for.

This city has an unmatched energy, and somehow, it always soothed the chaos in my soul until I met my wife.

A woman who changed me in a lot of ways, and some of them I'm not proud of; however, the fact remains.

If there is a woman who can put a King to his knees, it's Phoenix.

"It's pretty, isn't it?" someone asks me, and I look to my right to see an elderly woman wearing a thick blue coat standing next to me while she sighs at the view. "Despite being here many times, I can never get enough of it."

"Yes. I guess it's one of a kind." I glance at my wristwatch. Phoenix should have been here thirty minutes ago based on the message I got from the kids who agreed to be my little helpers.

I know everyone believes I should be more stern with them, but how can I be that when these little ones remind me that second chances are possible, and sometimes they are worth all the pain you've experienced?

"My husband proposed to me here." She burrows her face into her coat's collar. "Almost forty years ago." The sadness along with the wistfulness lacing her tone leaves no doubt he died. "We had this little tradition of coming here every year to celebrate our anniversary. I'm not sure it can be called that, but that's what we called it."

"That's very romantic," I tell her, my heart flipping inside my chest a little at the loneliness she must feel right now, and the devastation rushes through me at the prospect of losing my wife.

I might have survived it once, but I won't survive losing Phoenix, so when our time comes, I hope I'll be the first to go.

"He was like that. Romantic." She shakes her head and then grins wider, her blue eyes glistening with mischief when she points at the flowers in my hands. "You must be waiting for someone."

"I am." I drop my voice to a hushed whisper. "She's very special."

"I bet." She wiggles her finger at me. "Just make sure to wait and don't go." She leans closer and taps on my watch. "Noticed you checking the time. If you leave early, you might miss each other."

A laughter slips past my lips, and she shares it, probably thinking I find it hilarious while in truth we've already missed each other once.

I have no intention of letting it happen again.

"I won't," I promise her, and she pats me on the shoulder before heading to the elevator while I put my hand on the railing, leaning on it and drinking in the sight in front of me.

Once upon a time this place changed everything for me and Phoenix in ways we didn't expect.

Because we didn't wait.

This time around, though...

This time, I will wait, no matter what it takes.

As there is one more wound we need to heal.

. . .

*P*hoenix

"Oh my God, this is a nightmare," I mutter as the car moves at a snail's pace, barely making any progress while several other cars honk around us, announcing the drivers' mutual frustrations. "Jim, is there any other way?"

"I'm sorry, ma'am. There was an accident."

I huff in frustration, groaning at the clock because I've spent almost three hours in a car when the ride should have taken me forty minutes max.

What Zach planned for us is probably ruined at this point, and for whatever reason, it sends pain all over my system, polluting my soul with desperation and a sadness that confuses me.

I shouldn't be sad because this didn't work out, but...

I exhale heavily again. "How much longer do you think it will take?"

He checks something, and catches my gaze in the rearview mirror with an apologetic look on his face. "Around thirty minutes, ma'am. Give or take. I'll do my best, though."

Yeah, not sure how he plans to do his best. Since the streets are so narrow and there are so many cars, it's impossible to get out from this traffic, which only adds to my frustration.

Gasping for air, I press on the button, letting the window slide down and allowing for the wind to slip in, and that's when I look through it, studying my surroundings.

An idea pops into my head.

"I'll walk the rest of the way, Jim."

He looks over his shoulder at me and manages to say, "Are you sure —" Before I'm already out of the car and shut the door, my heels clicking soundly on the concrete as I pass by the cars who honk at me, and I just wave at them, running to the sidewalk.

The wind slaps me on the face hard, the cold nipping on my exposed skin since I didn't bother to button up my coat, but I don't care.

Instead, I turn to the right, crossing the street to the other side, and then run toward the building, excitement mixing with worry inside me at the prospect of seeing my husband but also being afraid that maybe he has left.

Wouldn't be the first time we missed each other on that particular viewing platform.

And it's not like today the stakes are high. If we miss each other we can still see each other and probably have a good laugh about it but something urges me to speed up my pace, the need to see him standing there because...

We missed each other all these years ago and it still leaves a bitter taste in my mouth, and I want it to be different this time, although a part of me prepares myself not to experience disappointment if my husband leaves.

He's a busy man, after all.

My entire body buzzes with anticipation as I finally reach the building. Racing inside, I press on the elevator button, waiting with countless other people to go upstairs while trying to catch my breath from all the running.

A man next to me holding a camera smiles, shifting closer when someone pushes him from the side. "Hot date?" He scans me from head to toe. "Are you late?"

"You could say that." I linger on his camera. "Do you have a date as well?"

He clicks his tongue. "Nope. I'm a photographer who adores this city, so once a month, I come here and forever capture the beauty that's New York." He shrugs. "Born and raised here, so I'm biased."

"Oh. Well, there is nothing like this city," I admit because love pours from me when it comes to it, but not because I grew up here or anything. Although that plays a part too.

I will forever love New York because this is where I fell in love, gave birth to my children, and built my life. Everything good and bad happened here. The city has witnessed all my ups and downs, and serves as a kaleidoscope of my memories.

As we enter the elevator with ten other people and press on the button so it will go up, I ask, "Do you have a business card?" Maybe it will be nice to buy some pictures and hang them in our living room since this place plays such a pivotal point in our lives.

"Sure." He fishes inside his pocket and gives me one, winking as the elevator dings. "Have fun on your date." With this, we all walk out, and I look around for Zachary among cheerful people who either snap pictures, shoot videos, or gaze at the city on the viewing platform.

However, among all these happy and thoughtful faces, I don't see the one I love the most, and with each second, my excitement slowly dies inside me, replaced by dread and a familiar pain echoing the one I experienced here all these years ago.

I should have expected it, though, right?

I'm late by three hours, the weather is cold as hell, and why should he wait for his own wife when he can see her anytime...

My mind comes to a halt when I spot him on the farther left, leaning on the railing, exceptionally handsome in his gray coat accentuating his emerald-green eyes as his dark hair glistens under the sunlight, and he holds a bouquet of orchids in his hand.

I notice how several women glance his way, and why wouldn't they, right?

He's the epitome of hot and all mine.

A relieved sigh slips past my lips at the sight of him, and laughter bubbles up inside me as I dash toward him, and that's when he turns my way, grinning at me. "You're here."

"Where else would I be?" he asks, puzzled, and then extends his hand to me when I come several inches away from him. "These are for you. I bought orchids all these years ago too. I knew they were your favorite." With trembling hands, I take them, breathing in their scent as the soft petals tickle my nose and our gazes meet while he continues, "And now I understand why." Softness coats his voice as he reaches for me, his cold thumb gently caressing my cheek while I step closer, the tips of my boots bumping against his shoes.

"Why?"

"You are very resilient. Orchids can survive without water for a long time, preserving their beauty. And that's what you did when you lived in hell. Preserved the beauty of your soul by filling it with love and not allowing the hate to consume it. How can I do anything else but admire it?" He brushes away the single tear sliding down my cheek, smiling at me, although his eyes stay serious and speak a story of their own. "Have you ever thought about what would have happened if we met on this platform back then?"

Pressing the bouquet to my chest, I nod while he still continues to caress me. "Yes. I mean, that's our what-if, right?" A burst of laughter escapes me. "I thought what we have now is our what would have happened."

"Me and you...we were so scarred by our pasts that I think we needed to learn how to love and then experience a heartbreak in order to cherish what we have with everything in us."

I close my eyes, thinking back on everything that happened up to this moment that shaped us into the people we are today.

Falling in love and breaking up is one thing, but when you fall in love and then lose it the way both of us did...it creates a certain kind of wound on your soul that's almost impossible to heal. Because after a heartbreak, you can withstand almost everything except...

Falling in love again as it makes you vulnerable to pain and devastation that multiplies by a thousand when you open yourself up to love again.

The kind of connection we have...the desperation we feel for one another...the love that's constantly present...it all happened because, once upon a time, we missed each other here and had gone off to build our separate lives.

Lives that somehow entwined after all these years and, as a result, gave us a second chance.

Zach wraps his arm around me, hugging me, and his scent envelops me while his lips are inches from mine. "I love you, Phoenix." My heart stops and then speeds up, beating so fast I'm surprised it doesn't jump out of my chest. "And I will love you till my last breath because I won't survive losing you. You're it, darling. My reward and atonement in this world." He places his mouth on mine in a butterfly-like kiss and leans back. "You're the love of my life. Thank you for giving me a chance and making me the happiest man alive."

The bouquet gets squished between us when I circle his neck with my free hand, "I love you, Zachary. Thank you for being so unapologetic." He chuckles, and then we both exhale. "You're the love of my life too."

After all, we've known each other since we were kids, shared our deepest secrets, showed each other our vices, and experienced the magnitude of emotions toward each other that not many get a chance to experience in one lifetime.

Rising on my tiptoes, I kiss him hard with the wind whooshing over us, my hair covering us from anyone else as he squeezes me so tight nothing but him matters at this moment.

A camera shutter sounds, and we both look to the side at the guy I saw earlier. "Felt like a special memory that someone needed to capture." He shakes his camera. "Call me for the picture." He points at Zachary. "Awesome first date skills, man," he says with admiration and then moves to the other people around, snapping several photos while we look at each other and burst out laughing.

First date. If only he knew how much has happened between us.

"Come here, darling." Zach pulls me toward the railing, turning me around so my back bumps into his chest as he places both of his hands on either side of me, caging me between him and the railing. "Let's look at the view before we go back home to our little ones."

He rests his chin on my shoulder as we drink in the beauty, content and peaceful in ways we haven't ever been before.

Today on this platform, everything comes full circle, and the reaming gap we had is closed and healed permanently.

No one expects their childhood friend turned pen pal to become their worst enemy.

But more importantly?

No one expects to fall in love with their worst enemy, but I did.

And thank God for that.

EPILOGUE

"Take me to the land where sinners love..."
Zachary

*T*welve years later

*P*hoenix
    Zachary wraps his arm around my waist, pressing my
back to his front, and kisses me on the neck while a smile curves my
mouth when he murmurs over my skin, "We've done it." I bite my lip
to hold back the laughter threatening to slip past my lips at his
strained and slightly annoyed voice. "Someone give me a fucking award
for staying civil all this time."
    Placing my palm on his arm, I pat it gently and can't help but tease
him, "If you behave yourself, a gift might wait for you tonight." He
stills at this; however, his grip on me tightens, his fingers digging into
my side. "And you'll get to unwrap it too."

He sucks in a breath and the action alone sends hot flashes through me, prickling my skin in the anticipation of what might come next. "Then I'll be on my best behavior," he promises me and then leans closer, pressing his lips to my ear and lowering his voice to a barely audible whisper, making sure no one hears him but me. "Prepare to be fucked hard, my darling. I want the screams and the moans."

My stomach dips under his touch while my head becomes almost dizzy from the picture he paints in my mind and for a second, I contemplate sneaking out from this party to indulge our cravings. "Remember what we did in one of the rooms here all these years ago?" My husband fuels more gasoline to the fire spreading in me in waves, urging me to focus only on his voice and nothing else. "We can still do it." A beat passes. "No one would even notice."

How can a woman forget?

I couldn't come to his father's mansion for years without blushing because, really, we should have had more restraint.

"Everyone would notice."

He chuckles, gliding his lips to the crook between my neck and shoulder and grazes his teeth. "Who gives a fuck? I can do whatever I want and what I want right now is my wife moaning my name as I make her come."

When he puts it this way...

A melodic and happy laughter snaps me out of my lust-induced haze, though, and I rest my head on my husband's chest and groan, "Stop tempting me. We need to be responsible adults right now."

"You started this, darling." And then his voice turns back to annoyed and even lethal when he growls, "It's hard to be a responsible adult when I want to smack that boy for touching my girl." He sounds almost miserable, and this time, I don't stop the giggle emerging from my mouth as the situation is very funny, all things considered.

My attention shifts back to the spacious room opening up to our view, brightening up with a crystal chandelier, seeding colorful crystals on the perfectly polished marble while the moonlight streaming through the open terrace door gives it an almost magical glow, inviting everyone to participate in this magnificent party.

Where only the richest of the rich were invited to celebrate this occasion with us all, some even demanding their invitations as they didn't want to miss the engagement of the year, as they called it.

As a result we have countless people either walking around, engaging in conversations with each other, or just admiring the house around us, wearing expensive jewelry and designer dresses to showcase their power to everyone.

Servers move smoothly through the crowds, holding silver trays with different drinks while several tables are spread all over the perimeter with food and snacks.

Some people even get out on the terrace, probably to enjoy some fresh air along with the view, as my father-in-law's garden is an art itself that's so mesmerizing I'm amazed he manages to get any work done.

However, all this pales compared to the gorgeous couple standing right in the middle of dance floor, swaying slightly to the music and wrapped so deeply into each other, leaving no doubt to everyone around them that they are in love.

"Ah, they look happy," I say, my heart fluttering at the sight of my daughter with her dark locks cascading down her back while the navy-blue dress shimmers under the light, bringing attention to her slender and graceful form.

"That boy" as Zach so eloquently put it, and who also happens to be Emmaline's fiancé, pushes her a bit to the side and catches the tip of her fingers before swirling her around and she ends up in his arms again, circling his neck and kissing his cheek to the loud applause of the onlookers. He's quite a dashing prince with his blond hair, and brown eyes gazing at her with so much adoration you can almost touch it.

Zach grabs a glass of whiskey from the passing servers and takes a larger sip. "I don't understand why they couldn't wait."

Rolling my eyes at this argument once again, I turn around to face him and cross my arms. "They're young and in love. Why should they wait?"

"My point exactly, darling. They're both twenty-one and still in college, Emmaline has a chance to become a prima. The last thing she needs right now is a husband."

I might have agreed with him under different circumstances; however, Anthony and Emmaline have known each other since kinder-garten and have been dating for years. That boy lives and breathes for her, and always supports her during all her performances. Even other dancers on the ballet team love him, not to mention Emmaline always does her best to show up to all the functions for Anthony.

While the boy still studies business in one of the most prestigious universities in the country, he has certain responsibilities that his family name gives him. His father probably would have never allowed this union if Emmaline wasn't a King.

Truth be told, we never much liked Kurt, especially with the way he always managed to dismiss his wife and made backhanded comments about Emmaline's future.

The asshole fully expected her to give up her dancing once she got her degree from school to be the perfect wife for his offspring because, according to him, a woman's place was with her husband, always. My blood boiled every time he mentioned it, but I kept my mouth shut under my daughter's begging gaze.

He toned down a bit lately, and I suspect it had to do with Zach "accidentally" hitting him in the gut with a golf club during their last game. Somehow, the man's demeanor changed almost instantly.

Despite objecting to this wedding and thinking it was too fast for them, Zachary supported and helped to plan the whole thing while showering our daughter with nothing but love.

However, there was always this unexplainable resentment in his eyes whenever they landed on Anthony, and while at first I thought it had to do with the fact that his little girl was finally growing up...I'm starting to doubt that with each passing day.

It seems as if my husband just doesn't want for her to marry him, period.

Looking around and making sure no one pays us any attention, I lower my voice and ask him, "You always liked the kid. What seems to be the problem now?"

Darkness settles over his features and I glance over my shoulder to see Sebastian slapping Anthony on the back and hugging him before he kisses Emmaline on the cheek. "Sebastian thinks he's the perfect match for our daughter. You know why?" Instead of answering my question, Zachary fires his own but doesn't wait for me to reply. "Because Anthony is exactly like him." Dislike coats his words, making me blink several times, wondering where he sees any resemblance between the two.

I open my mouth to elaborate on this rather cryptic and disturbing statement, when our twin sons walk toward us, grinning wildly, their identical gray suits fitting them perfectly and only emphasizing their muscled frames.

At eighteen they are as tall as Zach and have just started college in Boston. They chose to go into law, although with the amount of mayhem they cause and the wild parties they love to attend, I wonder if they'll even get the chance to finish it.

We love our boys to pieces, but they are destined to drive people around them insane with their antics. And the worst part about it?

Zachary finds most of them hilarious, which doesn't help much with the matter.

Despite all that, though, they are very responsible and respectful, so I guess we can call it a parental win and pray they won't come up with some shit that will result in their college being burned down.

"Hi, Mom," Wyatt greets me right before wrapping his huge arms around me and lifting me up a little. "We missed you," he says, leaning back, and I pat his cheek. "You look beautiful."

"True story," Ian agrees, kissing me on the cheek and winking at me while Zachary frowns at them.

"Your mother always looks beautiful." He pushes them away and his hand settles on my waist again, gluing me to his side. "And she's all mine."

Collective groans fill the air.

"Come on, Dad."

"Can you cool it just for tonight?" Wyatt waits a beat and adds, acting outraged, but the mischief dancing in his eyes gives him away, "Have some manners. There are kids around."

"Funny. When I had to bail you out just weeks ago for throwing a party with alcohol in it, you didn't seem like kids to me. In fact, the mug shots say otherwise."

"Mug shots?" I say in horror. Was this why they called us in the middle of the night?

Zach just kissed me and told me not to worry about it because he had it handled.

"Busted," Ian murmurs.

Wyatt glares at Zachary. "Thanks a lot, Dad!" He shifts his focus on me, his voice becoming more gentle. "It's not as bad as it sounds."

"Not as bad as it sounds? You—" Exhaling heavily, I shake my head and point a finger at them both. "Tonight is about your sister. We'll get back to this after the party. You both better be on your best behavior or I swear!" I've never punished these boys in my whole life so my threats probably aren't that scary. However, they are their father's sons.

Which means they hate to upset me.

They each quickly come to my other side, trapping me between them and Zachary. "Hey! It's okay, Mom. We didn't get in trouble."

"Yeah, just one little misunderstanding that resulted in an arrest. It's not even on our records. We were practically witnesses." Ian has the audacity to sound offended about my lack of faith in them. "I mean, think about it, Mom." He looks me straight in the eyes. "If it was us, they'd never catch us."

I just groan at this, because my son truly thinks he just reassured me, as if admitting to the fact that they are good at covering up their tracks should calm me down and swipe all this under the rug.

"Oh, you'll be great lawyers one day."

"We'll take it as a compliment."

"Don't."

My lips twitch at Zach's reply while the boys just laugh, finding it hilarious, and that's when we notice Emmaline waving at us while the event photographer prepares the camera, probably ready to take all the family shoots.

Our family has already joined her, taking small snapshots, and I push at the boys. "Go to your sister and make sure to take good pictures. And remember. Best behavior. No funny business."

"Of course not," they reply in unison, and then dash toward their sister.

We watch Ian swipe her and spin her around in his arms to her loud laughter. No matter the distance between them, the kids stayed close and call each other daily. It also helps that Emmaline knows about all the antics in advance and stops them if it really sounds dangerous.

Wyatt bows to her and hugs her once Ian puts her back on her feet, murmuring something in her ear, and she squeezes him hard.

I don't miss how both of my sons barely spare Anthony a glance, clearly sharing their father's sentiments on the matter. And they don't even bother to hide their emotions.

Then they spin around, squishing Emmaline between them and motioning for the photographer to snag all the photos, the flashlight going on their faces and temporarily, I forget all the worries as warmth settles into every cell in my body.

Because my kids are living and breathing proof that atonement and love exist even after hell on earth.

"I love you, Zachary King," I say, tilting my head back and meeting my husband's stare. "Thank you for all this."

He grins, cups my cheeks, and then tips my chin up, connecting our mouths in a sweet yet passionate kiss, staking his claim all over again while cementing this connection that grows stronger with each passing day. He finishes the kiss with a glide of his tongue before resting his forehead against mine. "I love you too, Phoenix. I love you more than life itself."

Right at this moment, my happiness knows no bounds, and I intend to soak all the emotions around me while my girl makes the biggest decision in her life.

And hope that the man she has picked would love her as much as her father loves me.

"Dad!" Emmaline's voice breaks through our bubble, and we both turn our heads in the direction where she motions for us. "Come on! Let's take all the pictures!"

"Let's go, darling." He laces his hand with mine, pulling me right along with him, but I halt his movements, tugging on my hand. "What's going on?"

"You go now. I'll grab the bouquet." I point at the table several feet away. "And be right back. You know Emmaline wanted pictures with it."

He leans down to give me a kiss and then squeezes my hip. "Don't take long." He strolls to our family while I dart to the table, still in awe at how the designer managed to capture exactly what I wanted.

The composition consists of several open pomegranates with the ripe seeds put together on a stick, imitating the flower's stab, and bonded together with a red ribbon creating a rather mysterious yet alluring art. At the same time, though, still keeping the fruit fresh and ready to eat whenever anyone wishes. A special, almost invisible foil protects it from any dust or dirt.

My girl loved pomegranates since her conception as even during my pregnancy I ate them like crazy despite my doctor advising me other- wise. As a result, not a day went by without us having the said fruit at home because we never knew when the craving would hit her.

Smiling at the memories, I place my hand on my chest as my heart contracts inside me, and I think about how my little girl is all grown up now and about to get married to the man of her dreams.

Yes, it's a good day, and I'm sure Zach would come around too. They say one of the hardest things a loving father has to do is let go and the idea must scare him enough to question Anthony's character.

I reach for the bouquet, picking it up, and whisper, "Oh no!" when it's about to fall as the heavy pomegranates send it flying forward. Mortification fills my every bone. However, before the disaster can strike, a muscled, tan hand catches it and keeps the balance.

I zero my focus on the gray sleeve. My eyes travel over the arm toward one of the most handsome men I've ever seen, and considering who I'm married to...that's saying something.

He adjusts the bouquet in my arms, and his mouth curves in a grin, bringing attention to his symmetrical features and emerald-green eyes that are so hollow, without thinking I take a step back as they promise me nothing good.

"Thank you," I say, finally finding my voice but still staring at the man in confusion, racking my brain for his name.

We've personally checked every invitation sent out because we didn't want some strangers at the party or only those who wished to elevate themselves.

Business associates, friends, and family only.

Try as I might, though, I cannot remember his name, although his face looks oddly familiar. "You're welcome." His eyes flicker to the pomegranates for a fraction of a second before he focuses back on me. "Unusual choice for a bouquet."

Despite the odd tension emitting from him that raises all my hackles, I keep my voice light. "Yes. Emmaline loves them."

Something flashes in his gaze, but it's quickly masked with hollowness once again. "Like Persephone."

"What do you mean?'

"Persephone ate the pomegranate seeds and got trapped with Hades for eternity."

I still at this comparison, my brow furrowing and not liking it because in the myth, the poor girl gets captured by the god of the underworld, who keeps her there against her wishes, and it turns into a whole power play.

He even uses trickery in order to keep her there.

"I don't think it was ever said that the fruit happened to be Persephone's favorite." I press the bouquet firmer to my chest, ready to end this conversation and go to my family. This man seems to be trouble, and I want to be as far away from him as humanly possible.

He takes a sip from his glass, whiskey judging by the color, and replies, "Favorite or not, that decision forever changed the trajectory of her life. Funny, isn't it? No matter what we do, and who we love, all decisions we make have consequences. And sometimes these consequences demand that your soul burns in hell every single day." A beat passes. "Wouldn't you say, Dr. King?"

Silence falls between us after his softly spoken words laced with distaste and weird anticipation as if he knows more than I do.

Who is this man, and why does he allow himself to speak in such a manner to me during the engagement party? I would have thought he might be a paparazzi who sneaked inside, but the expensive suit and the aura of dominance swirling around him leave no doubt the man possesses wealth and status rivaling our own.

And if life has taught me one thing well, it's to never engage in a fight with such beasts without having a backup because they thrive on causing chaos.

So plastering on an even bigger smile, I clear my throat and say, "I'm afraid I don't have time to engage in this philosophical debate. I have to go, but I hope you'll enjoy the rest of the party." Without even bothering to wait for this reply, I spin around and walk toward my family, when his voice stops me.

"Some things in life are inevitable, Dr. King. Maybe if Persephone's mother, Demeter, knew it in advance, she wouldn't have been so hurt."

Half turning to him, I ask, "Who are you?"

Who is brave enough to come to my family's home and throw a threat in my face? Unless he thinks he's so subtle that I wouldn't catch it?

He finishes his drink and places it on the nearby table, while sending a grin my way that promises me nothing good in the future. "Rafael Wright."

I freeze at the name and open my mouth, only to shut it when he heads to the exit. After dropping this information on me, I quickly glance at my daughter and husband, sighing in relief that they haven't noticed the man.

The knowledge does little to soothe my fear, and panic slowly slides through my veins and pollutes my cells with horror at the realization.

Because he's back.

And this time, he won't leave unless he gets what he wants, and what he wants is clearly the suffering and blood of the person who ruined him.

My daughter.

Oh, no.

Rafael

They say revenge is a dish best served cold.

I disagree.

Revenge is a dish best served when no one expects it.

Once upon a time, a little girl destroyed my life in ways I never anticipated.

She took away everything from me because *she lied*.

The time has come for payback.

After all, they call me the King of Heartbreak.

And I won't rest until Emmaline Katherine King's heart shatters, leaving nothing but hollowness and despair in its wake.

ALSO BY V. F. MASON

Dark Romance

Sociopath's Obsession

Sociopath's Revenge

Psychopath's Prey

Lachlan's Protégé

Micaden's Madness

Callum's Hell

Madman's Method

Madman's Cure

Arson's Captive

The Land Where Sinners Atone

Santiago's Conquest

Lucian's Reign

The Professor and His Obsession

Remi's War

Beauty and the Villain

The Heart of a Villain

Mafia Romance

Pakhan's Rose

Pakhan's Salvation

Sovietnik's Fury

Brigadier's Game

Kaznachei's Pain

Free Books

His Broken Princess

ACKNOWLEDGMENTS

First, I want to thank God and my family for allowing me to write and make this dream possible. The support means so much to me, and I understand that sometimes it drives you crazy, especially when I try to meet my deadlines and seem unavailable to you. But I love you guys and appreciate everything you do for me.

This book...I loved writing it and I hope you enjoyed reading it.

Thank you to Jenny Sims and Rumi Khan for editing my book.

Thank you to Hang Le for the fabulous cover.

Give Me Books thank you for hosting my release blitz.

Thank you to my reader group, you are amazing!

Thank you to all the bloggers for spreading the word about The Land Where Sinners Atone and The Land Where Sinners Love and leaving reviews.

And finally to all the readers who took a chance on this journey of love between Zachary and Phoenix. Thank you to each one of you.

CONTACT

Keep in touch with V.F. Mason!

Join Author V.F. Mason's Intense and Twisted Corner

Sign up to V.F. Mason's Newsletter

Like V.F. Mason's Facebook Page

Follow V.F. Mason on Instagram

Follow V.F. Mason on Bookbub

Made in United States
Troutdale, OR
01/13/2025

27902012R10137